CW00431088

The Impending Sausage Sandwich of Doom is a work of fiction and any resemblance to actual persons, living or dead, is purely coincidental.

ISBN – 9781521225769

The Impending Sausage Sandwich of Doom

For George & William

Chapter 1

Interactions with The Flash

'I'm getting an angry man here,' announced Jeremy Flashman as he entered the darkened room, a television crew trailing surreptitiously behind him. The soles of his crocodile skin shoes fell hard on the stone floor, the echoes rebounding from the gloomy brick walls and transmitted onwards to the millions of viewers watching from home. A glimmer of light caught the gold medallion which sat nestled in Jeremy's chest hair, proudly on display courtesy of his partially open shirt with exaggerated collar. The reflected beams struck out in a multitude of directions, forcing the camera to pan away and onto Jeremy's fellow presenter.

'Can you give me a name?' asked Carol, trying desperately not to appear in awe of her counterpart. Her role in this charade was both well practiced and finely honed from the many years they had worked together. Jeremy would reveal a dark, hidden secret gained via his exclusive powers of mediumship. Carol would accordingly appear amazed. The underlying truth however was that more accurate predictions could be guaranteed from fortune cookies acquired from Chinese restaurants where chicken omelette and chips feature heavily on the menu. Still, as producer, host and autocratic dictator of the hit television show Ghostbusters UK, Carol had long since worked out the most successful format. Jeremy was the resident psychic with the questionable fashion sense and immoveable hair, she was the pleasantly attractive presenter. At the age of fifty-eight and with said appeal in swift decline, the thousands of husbands watching at home couldn't quite explain their continued fascination with Carol Swanson. Of course, they were also unaware of the empirical equation that governed them: Beguilement of Carol Swanson *equals* number of golf clubs acquired *divided* by seats available in recently purchased sports car.

'A name?' Jeremy mused, gathering the information from a realm with which he alone could communicate with: his imagination. 'Yes, it's coming to me. It's quite hard to make out. Donald or Daniel I think.'

'And what sort of time are we looking at here?' enquired Carol.

'I'm getting the number one. Yes, it's a year with a one in it.'

'That's fascinating Jeremy!' Carol interrupted. 'In 1702 there was a murder in this *very* house. The victim was called Duncan, which I think we can agree on is close to what you're channelling. But I don't want to give too much away now, please go on.'

'He's clearer now. I'm getting a name. He's calling himself Duncan. I'm getting a word as well, starting with M, it's …. it's …. oh no, he saying murder! He's saying murder, Carol! Murder!'

'That's amazing! You have yet again discovered a horrific truth,' Carol affirmed before turning to address the resident scientist nearby. 'What do you make of this Rupert?'

'Well I would like to see if Jeremy can pick up a surname?' Rupert asked, tugging nervously on his hand knitted jumper.

Jeremy brushed his nose casually with his finger in response. Carol, catching the signal in the corner of her eye, recognised what to do next.

'After the break,' Carol announced, 'Jeremy Flashman will attempt to find out the surname and actually solve the mystery of the murder of Duncan. We will also be going down to the cellar which is said to be the most haunted room in the house. Will the ghost of Duncan appear to us? Find out after the break!'

*

Life for Elliott Rose was anything but unexciting. Poorly paid? Absolutely. Unexciting? Not if one judges success as being employed as the official stooge on Ghostbusters UK. When Jeremy, Carol and the rest of the crew were being scared by stones being thrown in the darkness, Elliott's hand was the one that threw them. When a door opened of its own accord, Elliott was the unseen force pushing it before retreating stealthily back into the shadows. Yet his employment on the show was a fiercely protected secret. Carol had him tied up in a contract that even Satan would find a bit tricky. Besides, Elliott reasoned, what was the point of revealing the truth? One of England's infamous tabloid newspapers would gladly have paid him to disclose the secret. But what use is that when you're unemployed and being stared at in court by Carol and her team of lawyers from the underworld.

Tonight's show was no different from usual. Elliott flitted unseen between the carefully placed television cameras on his way down to the cellar. His soft soled trainers hardly made a sound as he glided across the stone floor. With his lean frame clothed entirely in black and his shaggy blonde hair concealed beneath a dark grey beanie hat, he was all but invisible. Elliott Rose was a ghost, a shadow intent on deception. And Ghostbusters UK had every intention of helping him maintain this supernatural façade. Cameras were expertly placed, creating blind spots for the audience at home. Any sounds recorded were transmitted onwards to the millions watching by the tiny microphones attached to Carol's revealing dress and Jeremy's oversized lapel. For effect they would no doubt be accompanied by Sinclair, the youthful sound man who bowled into rooms with his bulky equipment slung over his shoulder. The extended microphone that could have doubled for a fluffy murder weapon certainly looked authentic, but turned on … Well that's another matter.

The door opened with a sinister creak as Elliott pushed it gently. For some, having a wasp sandwich shoved up their nose would have been preferable to entering the eerie cellar with the menacing shadows lurking just beyond the door. Elliott however, having previously been in so many of these supposed haunted houses, knew there was nothing to fear. In all his years of working on the show, not once had he seen anything that could be considered supernatural, at least not anything that wasn't of his own creation. He had soon learnt that the only thing to be scared off in darkened rooms were the unwelcome sexual advances from Carol. She seemed to regard him as a potential sexual plaything first and employee second.

Elliott flicked on his small torch, casting a beam into the room. The dust particles from four hundred years of history danced in the light as it fell on each corner in turn. Within seconds Elliott had found his prearranged position, just to the right of the door. When Jeremy and Carol entered, the newly opened door would further conceal him and the viewers would have little clue as to the the truth. Now all he had to do was wait. Time to think.

As his girlfriend Simone would often tell him, his was an enviable job. At first Elliott had felt the same. It felt good to do something secretive, something different, but as time passed the monotony of the job had begun to grate. Every week Carol would instruct Elliott, with predictable menacing vigour, that anything *too* outrageous, anything *too* paranormal would not be welcomed. And if such a thing did happen, and for his sake she sincerely hoped it didn't, he would find himself sacked without hesitation. One week it might be a gentle knocking on the wall or floor, the next maybe the throwing of an object. Tonight was Object Night. During his time on the show Elliott had become quite the expert, mastering the flick, the underarm throw and one night, in a fit of irresponsibility, a full blown cricket bowl. Unsurprisingly Carol and her megalomaniacal empire had disapproved of such off-script improvisation, his enthusiasm rewarded with a written warning. Once more and he was out. Well, at least he could still flick stones at Flashman's head, ricocheting them off his coiffured hair, set solid by Venezuela's annual supply of hairspray.

Elliott flicked on the torch to look at his watch, sighing as he realised it would be ten more minutes until they arrived. Whilst they were upstairs, pushing a glass around a table (the only powers present being that of poor spelling), Elliott would be down here, waiting. Still, he knew the plan. He flicked the torch off and stood silently in the darkness. Listening to his breathing, slow and purposeful, his attuned ears suddenly heard something else. As Elliott attempted to focus on it, it faded away almost as suddenly. An eternity seemed to pass before he heard it again, but when he did he was ready. He listened intently as the faint sound rose and fell, trying to work out where exactly it was coming from. It sounded like a bell being struck in the distance: a church bell perhaps, the sound rolling across the mist draped fields outside? The bell rang again, louder this time. It didn't sound quite right. Church bells ring true of the metal they're cast from, a reverb that infiltrates the very fabric of history. This bell however was sharper, higher in key, nearer perhaps. Maybe the silly buggers upstairs were doing something? Elliott wasn't convinced. He was sure it was originating somewhere from the other side of the cellar. Why was a bell chiming in the very room in which he was standing? It made no sense. Unless of course … no. Elliott didn't believe in any of that.

Ding!

The sound passed straight through Elliott; through every defence, through every argument he had ever formulated.

Ding!

There are no such things as …

Ding!

Get a grip, Elliott thought. There is no bell …

Ding! Ding! Ding! Ding!

Elliott's hands began to shake. He cast a look towards the door and his means of escape. Screw this job, he thought, I don't get paid enough for this. His left knee was twitching, ready to run.

Suddenly the chiming came to an abrupt halt and silence prevailed throughout the room. As Elliott listened, he could only hear his own breathing, quicker and more frantic than before. His fists began to unclench, his eyelids allowed to blink once more. Relaxing slightly, he allowed himself to think. Just an exaggerated imagination, he proposed, a trick of the darkness and the solitude.

This was quickly proven to be a horrific misjudgement as a ghost of terrifying proportions manifested itself mere feet in front of him. A swirling mass of whites and greys seemed to twist its way into this world, quickly resolving into the broad form of a man that towered above him.

Elliott did the most logical thing he could think of.

'Fuck me!' He shouted and every atom of his body made a break for the door.

Chapter 2

The rewriting of history at Croydon Leisure Centre

Mrs. Vivian Cole had walked the earth for seventy-three years. Technically only fifty-two of these years was spent actually walking, the last twenty-one being primarily concerned with sitting in an armchair wielding a cup of tea and an outrageous sense of prejudice. These qualities had already sent two husbands to the grave willingly, and caused the suspiciously named Uncle Pete to relocate to Canada. Yet none of this had ever been considered suspicious by Gordon Cole, her forty-three-year-old unmarried son who still lived at home.

'Gordon, when are you going to work, dear?' Mrs. Cole muttered in a quivering voice directed towards the kitchen. It was a deliberate and well-practiced tone to accentuate her fragility.

'Soon mum. I'm just making a sausage sandwich,' Gordon replied, all six foot four of him with a protruding stomach.

'Don't forget my tea Gordon.'

'No mum, I won't forget,' Gordon sighed, turning the sausages over as the sizzling fat leapt from the pan and splattered itself on the calendar for 1983.

Five minutes later Gordon entered the front room with his mum's tea in one hand and the sandwich in the other, a combination of brown sauce and fat oozing from the side and pooling onto the plate. After placing the cup down onto the heavily varnished table beside his mother he made his way over to the lime green sofa opposite. A worrying groan emanated from the wooden frame as he sat down.

'Gordon?' Mrs. Cole murmured, taking a sip of her tea.

'Yes mum?' Gordon replied, suspicious at the speed with which she had picked up the cup.

'What time will you be home tonight from the factory?'

'I would say ten, maybe.'

'Oh, I do wish you didn't have to work in the evenings, especially on a Saturday. I get so lonely.'

Gordon looked up and found himself offering an apology before he'd even realised he was doing it. Mrs. Cole crinkled her nose in dissatisfaction before turning back to Crossroads on the television. If only Mrs. Cole knew the truth.

Gordon Cole had been living a lie for the best part of fifteen years. In all that time his mum had never once questioned how he had paid off the mortgage on their two-bedroomed terraced house in Derby. Nor had she enquired how they always had enough money to afford the most up to date items for the house. Only last week Gordon has come home with a brand new Betamax video recorder and she hadn't batted an eyelid. Still, if she wasn't asking then he wasn't telling. How he managed to acquire such money was known only to a select few. And tonight would be no different. From their house in the Midlands he was going to drive south to Croydon, and someone was going to suffer.

*

The blue Austin Maestro drove leisurely along the dual carriageway before exiting at the Croydon turn off, decelerating as it approached the traffic lights. Gordon shifted uncomfortably in his seat, the drive from Derby having been a long one. The car simply wasn't designed for a man of his physique. His large frame contained the strength of many men alongside a history of many sausage sandwiches consumed. It would only be a few more minutes before he arrived.

You couldn't really call his chosen profession a job as such, more a calling in life. It was a secret he fiercely guarded. Once a week on a Saturday afternoon Gordon Cole became an icon to millions. Except that nobody actually knew who he was. Without the dragon embroidered mask, he was simply a forty-three-year old man from Derby. With the mask he became Hapkido Valentine, British wrestling star: a hero to some, a villain to most. If the All-Star UK Wrestling Federation was to be believed, he had also trained in a multitude of martial arts, aided by mysterious spiritual powers. Hapkido Valentine was a man of mystery; sinister and intriguing in equal measure. Some claimed that he hailed from a secret island that lay hidden in the impenetrable mists off the Japanese coast. Others stated that he was brought forth by dark magic from another dimension. The truth was that the nearest Gordon Cole had ever been to Japan was when he'd once watched Enter the Dragon.

Gordon turned the Austin Maestro into the car park of Croydon Leisure Centre and became Hapkido Valentine.

Finding a space in the car park well away from any other cars, Gordon levered himself out from the driver's side door and slowly walked around to the boot to remove his bag. There were around twenty fervent autograph hunters at the door as he approached. A few murmured amongst themselves as to whether the approaching man was anyone they recognised. With a resounding consensus of no they let him pass without hindrance. Yet if they knew that within his bag he carried the attire of Hapkido Valentine things would have been so very different. Still, it was the price to pay for being the greatest masked wrestler in Britain, even if the lack of recognition grated week in, week out. Hapkido knew that for the greater good his two worlds must never meet. The public continued to be fascinated by the mystical warrior from the Far East and not by a man with a receding hairline and substantial sideburns.

Once inside Gordon made his way along the narrow corridor towards the main changing room. The sound of activity up ahead grew ever louder, voices interspersed with the sound of heavy items being moved about. Suddenly a man emerged from one of the doors to the side, instantly filling the width of the corridor and blocking out the light from up ahead. The forty-stone frame of British Champion and beloved wrestling star Gentleman Jim had emerged from his dressing room. Hapkido felt the air in the corridor shift as Jim came to a halt and turned to look at him. Already dressed for his bout, Jim's costume was even more recognisable than his own. His size fifteen leather boots were a pristine white and of immaculate shine. His red and blue skin-tight leotard was accompanied by a Union Jack cape which sat attached to his shoulders.

'Alright there Gordon!' Gentleman Jim boomed in a strong cockney accent.

'Hello Jim. How's things?' Hapkido asked, coming to a halt.

'Good, good!' Jim thundered at a volume befitting a man of his size. 'I see you're fighting Stardust Simpson today.'

'Aye,' Hapkido replied, his mind starting to drift.

The relationship between Hapkido Valentine and Gentleman Jim had always been a little strained. He didn't hate Jim, in fact he rather liked him. But Hapkido felt that he never had a fair shot at the title whilst Jim was around. They had fought on many occasions with Hapkido always cast as the villain. Yet Jim always won because any other result would have been unthinkable for the viewing public: that was how it worked. However, over the last couple of years the younger wrestlers didn't seem to accept this unwritten rule, especially Stardust Simpson. His match with the great Hapkido Valentine tonight would be his biggest yet and by all accounts he wasn't too happy with the plan for him to lose to the more established wrestler. Hapkido had seen it all before though, a steady stream of wrestlers wanting to achieve everything too quickly. Longevity in the sport wasn't a result of athleticism or technical ability, it was appeal. The public loved Hapkido Valentine – well actually they hated him but the two concepts were almost indistinguishable. These new wrestlers didn't concentrate enough on winning the crowd. Stardust Simpson was just another name that would soon fade, Hapkido ruminated. They all did eventually.

'Good luck with the match Gordon.' Gentlemen Jim commented, manoeuvring himself back into his dressing room. Just before he closed the door he gave Hapkido a subtle wink, confirmation enough for Hapkido that what he had planned would meet with Jim's approval.

Hapkido walked into the crowded dressing room. Fellow wrestlers filled the small room, trying to find enough room to squeeze into their costumes, the air thick with the heavy scent of body odour and cigarettes. Towards the back of the room he found his table with a small tarnished mirror perched on top. A chair, no doubt meant for him was off to the side. Draped over the back was a green leotard.

'Sorry, Gordon,' a nearby wrestler commented, reaching across and retrieving it.

Finally sitting down, Hapkido looked at the reflection in the mirror, stunned by the face looking back. There was no denying it, he was starting to look old. Easily fixed though. Reaching into his bag he pulled out the mask, the dragon embroidered across the front in red and yellow silk. As he pulled it over his head, tying it securely at the back, the last vestiges of Gordon Cole slipped away, Hapkido Valentine lived.

The reflection in the mirror belonged to a mystical warrior, trained in the ancient martial arts of Karate and Judo. Yet these skills paled into insignificance compared to a power that he could draw upon. And he wasn't afraid to use it. Hapkido Valentine could hypnotise a man just by looking into his eyes, their souls drowning in a world of submission. At the beginning it had merely started out as a stage trick, but Hapkido knew it was now much more. He had spent years, with the assistance of the East Midlands library service, researching the power to control a man through hypnosis. On numerous occasions back in Derby, Gordon had even tested it on his own mother. Without fail she would go into a trance, albeit one with snoring.

Two months ago things started to change. At a match in Luton against Terry Waters, Hapkido's powers of hypnotism were called into play as the script demanded. Terry was rebounding off the ropes, careering towards Hapkido who stood resolutely in the middle of the ring, his gaze fixed solely on Terry's eyes. Terry came to a stumbling halt, mere inches from Hapkido's face. There was a vacancy in Terry's eyes: more than acting, he was no longer in control. It was only meant to last thirty seconds. Not even Hapkido expected Terry to be taken from the ring on a stretcher, staring blankly at the ceiling. That was when Hapkido Valentine knew. Afterwards, Gordon had tackled Terry about it in the pub. He claimed he couldn't explain it either. Initially Gordon couldn't quite tell if he was being wound up but what if it were actually true? Were the two worlds of Gordon and

Hapkido actually coming together?

Hapkido snapped out of his memories of the past. Reflected in the mirror, far across on the other side of the room was Stardust Simpson. Dressed in a gold jumpsuit, his blonde hair was permed into tight curls.

Hapkido had been deliberating on his powers for some time, not sure if the world was truly ready. Now everything seemed to make sense. Here was the perfect opportunity, a chance to prove that youth and fitness was no match for the mystical powers of the East. Hapkido Valentine was something new, and tonight the world would finally see.

Chapter 3

Politik Bureau ring dynamics

Hapkido was well over six foot of pure wrestling terror. As befits a man who'd struck fear into the hearts of a nation for fifteen years, his outfit was equally as notorious. Old women in the crowd had been known to drop their corned beef sandwiches when they caught sight of his attire as he entered the ring. Calf-hugging boots were worn over a skin tight black costume, adorned with a woven red and yellow design in the finest of silk. Originating at the stomach, the threads coalesced into the form of a flowing dragon that coiled and swept across the chest, before coming to a fearsome end in the form of a snarling dragon's head on the shoulder. Along the arms two trails of flame wound their way down towards Hapkido's large purposeful hands. Another flame twisted its way across the collar bone, tracing its way onto the left-hand side of the mask, morphing into the image of a dragon as it did so. It was a costume famous the country over, even if the face within was anything but. Gordon Cole was now just an echo: Hapkido was alive.

His boots spun on the floor, turning towards the doorway in the distance and strode with authority towards the arena. He saw the other wrestlers watching him as he moved amongst them, knowing that they considered him with a mixture of admiration and envy. As he passed it was imperative that he avoided the eye contact of others, regardless of whether they were long time compatriots or rivals. At the far end of the room he paused, his hand lingering on the handle of the door. Beyond lay the battleground, the baying crowd waiting. They might not like him, but they certainly needed him. Who was he to disappoint. The villain of British wrestling was about to show the crowd exactly what they had been waiting for.

'Gordon,' interrupted a voice from behind.

Hapkido heard the name, incensed as to the nature of the

greeting. There was no Gordon, only Hapkido Valentine. He turned around slowly, fixing his stare upon the person who had addressed him.

Bernie Subiaco, president of the All-Star UK Wrestling Federation, stood diminutively in front of him. He was a good foot shorter, his closely cropped black hair streaked with grey and dressed in a cheap grey suit with kipper tie. It had long been postulated by most of the wrestlers that the grey in his hair was a direct result of having recently married a Russian woman. By all accounts she was as fearsome as any of Bernie's employees.

'Bernard,' Hapkido replied distantly. It was a rarity for the great Hapkido Valentine to speak. He was an enigma when fighting and an oddity when not.

'Listen Gordon, sorry Hapkido. I need to tell you about a change of plan,' Bernie began to explain.

'A change?' Hapkido muttered slowly, not quite following.

'Sorry to leave it so late. The result of tonight's match has had to be changed. I knew you would understand, you being such a professional and all. Anyway, at the point where it looks like you are beaten and then you … you know … turn it around with some of your ... powers? Well at that point we need you to lose. Imagine the shock! Imagine what they'll say. The great Hapkido Valentine, beaten by the young pretender. It will be huge. It will be massive. They'll love it. They'll love you, more than ever!' Bernie announced with a flourish, desperately trying to conceal his fear as to Hapkido's reaction.

Hapkido rolled the words around his mind. Was he actually being asked to throw the match? He was familiar with the concept of allowing Gentlemen Jim to win. But to actually lose to someone else? To lose to Stardust Simpson? The impact sent seismic waves through his being. A small crack appeared in Hapkido's psyche, just wide enough for Gordon to re-emerge.

'You want me to lose?' Gordon replied incredulously, the exasperated tone set against a thick Brummie accent. 'You actually want Hapkido Valentine to lose against … Stardust bloody Simpson?'

'I'm afraid so Gordon,' Bernie replied, taking a step back.

'Hapkido!' The wrestler corrected, infuriated.

'I'm afraid so … Hapkido. The crowd love Stardust. He's new, he's exciting, he's ... well how can I put it?'

'The future?' Gordon speculated.

'Look, Hapkido. It's a one-time thing. We're spicing things up a bit. Imagine it, the great Hapkido Valentine beaten by the young upstart! Imagine the shock. Imagine the rematch!' Bernie explained confidently, enthused by the idea.

Gordon stood stock-still and considered everything he had heard. He couldn't deny its magnitude. After all, he was the great Hapkido Valentine. No one beat the great Hapkido Valentine! Yet he knew what it really meant. All those years of being thrown around a ring, all those years of pain and injuries. For what? To be discarded in favour of the next generation. Of course it was inevitable; he'd known that for years. He could stop a man twice his size but he couldn't stop time. To be confronted by it however, to actually hear someone say it, it was a crushing blow. He might win the rematch (although he doubted it), but sooner or later he would be asked the very same question again.

'So Hapkido, you okay with this?' Bernie asked tentatively.

The wrestler exhaled heavily, his body language more submissive.

'I understand,' Gordon replied, his voice heavy with resignation.

'Just a one-time thing, honestly,' Bernie reaffirmed.

Gordon Cole turned and opened the door. As it closed behind him, leaving Bernie and the rest of the federation on the other side, Hapkido Valentine adjusted his frame, standing taller than ever before.

'Hapkido Valentine never loses,' he whispered, striding towards the arena more purposefully than he had done in years.

*

'Ladies and gentlemen,' the announcer roared into the microphone, his voice reverberating off the back wall. Its volume was more than adequate for a consortium of old ladies to stop knitting and look up in anticipation.

'It is my great pleasure,' the announcer continued, 'to introduce a wrestling match of stupendous proportions. In the blue corner, from Grimsby, the one, the only, Stardust Simpson!'

All eyes in the crowd moved towards Stardust with a sense of excitement. Taking a bow Simpson embraced the admiration, running his fingers theatrically through his immaculate perm. The future never looked so dazzling.

'And in the red corner, hailing from the mystical lands of Japan, the man you love to hate, Hapkido Valentine!'

Hapkido stood firm, his muscles flexed, holding a wild stare. His eyes only slightly flickered as a half-eaten corned beef sandwich flew mere inches in front of his face.

Some say it was the bloodiest match ever witnessed. It certainly wasn't appropriate for Saturday afternoon television. If those responsible for scheduling had known that the lines between fictionalised violence and actual bodily harm would become so blurred then they would never have allowed it.

It started exactly as expected. Stardust was the first teetering on the brink of defeat, pinned, one, two, shoulder up, safety! Then Hapkido found himself in a submission hold with seemingly little hope for escape. Spurred on by the crowd he searched deep for the supernatural strength required to break the hold. Back and forth, the winner impossible to call. And then came the turning point. Under normal circumstances the crowd knew full well how it would finish. In an act of complacency, perhaps misplaced bravado, Stardust Simpson would have stared into the eyes of the great Hapkido Valentine. From that point onwards he would have been lost, those deep-set eyes claiming another victim. From this induced hypnotised state, defeat would have swiftly followed. But Bernie Subiaco hadn't wanted that. No, Bernie wanted Stardust Simpson to break the trance, to fight back. A new hero would have been born that day. The crowd would be welcoming a fresh champion into their hearts - Stardust Simpson, conqueror of evil, the man who vanquished a terrible foe and avenged all those who had fallen before. Hapkido in the meantime would be a broken man lying on the canvas, the only path remaining for the mystical warrior being the one towards ignominy. Hapkido however had other ideas. Since that match with Terry Waters it was apparent to Hapkido that his one-time stage trick had become a reality, a trait of the warrior within. He simply didn't know how far his powers went. It was time he found out.

Stardust bounced theatrically from the ropes and threw himself across the ring, a blur of gold thundering towards his opponent. Hapkido was ready, standing firm, fixing his stare. At first Stardust slowed, his feet beginning to drag as he ran. Within a few steps his legs had become heavier, lumbering across the canvas now, his body reluctant to carry him any further. Coming to a halt mere inches in front of Hapkido, Stardust's body finally submitted to the transcendent powers focused upon him. His mind was absent in the face of adversity and despite the pleas from the crowd, there was little hope. Many had met with a similar fate, and Stardust was deeper than anyone had ever been before. Hapkido took in the sight before him. He leaned closer, listening to the rapid breathing of his rival, ensuring he was truly gone. Nothing. Lost. No way back.

The crowd gasped, Stardust Simpson, the great young hope of British Wrestling had been beaten, falling into a deep trance from which there was no escape. Hapkido let a thin smile creep across his lips, barely noticeable to even those in the front row who sat there with their jaws open in disbelief. Hapkido turned and took in the sight of the crowd, booing and hissing at him. They may not like him but they would remember him as the one true warrior. Accompanied by a renewed bout of jeering he ran across the ring, twisting his body and bouncing off the ropes, propelling himself through the air towards Stardust Simpson. Twenty-something stone of considerable bulk connected with the chest of his opponent and they went crashing to the canvas, the sound of the collision echoing throughout the arena. Amid the wreckage lay Stardust Simpson, steadfast in his trance, unaware of the calamity that had occurred. Sprawled across him, pinning him down was Hapkido Valentine, his entire weight bearing down on the man beneath him.

From the corner the referee looked on, not quite sure what to do. He'd expected the match to develop somewhat differently from what he was now witnessing. After a few furtive glances to the sides in the hope of finding further instruction, he was disappointed to be met only with blank stares in return. What else could he do? He did the one thing that seemed to make sense: follow the rules. These guys obviously knew what they were doing even if he didn't. Sliding onto his knees to the side of the two wrestlers he began the count.

One...

Stardust lay motionless.

Two...

Suddenly Hapkido felt a push from beneath him.

Stardust was obviously not quite in as deep a trance as Hapkido had hoped. The hypnotism was obviously wearing off. The truth however would have hurt Hapkido more.

Stardust Simpson had missed his cue. Only when he went crashing to the floor with Hapkido on top had he remembered that he was meant to break the trance before the pin. Regardless, the minor details didn't really matter as both he and Hapkido knew who the winner was meant to be. Yet as he pushed the man on top he was met with force in return. He's not moving, he's not bloody moving! Stardust realised a lot in the short time that followed. He had wanted the match to be a classic, one that would be talked about for years. He would be the great Stardust Simpson, the one man who beat the legend Hapkido Valentine. His push from beneath should have been the signal for his opponent to allow him to escape. And here he was, resolutely pressing him to the canvas, quite unlike a man who was resigned to losing. Obviously Hapkido had decided to go with his own plan for the fight. Maybe he was trying to humiliate him, trying to bow out on a high? Well, if that's the way he wanted it then so be it. Now all he had to do was escape the hold of the man he could hear breathing heavily above him.

In the history of mankind a count to three had never taken so long as it did in the ring that day. As Stardust pushed with every essence of strength, Hapkido continued to hold him down.

Three!

The bell rang, the match was over. In response Hapkido's resolve lessened, knowing he had achieved what he had planned. It was just enough for Simpson to lift him a few inches and with lightning speed scramble out from beneath.

Both men staggered to their feet, looking unsteady as they did so. Stardust Simpson looked at his opponent with a disbelieving look. Hapkido in response gave a sly grin. Had he thought ahead, Hapkido probably should have expected what came next. Stardust Simpson, his face full of fury, launched himself across the ring. As their two bodies met their arms became entwined, each man trying to find something to hold, something to gain an advantage with.

'What are you doing?' Simpson exclaimed. 'You were supposed to let me win!'

Hapkido didn't respond. Instead he attempted to catch his opponent's eye but after a few seconds it became apparent his powers had been dampened by some unknown force. Reluctantly he would have to resort to more traditional methods. Using his superior strength, focusing every ounce of energy available he pushed his opponent away from him. Unexpectedly Stardust found himself stumbling backwards, falling onto the ropes before being flung back towards the centre of the ring where Hapkido was waiting. There was nothing elaborate in the move that sent Stardust Simpson back to the canvas. Technically it wasn't even legal. Hapkido delivered a punch straight to the face, the sound of his fist connecting barely concealed by the gasps from the crowd. At this point Hapkido could feel his energy spent. The fight had gone on for ages, and his age was finally catching up with him. The end of his career was nigh but he still had the advantage, he still had the opportunity to go out on a high. Hapkido's signature move, post onset of trance was a flying body slam from the top of the corner buckle. On this occasion the trance had been replaced by a punch but the effect was much the same. As Hapkido walked towards the corner the crowd started to boo him. It would have been nice, just this once, to have been cheered. Still, he was going to miss them and whether they knew it or not, they were going to miss him too. Once on top of the buckle, swaying a little unsteadily as he turned, Hapkido faced the ring. However Stardust Simpson wasn't exactly where he had left him. To be precise he was now standing directly below him, blood streaming from a cut on his lip. Stardust reached up, grasped a handful of costume around Hapkido's chest and pulled him back into the ring. The canvas shook as Hapkido Valentine came crashing down.

Before Hapkido even had time to contemplate the situation, he could feel his adversary holding him to the floor with a knee pressed hard to his back. Then his mask tightened as, from behind, Stardust attempted to untie the laces. He could hear the clamour of the crowd rising. They could sense a momentous event in British wrestling: the unveiling of the true face of the warrior. But he was not a broken man yet.

With one final surge of vigour he propelled himself upwards and into a standing position, sending his rival falling backwards. His knees hurt, his breathing frantic, struggling to remain standing. He just needed one final assault. Turning, he ran back across the ring to where Stardust was now standing. Twenty years ago it might have worked but the man in front of him now was more than ready, sidestepping Hapkido as he careered towards him. Colliding heavily with the corner, Hapkido bounced back towards the centre of the ring, his feet going from beneath him. It was not the canvas that Hapkido felt next but a hand on his shoulder. Stardust swivelled Hapkido round, the faces of the crowd blurred as he spun involuntarily. With an arm reaching beneath Hapkido, the other looped over his shoulder, Stardust Simpson started to lift him from the canvas. With some considerable effort he was spun around in mid-air so that he now faced downwards. But he wasn't falling, he was being held, upturned with his face staring out at the countless rows of upside down faces of the crowd. The view wasn't to last forever, Hapkido felt himself being driven downwards.

Chapter 4

The transcendent passage

The crowd didn't quite know how to react. They had long been content to witness the brutality of wrestling from their distant viewpoint, where the good guy won, the bad guy lost and everyone went home happy. The violence wasn't real: it began and finished with the ringing of the bell. Yet here they were, reluctant observers to a situation where theatrics and reality were indistinguishable. They winced as Hapkido's head hit the canvas at speed, they sat in shock as his giant frame slumped to the floor. Was this really part of the show? Were they meant to cheer? The realisation came slowly. This wasn't an act. Any notion of performance was quickly dispelled as the bell rang frantically, the chiming incessant and urgent. A man raced down the aisle, clambering into the ring whilst holding a small leather bag. He didn't seem part of the show, even more so when he began gesturing to others to help. Soon a crowd of people surrounded the motionless body of Hapkido Valentine. Stardust Simpson meanwhile backed into a corner, looking confused, disbelieving that the unfolding events were a consequence of his actions.

The crowd that surrounded Hapkido grew more animated, shouting desperately for someone, anyone who knew what to do. Eventually, no doubt after a phone call had been made, two ambulance-men raced towards the ring. The crowd looked on expectantly, optimistically. They were to be disappointed. After a few minutes the house lights turned on and the announcer came over the speakers in a solemn tone to request the crowd to leave. As they filed out, some in tears, their last sight was that of a white sheet being draped over the lifeless body of the great Hapkido Valentine.

For Hapkido things didn't seem to make sense. He couldn't

quite separate the reality … the dream. A terrible darkness seemed to be clawing at the edges of his vision. It wasn't so much that his body was numb, more that it didn't belong to him. His eyes stared upwards towards the ceiling but he wasn't sure that it was actually his eyes that were seeing. He knew he was still there in the ring, lying on his back but also at the same time he was anywhere but there. He felt light, floating almost, his connection to his physical body tenuous at best. There was an urge to rise yet something was holding him down, an unknown weight attached to him by small ethereal strands that he felt stretch and break one at a time beneath him. Not long now, he found himself thinking. Not long now.

The darkness seemed to be all around him now, reality becoming distant. Every moment of joy or pain, every memory of the life left behind resided as a small point some way in the distance, moving ever further away. The voices that belonged there became muffled, distant, the ringing of the bell fading. In time the point became harder to see; flickering, as if something or maybe someone was passing intermittingly in front of it. The darkness surrounded him, holding him, carrying him away from the point of light. The more he tried to concentrate the harder it became. His last thought, if he could call it that, was the urge to sleep: to release himself from the burden of the man he once was, to forget the world he once knew. And then there was nothing.

How long?

That was the first thought that roared through his being as he became aware. A million neurons flashed and crackled back into life.

How long had he been asleep? Was he even sleeping? Where was he?

It was so dark. He couldn't feel his body, merely a sensation of floating.

Could he see? Yes, he could see. Something up ahead? A point, small, distant, seemingly important.

A light…. It's a light, thought the wrestler.

It's getting nearer, pulling me towards it. He couldn't tell which way was up or down, but he could sense forward.

As the light grew larger he could just about make out a figure somewhere within it. Finally he understood. The figure ahead of him wasn't only separated from him by distance but also by time. A thousand answers to a thousand questions lay ahead, purpose directing the movement towards it.

Heaven! Hapkido resolved, rolling the thought around his mind. This must be Heaven!

The light grew ever nearer, a brilliant white. Yet the light itself seemed to lack depth, rectangular almost in shape. The figure he had previously seen was now a shadow cast onto the white from the other side, moving, running maybe, close, yet so far away. The details were so difficult to grasp.

He was close now. What he had mistaken for a light initially now seemed to be something, he just wasn't sure what. The tones were a multitude of whites and light greys, shadows in the folds of the form. Arching his head back, for it seemed that he had a head now, he watched fascinated as the shape passed over him. Slowly it fell gracefully onto him, draping itself over his head and shoulders. Then came the tactile sensation of it on his palms, cold with the contact. His face, for he definitely now had a face, felt the form fall across it. It felt light, like a thin sheet. Sounds began to filter through: at first a multitude of distant whispers before one voice cut through the rest. It was somewhat of a surprise to hear the words being said, shouted even.

'Fuck me!'

This wasn't quite how he'd imagined heaven would be.

Chapter 5

Special offer on one flux capacitor, used

Perhaps it was sudden bravery that made Elliott Rose hesitate as he reached the door. More likely it was the fact that the ghost he'd glimpsed from the corner of his eye seemed to be wearing a white sheet. It was classic Scooby-Doo, enough for anyone to stop and think about it.

'Ha, nice try mate,' Elliott declared, coming to a halt. His hand slowly inched away from the door handle.

As Elliott turned back to the room he looked the figure up and down. If someone was going to go to the effort of trying to scare the life out of him, they could have at least tried a bit harder. It wasn't exactly original.

'Sinclair is that you? You could've least tried to look a bit more convincing,' Elliott stated.

The figure started to sway.

'Come on Sinclair, take that bloody sheet off and stop dicking about!' Elliott demanded, his voice full of frustration.

'Where am I?' The form whispered from beneath.

'Where are you? About two minutes from the dole queue! Come on mate, you know that idiot Flashman and the sex maniac are due in here at any moment. They'll do their nut if they come walking in here with their cameras and everything and you're just standing there with a sheet over your bleeding head.'

'I was only just … Where am I? I thought I was ...' the form muttered, confused.

'Sinclair, will you stop being an idiot!' Elliott shouted, crossing the room and reaching out with his hand to pull away the sheet.

'No!' The figure responded forcefully, projecting its arms forward to signal Elliott shouldn't come any closer. The sheet drew back slightly to reveal two muscular hands underneath.

'I've had enough of this. Just take the bloody sheet off!' Elliott implored.

'I can't,' the figure emotively replied. 'Because .... because I was somewhere else. I thought I was ...'

'Take the bloody sheet off!' Elliott shouted, casting a nervous glance back towards the door.

'I can't,' the figure stuttered. 'I think I might be disfigured. I think I might be dead. I was somewhere else.'

'This joke has gone on far enough. Well done, you got me. Now take off the sheet you stupid bastard!'

'So be it.' The figure announced, a hand reaching upwards.

Grasping the sheet from around the chest, the figure pulled at it so that it slid over the top of his head and fell crumpled to the floor. Elliott in return stood with his mouth open wide.

'What is it? Am I horribly disfigured?' The emergent figure asked.

'No dude, it's just...' Elliott hesitated '...it's just you're dressed as Hapkido Valentine.'

A silence permeated the room as both men looked at one another. In that time Elliott considered the facts. The figure that stood before him was over six feet tall with arms that looked like they could rip a man in two. Sinclair was a short man, five foot six at best, with a mop of unruly hair. It was obvious that they were not one and the same. And that wasn't even taking into account that Sinclair rarely, if ever, went around dressed in a skin-tight leotard. But if this wasn't Sinclair then who the hell was it?

'Who are you?' Elliott questioned, starting to suspect a fan of the show with a stack of mental issues to boot.

'I am Hapkido Valentine.' The figure declared. 'Five times challenger to the British heavyweight wrestling championship, master of the mystical arts of Japan.'

'I know who Hapkido Valentine is mate,' Elliott replied. 'Perhaps what I should have asked is how the hell you got in here? And what's the number of your care worker?'

'Care worker?' The man dressed as Hapkido Valentine asked.

At this point Elliott heard a door being opened nearby: not to the cellar itself, but not too far away either. The twin voices of Carol and Flashman were instantly recognisable, and they were getting nearer. Panicking, Elliott raced over to the man and reached out to grab him by the forearm. He didn't exactly know what he was going to do but he had to do something.

'No!' The man shouted, a little too loudly for Elliott's comfort. 'No one touches Hapkido Valentine!'

Elliott withdrew his hand instinctively. Realising that the man was in no fit state to be dragged willingly, he had to resort to other tactics.

'I need you to come and hide behind the door with me,' Elliott requested calmly, although he was anything but.

The man showed no signs of moving, despite Carol's and Flashman's voices increasing in volume. Elliott, unnerved, did the only thing left he could do: save himself and hope for the best. Rushing into the shadows of the alcove behind the door, he desperately hoped that the man would follow. He only just made it before Carol and Jeremy entered.

'So are you getting a presence Jeremy?' Carol asked as she entered the cellar first, making sure her camera was directed away from the alcove.

'I'm getting something. It's a voice. He's trying to warn us not to come in here,' Jeremy Flashman replied, every ounce of drama magnified tenfold.

'And is this the same spirit you detected downstairs Jeremy?'

'Yes, it's the murder victim, Dominic.'

'Did you mean Duncan?' Carol replied, tilting her head to one side to illustrate to the resident medium that it shouldn't be so hard to remember at least one name per episode.

'Yes Carol. Duncan is here too.' Jeremy replied after briefly hesitating.

Other members of the film crew entered the cellar behind them, led by Sinclair who positioned himself at the back and arched the boom microphone over their heads.

'Shall we try and connect with him?' Carol asked as Rupert the resident scientist and inexact sceptic filed into the room belatedly.

'I have the equipment ready.' Rupert declared, twiddling a knob on one of his unfathomable detectors. As he did so he wondered how exactly a third in Business Studies from the University of Swindon had led him to be standing here.

'Okay,' Carol announced loudly. 'Are there any ghosts here? Any members of the netherworld? Anyone who wants to make contact with us?'

A silence filled the air as they collectively peered into the darkness. The night vision cameras scanned the room and found only the faces of Carol, Flashman and the rest of the crew cast in an ethereal green hue. Not a sight of anyone or anything else.

'We know you're here, Duncan.' Carol announced. 'We know what happened to you. Why don't you show yourself to us? Can you throw something, Duncan?'

The silence continued.

'Come on Duncan, throw something!'

Still nothing.

'I said...' Carol started, her voice frantic at first before settling down, 'it's now time to throw something.'

Carol's request was not so much for Duncan (who unsurprisingly wasn't present) but for Elliott to actually *do* his job. Elliott on the other hand had no such intention of throwing anything. He was amazed that they hadn't seen the man he had encountered moments before. In fact he didn't have the slightest clue where the man dressed as Hapkido Valentine was but he had no intention of throwing something that might annoy someone whose mental state was already in question.

'Well, it's obvious that any activity down here has passed. So back to the studio for an update, and then we'll be moving on to the library.' Carol announced, a hint of frustration in her voice.

A few seconds of complete silence followed until Carol was sure they were no longer on air. Angrily she flicked on her torch and swung it around in the direction of the alcove. Elliott Rose stood illuminated in its beam.

'What the hell was that!' Carol shouted in a stentorian tone.

'You idiot!' Jeremy Flashman added. 'You almost ruined everything.'

'Look, I can explain. You see ...' Elliott replied, nervously.

'This better be good, Rose.' Carol threatened. 'If you don't have a damn good reason why there was a distinct lack of paranormal activity in here then there will be trouble.'

'If you'll just let me explain,' Elliott began, 'I was down here waiting, when suddenly this nutter turned up. I have absolutely no idea how he got in here but I hardly thought you'd want me throwing stones at him and risk him going crazy on air.'

'What the hell are you talking about?' Carol asked, her fury growing exponentially.

'Use your torches. Have a look. He's in here somewhere.'

In response a multitude of torches flicked on and cast their beams across every inch of the room. It was soon evident that there was no one besides themselves in the room.

'I don't understand. He was right there, dressed as Hap...' Elliott stated, stopping mid-sentence as he considered what he was saying.

'Elliott, listen very carefully to me,' Carol whispered.

'He must have walked out when you came in,' Elliott protested.

'No one passed me,' Sinclair confirmed, rather unhelpfully.

'Elliott, it's important you understand this,' Carol continued.

'But ... he was just ...' Elliott muttered, confused.

'You're fired!' Carol shouted, unsettling the dust from the very walls which surrounded them.

Chapter 6

Dickie Davis, a legend in fourth gear

As Elliott descended the front steps of Chegwinton Manor, he emerged into the breaking dawn. A muted sun was beginning to creep above the horizon, illuminating the wispy clouds that hung high in the morning sky in a spectrum of pastel hues. The aged trees either side of the gravel driveway swayed gently with the breeze, a solitary leaf capering a momentary dance before brushing against the wheel of Elliott's car in the distance. Making his way towards it, Elliott, dejected and solemn, dragged his feet across the gravel, barely lifting them from the ground. So here I am again, Elliott reasoned, out of work, and this time it wasn't even my fault. Whose fault was it though? That was an answer he couldn't quite determine. A hallucination perhaps? Or was he right first time? An overenthusiastic fan of the show, albeit one with amazing powers of escape. Elliott opened the car door and sat down in the driver's seat.

The white Renault Clio turned from the main driveway and onto the road that ran through the village. A charming row of terraced cottages passed by the driver's side whilst Elliott thought of those inside. As they slept serenely within, he was busy making his way home: an hour's drive back to his flat in Croydon. That in itself would be something to look forward to if it weren't for what awaited him there … or rather who. Simone always woke when she sensed him climbing into bed alongside her. And as usual she would want to know how it had gone. Yes, he had thrown something. No, Carol wasn't happy with his performance. Yes, he knew it wasn't a proper job. No, he hadn't suddenly been promoted to chief stone-thrower or whatever. He did love her, but Christ she could moan. Now he had to go home and tell her that he had lost his job and it was safe to say she wasn't going to like it one bit.

'So I'm guessing I got you in trouble,' declared Hapkido Valentine from the passenger seat.

'Jeeeeeeesus!' Elliott screamed, realising with abject horror that he wasn't alone. The car swerved violently to the right as the shock raced through his body with a terrifying shudder. His eyes caught sight of a bollard in the road directly ahead just in time. Instinct took over and Elliott swung the steering wheel hard so that the car darted back to the left-hand side of the road, the yellow and white bollard whistling past his door.

'It's you, but ... but how?' Elliott blabbered.

'In Japanese folklore, the ninja is the master of stealth.'

'What?' Elliott asked, one eye on the intruder, the other on the road ahead. It was around this point that his heart started beating again.

'I said in Japanese folklore, the ninja ....'

'I heard what you said!' Elliott interrupted, his mind in complete disbelief about what was happening. 'I mean, how the hell did you get in here? Were you hiding in the back seat or something?'

'Hapkido Valentine always rides in the front.'

'One minute there was no one sitting next to me. The next thing I know the lunatic who cost me my job is sitting right there!' Elliott exasperated, confused beyond all reason.

'I do apologise about that. You see, I hadn't planned to manifest in that cellar but my skills are not quite as honed as I would have wished. The first attempt at transition is always fraught with potential difficulty.'

Elliott in response desperately tried get a grip on the situation.

'This is not real. This is simply my imagination!' Elliott reasoned frantically. 'There is no way that you could have climbed into the front seat without me noticing. Therefore it's not possible that there is actually someone else in this car with me. And most defiantly not someone dressed as Hapkido Valentine.'

'I can understand why you would be nervous about meeting me. I am after all one of the most famous wrestlers in Britain. It's actually quite rare for me to speak, but I suppose I did cost you your job so it's the least I can do.'

'This is not real,' Elliott continued, trying desperately not to look at the figure next to him. 'This is some sort of hallucination; happens to people all the time. I am obviously having some kind of nervous breakdown!'

'Would you like my autograph?'

'There is no one else in the car,' Elliott persisted, taking one hand from the wheel and running it through his hair. Grasping a handful of his blonde hair he pulled it tight and began talking to himself as calmly as possible.

'This, Elliott, is your imagination. There is no one in the car with you. That man that you can see dressed as Hapkido Valentine is not actually there. It is not possible that anyone could hide in the car and then get into the passenger seat unnoticed. Therefore if it's not a real person that only leaves two alternatives. One is that you are mid-breakdown and the other, well that's not possible. You are not having a conversation with the ghost of Hapkido Valentine.'

'A ghost?' Hapkido questioned with genuine surprise. 'I'm not a ghost. Why would you even think that? I simply managed to transport myself across the astral plane and materialise here. It's an old trick of the samurai warrior when in danger.'

'What!' Elliott automatically questioned, despite his previous statement that there was no one actually there.

'Oh yes, quite rare I admit, but if a samurai achieves the necessary state of enlightenment he can attain abilities of quite unimaginable power.'

'Putting aside the fact that you have just appeared out of nowhere, you know, as is the wont of ghosts,' Elliott asked, trying to clarify matters, 'are you actually saying that you've teleported here, you know, like in Star Trek or something?'

For all Elliott's confusion, he was starting to feel something other than fear. Best to understand what was actually happening before he went and checked himself into the nearest asylum.

'You see,' Hapkido continued, 'I was in this match with Stardust Simpson. Faced with his own inevitable defeat, he decided to use a move that could have seriously injured me. Quite against the rules of course, but then you wouldn't expect anything less from someone like him. It's obvious that given the dire situation I found myself in, my powers awakened. As a result I was able to transport myself here.'

'Can I just ask one thing?' Elliott requested.

'Go ahead,' Hapkido replied, expecting Elliott to give a glowing endorsement of his renowned wrestling skills.

'That was over thirty years ago. I was a kid when that happened. It's not something you forget when someone dies on Saturday afternoon television.'

'What are you talking about?'

'You're dead!'

'Oh, I see what you're thinking. No, you're mistaken. I've actually crossed the astral plane.'

'If, and it's a big if,' Elliott considered, wondering why he was still driving when it seemed to make more sense to stop the car and run for the hills. 'If I'm not actually having a breakdown and the real Hapkido Valentine is sitting next to me, then that definitely makes you a ghost.'

'No, you're mistaken,' Hapkido replied with a slight tremor in his voice.

'I remember it clearly. Hapkido Valentine died in the ring on Saturday afternoon television. It was on the news and everything.'

Hapkido was silent in return, allowing this revelation to soak into his consciousness.

'I died?' Hapkido asked, a sense of sadness in his question.

'You died.' Elliott clarified with an urgency in his voice.

Hapkido fell into silence again. Elliott meanwhile focused on the road ahead. If he could just get home he would be in a much safer place.

'Of course, it all makes sense,' Hapkido finally announced with confidence.

'What...' Elliott asked, closing his eyes in resignation, 'makes sense?'

'It's obvious. You said this happened thirty years ago. So this must be the year 2013.'

'A bit more than that,' Elliott corrected.

'Well, something must have gone wrong with the transition. Somehow, I have travelled through time as well.'

Elliott's eyes closed again, a fraction longer this time. When he opened them he saw the sign for the Croydon turning. That meant a dual carriageway, and dual carriageways were good. That meant speed. Speed would allow him to get back home quicker. Maybe, just maybe then the madness would stop. Elliott reached towards the gear stick as his foot hovered over the accelerator. As he did so his hand inadvertently slipped over the top of the stick and touched the leg of Hapkido Valentine. To Elliott's total astonishment his hand didn't hit Hapkido's leg, rather disappeared inside it instead. The sensation was a tingling on the fingers. There may have been more to sense but his brain wasn't interested in any of that. The sight of his hand disappearing into the leg of what until seconds before appeared to be a solid person was too much to comprehend.

'No!' Hapkido shouted. 'No one touches the great Hapkido Valentine, no one!'

'Shit, I'm sorry. It was an accident,' Elliott replied, whipping his hand back, reeling in horror that he'd touched a ghost. Yep, definitely a ghost.

With this sudden realisation Elliott began to scream.

'Do not do that again!' Hapkido demanded.

It took a full two miles before Elliott finally managed to regain his composure and stop screaming. It was another mile and a half before he felt he could continue the conversation.

'Can I ask something?' Elliott asked as his breathing returned to a normal pace. 'If you've just travelled through time, how come I just put my hand straight through your leg? You know, as if you were a ghost. If you were a figment of my imagination or an actual time traveller then surely you'd be solid?'

Hapkido shifted himself in the seat to get comfortable as he considered the question. Elliott couldn't fail to notice that the seat didn't move in response.

'It is evident,' Hapkido speculated, 'that perhaps the transportation hasn't gone according to plan. No doubt I haven't quite completed the transition yet.'

'Obvious?' Elliott replied, gesturing his disbelief at the ongoing conversation. Shaking his head rapidly he hoped he would wake up.

'There is indeed a lot to think about,' Hapkido pondered.

This was perhaps the first thing Elliott had heard his travelling companion say that actually sounded sensible. So much so he made a point of looking at his passenger. It was somewhat of a surprise to see that Hapkido Valentine, the great British wrestler who died in 1983, was no longer there.

Elliott's thoughts for the remainder of the trip lacked any definitive conclusion. Parking up outside his block of flats he concluded that at least it couldn't get any worse. He passed through the communal doors of the building and climbed the steps to his flat with trepidation. How the hell was he was going to explain this to Simone? Not only would she have to deal with a boyfriend who had just lost his job but also one who was now seeing ghosts of long dead wrestlers. Luckily an envelope fixed to his front door provided a distraction before he entered. Elliott peeled it away from the door and took out the note within and began to read.

Dear Elliott,

I'm sorry that it has come to this but I can't go on like this anymore. It just feels like we are going nowhere in our relationship. I've been thinking of leaving for a while now but recently I have come to the conclusion that we are stuck in a routine that we can't escape. This isn't helped by the fact that some nights I never see you whilst you go out and do your job. I call it a job, but you can't realistically describe eight hours sneaking around supposed haunted houses as worthwhile employment. I wouldn't actually mind if you were actually doing something credible, but you never even encounter any ghosts.'

Elliott paused for a moment, putting all other thoughts to one side to consider the irony of her statement before reading on.

'Maybe I could have done more to save our relationship. Unfortunately, I see no other option for us but to make a clean break. I'm sorry if this comes as a surprise to you. I've taken some of my things from the flat so there is no need for us to see each other. I hope we can both move on from this. Love Simone.'

'Well that's just brilliant,' Elliott proclaimed.

There had been a lot of things Elliott hadn't expected to happen this evening. Being fired. He hadn't expected that. Seeing ghosts. He definitely hadn't expected that. Simone leaving. He may not have expected it, but as he turned the key in the lock it didn't come as a total surprise either. He'd even considered leaving Simone on more than one occasion in the past. But faced with the fact that it was she that had left, and not the other way round, he couldn't help but feel more frustrated than upset. It was just one more disaster to have beset him on the strangest night of his life. But at least it couldn't get any worse. Walking through the door into the flat it seemed he had greatly underestimated the power of the universe to mess with him with one last time. When she'd wrote that she'd taken a few things, what she'd actually meant was that she'd taken absolutely everything. A sofa remained in the lounge along with the TV. The bed was still present in the bedroom, minus sheet and duvet. But that was pretty much it. It looked like someone had attempted a ram raid on the local Argos store but got his address by mistake.

'Fan...bloody...tastic!' Elliott exclaimed as he fell backwards onto the bed, incensed.

It was there he lay awake for the next couple of hours, unable to drift off. After all, he had a lot to think about.

Chapter 7

Come back Milk Tray Man, all is forgiven

Elliott awoke. His normal instinct would have been to check the time but as Simone had taken the clock radio this was proving difficult. Yet this wasn't his main gripe. He was more concerned with the light that the sun had sent in the direction of the Earth eight minutes previously. As Elliott attempted to open his eyes fully, each and every photon travelling through his bedroom window had the sole purpose of burning the retinas from his eye sockets. Curtains might have helped, if Simone hadn't taken these also. Elliott raised his head from the bare mattress and lifted himself from the bed, still dressed from the night before. It was probably around midday. Noon has a certain feel to it, and it felt like noon to Elliott. This was further confirmed by the theme tune of the lunchtime news blasting out of the TV next door, flowing uninhibited through the plasterboard wall that separated his flat from Mrs. Clarkson's flat next door.

Making his way from the bedroom, along the short corridor and into the front room he took in the horrifying sight that met him. Simone had been kind enough to leave the television, which was after all his, and surprisingly also the sofa. Obviously they were too heavy for the witch to carry. Next came an inspection of the kitchen, if you could call it that. Kitchens were usually defined by cutlery and the like. No such definition here.

As Elliott re-emerged into the lounge he inflated his cheeks and blew out in a masterful display of disappointment. It was bound to happen, he reasoned. In fact he was surprised it hadn't happened earlier. Still, it was a shame, they hadn't always been such a bad match. Elliott's mind began to drift to the better times they'd shared. The reminiscing came to an abrupt halt as he stared up and noticed she had also unscrewed the light-bulbs from their fittings.

'Well, that's just great,' Elliott exclaimed, wondering if life really could get any worse.

In the last twenty-four hours he had lost his job, his girlfriend and most of the items in the flat that weren't secured with six inch nails. On top of that he hadn't forgotten his rather disturbing encounter with the ghost of Hapkido Valentine. That was real, wasn't it? Elliott asked himself. That must have been some crazy dream, surely? Still, he had to be certain.

Remembering Hapkido Valentine's rather uncanny ability of appearing out of nowhere with the sole intention of making Elliott lose control of his bowels, he had to make sure he was alone. Walking back into the hallway he made his way over to the airing cupboard. If Elliott was going to hide somewhere, he would have chosen here.

'Ha!' Elliott shouted, flinging the door open to find only the boiler, a broom handle (minus head) and a coat hanger (minus coat). Elliott wasn't going to give in so easily though.

Concluding that the old 'under the bed trick' would be more likely he made his way back into the bedroom and approached the bed with some trepidation. Gradually, with one hand supporting him on the mattress, he lowered himself down to look underneath. Nothing, aside from a thick covering of dust and a map of Belgium — strange, considering he'd never been to Belgium.

As Elliott stood up he replayed the events of the evening before. The ghost of Hapkido Valentine hadn't seemed to want to hurt him. In fact, he was just as confused as Elliott had been. Therefore it was obvious that if the long dead wrestler was looking for answers, he wasn't going to find them in a flat on which squatters would soon have designs. Whatever happened last night was undoubtedly a one-off thing: there was no one in the flat aside from himself. And to think, in the time he'd been looking, he could've spent it doing something much more productive. Like going to the toilet as his bladder suddenly requested.

'Morning,' Hapkido Valentine boomed cheerfully as Elliott walked into the bathroom.

Elliott leapt involuntarily backwards, his sub-conscious

wanting no part of what it had just witnessed. The last thing Elliott had expected to see was the naked, hairy form of the wrestler taking a shower. That, and the fact that Hapkido still had his mask on. The spray from the shower travelled unhindered through the embroidered dragon mask and the rest of the wrestler's body, falling heavily at the far end of the bath. Despite this, Hapkido was going through the motions of washing, his hands moving across his hairy, protruding stomach before proceeding to underneath his arms. Opening his mouth to scream Elliott found no sound came out. Not knowing what else to do he simple backed away slowly and closed the door behind him.

The sudden awareness that the ghost of Hapkido Valentine had returned was hard to fathom as Elliott sat on the sofa, his head in his hands. How had he not heard the shower? Over the years he had become so used to waking and hearing Simone showering that it had become background noise. This morning had been no different, he hadn't registered the sound because he hadn't yet come to terms with her departure. Combine this with the sound of Mrs. Clarkson's television from next door — set at a volume that only the partially deaf and the Gods of Valhalla might tolerate — and it was all perfectly understandable.

Five minutes later Hapkido Valentine walked into the front room in his full wrestling ensemble, adjusting himself where the tight fitting Lycra outfit met spectral genitalia.

'Why me?' Elliott sighed as his hands slid from his face, his fingers tracing the hollows of his eyes before falling into a loose praying position near to his chest.

'What's your name by the way?' Hapkido asked, stretching as he did so.

'It's Elliott, Elliott Rose.'

'Good to meet you, my name is Hapkido Val...'

'...entine.' Elliott finished.

'Of course, I imagine you've seen me on television on a Saturday afternoon,' Hapkido stated, making his way across the room.

'Yeah, something like that,' Elliott replied.

'It is interesting that I find myself in your presence again,' Hapkido cogitated.

'I'm not sure *interesting* is the word I would use. *Terrifying* perhaps.'

'The time travel I've no doubt experienced appears to still be in its transitional stage. That would explain the fact that I don't seem quite solid just yet. When I do appear, I seem to be appearing in this time period. Each time I do so it seems to be in your presence.'

'I noticed,' Elliott sarcastically answered as his hand rubbed his forehead frantically.

'Somehow we seem to be linked.'

'Great,' Elliott sighed, his head tilting back to gaze at the ceiling.

'It could take some time to work this out. Any chance of a sausage sandwich?' Hapkido asked, his Midlands accent rising in scale.

Elliott's and Hapkido's attention was instantly diverted as the doorbell rang. Both exchanged glances, Elliott hesitating as to what to do next.

'Shouldn't you be getting that?' Hapkido suggested.

'But what if someone sees you?' Elliott replied.

'Oh I wouldn't worry about that.'

Elliott rose from the sofa and made his way along the hallway. Gingerly looking through the spyhole he saw Mrs. Clarkson, the critically deaf spinster from next door looking back.

How Elliott had come to be living next to an old lady was rather a long story. It wasn't just Mrs. Clarkson per se, the whole building was exclusively occupied by pensioners. It had been two years ago that he'd signed an extended lease with the landlord Mr. Smith. Quiet neighbours, he'd said. On hand security via a cord in the bathroom, he'd said. The one thing he had rather conveniently neglected to mention was that the flat was on the top floor of an old people's home.

'Morning Endsley,' Mrs. Clarkson announced as Elliott opened the door. In the two years he had lived there she had failed to get his name right even once. He would have corrected her but didn't get the chance as she slipped by him and into the flat with a combination of ninja skills and inappropriateness. It was a skill borne from the ancient trials of Saturday morning jumble sales.

'Morning Mrs. Clarkson,' Elliott replied frantically, trying to get between her and the front room.

She might be an intruding, name-forgetting old dear but he didn't want her to drop down dead from shock when she encountered the ghost of Hapkido Valentine in his front room. Unfortunately, she was heading towards her likely death willingly, weaving like a dysfunctional Exocet missile that flew with a strong fragrance of lavender. Elliott could do nothing but follow her into the front room, hoping that he could catch her when she fainted. She didn't. In fact she did nothing except tut loudly as she entered the front room. This was despite standing two feet away from the sofa upon which the bulk of Hapkido Valentine was now watching television. In the seconds Elliott had been away Hapkido had somehow changed channels to American wrestling which he was now watching intently.

'Is there a problem Mrs. Clarkson?' Elliott asked, hoping that maintaining a front of normality would explain away the strange scene within the room. She stopped tutting and turned around, her gaze passing by Hapkido without a flicker of recognition.

'Yes Endsley. I have a message for you from Simone. She's left you I'm afraid.'

'Okay,' Elliott replied, humouring her for the time being. He was amazed that she hadn't seen Hapkido.

'Last night, but it's probably best I don't go into details.'

'Please do,' Elliott asked, hoping to learn something further to the letter.

'I don't like to curse dear, but she said that you were a useless sack of shit.'

'Were those her exact words Mrs. Clarkson?' Elliott asked, taken aback by what he had heard.

'No dear, I toned it down for your benefit.'

It was at this point that Hapkido seemed to wake from his wrestling-induced trance.

'They call this wrestling? Not a patch on me in my prime!' Hapkido declared.

Elliott shuddered. Mrs. Clarkson carried on, regardless.

'Simone said you would understand why she had taken most of the things in the flat. Personally I thought she was taking too much and I said as much.'

'How exactly did she manage to move all the furniture on her own?' Elliott asked.

Elliott was prepared for the shocking news that she was seeing someone else, someone better. The ever helpful Mrs. Clarkson was happy to divulge.

'The furniture dear? I called my Grandson Trevor who was more than happy to help. He's such a good boy you know, twenty five now and ...'

Mrs. Clarkson was instantly drowned out by Hapkido Valentine making a statement from the sofa. 'I created that move in 19 bloody 76!'

'...still hasn't got a girlfriend though.' She finished, refusing to be interrupted.

'Well, thanks for coming round Mrs. Clarkson,' Elliott muttered as he tried to usher her towards the door. The attempt was pointless as she evaded the manoeuvre with ease, making her way across to the sofa. Elliott panicked.

'Mrs. Clarkson, please don't go over there. My friend is somewhat ...'

'What friend dear? You know I don't know why you watch this rubbish. I mean grown men, throwing themselves about like that,' she announced. 'Now Bargain Hunt, that's a good program.'

Mrs. Clarkson sat down slowly on the sofa. It wasn't a big sofa, and Hapkido wasn't a small man. He leapt with the agility of a man used to such sudden movements, perching himself on the arm of the chair, narrowly avoiding contact.

'Careful love, I was sitting there,' Hapkido stated as he stabilised himself.

Mrs. Clarkson settled back without a sense of anything untoward, switching the channel over.

'Didn't you see me?' Hapkido asked, annoyed.

Mrs. Clarkson didn't seem to hear this either.

'I do hope the red team wins today,' Mrs. Clarkson declared, all thoughts focused on the eccentric presenter with a wardrobe styled by the local lunatic asylum.

'I don't mean to be rude love, but is there a reason why you're ignoring me?' Hapkido asked, leaning over and giving her a deep meaningful stare from behind the embroidered dragon mask. It was a stare that had hypnotised hundreds, but its effect on Mrs. Clarkson was stunningly ineffective.

'You'll have to speak up, she's a little deaf,' Elliott clarified, forgetting for a moment that getting a frail old lady to communicate with a visitor from the netherworld was not a good idea.

'Who's deaf dear?' Mrs. Clarkson replied.

It wasn't the first time Elliott had experienced his next door neighbour's selective hearing which seemed to come and go when most convenient.

'No one Mrs. Clarkson. No one at all,' Elliott answered, shifting uncomfortably on his feet.

Hapkido meanwhile extended his gloved hand and waved it in front of her face. Mrs. Clarkson stared straight through, concentrating on the scene of an auction room on screen. The red team seemed to be making an instant loss on a poorly conceived purchase, or to give it its technical term, a piece of tat.

'Look, do me a favour and don't talk to her. This is already complicated as it is,' Elliott said towards Hapkido.

'Talk to whom dear? I know it must be hard to accept that Simone is gone but pretending she's still here won't help anyone. Now why don't you come and sit next to me and we can watch this together,' Mrs. Clarkson requested, patting the small space on the sofa next to her in an unappealing fashion.

Elliott would have done so if it weren't for two obvious reasons. The first was that he had no desire to watch daytime television with a (supposedly) deaf old woman. The second was that the space was already occupied by the boots of Hapkido Valentine as he sat on the arm of the sofa. It was already looking crowded over there.

'I'm fine thank you Mrs. Clarkson,' Elliott stalled, aware of how uncomfortable he looked standing.

'You know, I don't think she can see me,' Hapkido concluded.

Elliott had come to the same assumption but wasn't sure

whether this was a good or bad thing. If she couldn't see Hapkido then why could he? It wasn't easy to maintain a three-way conversation when the second person isn't aware of the third.

'I suspect that my transition from the previous time period is only apparent to certain individuals,' Hapkido surmised.

'It's because you're a ghost!' Elliott blurted out before realising he really should have kept quiet.

'A ghost dear? Who's a ghost?' Mrs. Clarkson asked, directing a stare towards Elliott. It was a gaze forged from a thousand bingo wins that had gone to someone else.

'A ghost...' Elliott panicked. 'A ghost of ... A ghost of Simone, it's like she's still here,' he cried, scrunching his eyes and hoping the over-dramatic display would convince her.

'No dear, didn't I mention it? She's left you.'

'It's an interesting development, her not being able to see me,' Hapkido commented. 'If my transition is not yet complete then that confirms that we are somehow linked. To complete the time travel something must be missing, something not yet discovered.'

Elliott was so desperate for this to start making sense that he found himself replying, regardless of Mrs. Clarkson, hoping that somehow he could muddle through the two conversations.

'Keep talking.'

'I wasn't talking dear,' Mrs. Clarkson answered.

'I know Mrs. Clarkson. It's just so nice to hear a woman's voice now that Simone has left,' Elliott replied, changing his focus back to her.

Elliott pursed his lips together, hoping it would indicate that he might burst out crying again at any moment. Such a poor display of acting would have seen him hounded out of an Australian soap opera as a disgrace to the profession. But this was all the invitation required for Mrs. Clarkson to review her trip to the corner shop last Tuesday. As she did so Hapkido continued speculating, his voice booming over the complaints about the price of bread.

'It is apparent,' Hapkido continued, 'that we have some important work to do. Once we deduce why we are linked then no doubt my time travel will become complete.'

'And then the doctor said my varicose veins weren't that bad!' Mrs. Clarkson unwittingly interrupted.

'I must admit,' Hapkido remarked, 'I'm finding it quite hard to concentrate with your friend here chatting about her continual health problems. Can't you get rid of her?'

'How?' Elliott asked.

'How, what did you mean dear?' Mrs. Clarkson asked.

'How.... did you find out about ...' Elliott flustered.

'My varicose veins dear? Well, it was in the bath six years ago,' Mrs. Clarkson continued, her conversation reinvigorated.

'I think I know a way I can make her leave,' Hapkido mused, a finger positioned over his lips. 'This transition between my time and yours has seen me pass through what I would describe as some kind of void. If I listen carefully I think I can make out the voices of other time travellers. I'm getting a voice coming through. I think his name is Ronald.'

'You're kidding me?' Elliott responded, pretty sure the only void Hapkido had travelled through was not inhabited by the living.

'Sorry dear, who am I kidding?' Mrs. Clarkson asked.

'Kidding about the price of bread,' Elliott replied.

'Do keep up Endsley, I was talking about that ages ago,' Mrs. Clarkson answered before launching headlong into an account of Mrs. Varney's haemorrhoids who lived down the hall.

'I'm hearing the voice clearer now,' Hapkido continued. 'He says his name is Ronald. It would seem he knows your next door neighbour. What's that? He was apparently her husband. Do you think she knows that he was a time traveller?'

Elliott sighed.

'What's that Ronald?' Hapkido asked. 'He says he's not a time traveller but ... well that's strange, he claims he's actually dead. Apparently he has a message for his wife that guarantees she will leave immediately.'

Elliott nodded his head in the wrestler's direction, suggesting that he would try anything at this point in time.

'Ronald's going to say it to me and I'll repeat it. You in turn repeat it to Mrs. Clarkson,' Hapkido instructed.

Elliott continued to nod.

'Dorothy,' Hapkido spoke clearly.

'Dorothy,' Elliott repeated.

'What's that dear?'

'I have a message from your husband Ronald,' Hapkido continued.

'I have a message from your husband Ronald,' Elliott stuttered.

'A message dear? From Ronald? I haven't the faintest clue what you are talking about?'

Hapkido began speaking and Elliott relayed a few seconds later, not contemplating the words he spoke.

'Ronald says he knows it wasn't really an accident. The electric fire that fell into his bath whilst plugged in — it wasn't really an accident. He forgives you for electrocuting him,' Elliott announced.

Elliott only realised what he'd said after he'd finished. He certainly wasn't prepared for the reaction he got. Mrs. Clarkson calmly got to her feet and approached Elliott, her face a model of serenity. The first Elliott knew of the slap was the stinging sensation across his face coupled with an overarching feeling of shock. Mrs. Clarkson, Elliott concluded, had obviously spent the last one hundred and forty years practicing the art of deploying her ring, attached to a vengeful hand, to maximum effect. Elliott raised his own hand and delicately checked for blood, surprised she hadn't cut the skin. Mrs. Clarkson was no doubt professional enough not to leave evidence. The action took Elliott less than ten seconds to complete but by that time Mrs. Clarkson had already stormed along the hall and out of the front door.

'Thanks a lot pal,' Elliott declared, rubbing his cheek as he turned towards Hapkido.

'I can't be held responsible for what is relayed from the void,' Hapkido replied. 'Besides, it was only a slap, I've faced much worse than that in the ring. There was this one time against Clive *'The Killer'* Morris when he had me in this head lock and ....'

Any chance of Hapkido finishing the story was interrupted by Elliott putting on his jacket.

'Where are you going?' Hapkido asked.

Elliott took a brief moment to stare at the ceiling despondently before replying.

'I need a pint.'

'Hang on. I'll come with you,' Hapkido announced.

'I thought you might,' Elliott replied, making his way out of the front door and closing it quickly behind him.

'Hey, what's going on? You've closed the door and I haven't even told you about how I escaped Clive *'The Killer'* Morris.'

Elliott picked up his pace, hoping that Hapkido's reluctance to accept himself as a ghost might extend to an aversion to walking through doors also.

Chapter 8

The Woodbine connection

Elliott had never wanted the lift to arrive sooner. Glancing back to the door of his flat, he fully expected the wrestler to emerge at any moment. Willing the lift to arrive he felt a trickle of sweat drip from his temple. After what seemed an eternity the lift arrived with a welcoming ping.

'Where was I? Oh yes, so anyway Clive has me in this headlock,' Hapkido announced, the doors sliding open to reveal his presence within.

'Oh for fuck's sake!' Elliott cried, throwing his hands into the air extravagantly.

A temporary silence ensued until Hapkido broke the quiet.

'So let me get this straight, you live in an old people's home?' Hapkido asked, gently chuckling to himself.

Faced with the inevitable outcome that whatever he did, Hapkido Valentine would be there regardless, Elliott acquiesced, moving into the lift alongside him.

'I suppose it's not too bad,' Elliott commented. 'The corridors aren't filled with arseholes trying to kill you, unless we're talking bingo night and they've taken some heavy losses. Plus I get a red triangle dangling in my bathroom in case I have a heart attack.'

'Yes but that's not very likely given you're at least fifty years younger than everyone else here,' Hapkido suggested, tapping his foot with a distinct lack of sound as they waited for the doors to close.

'I don't know, seeing as you've set up residency in my flat, the chances have somewhat increased I'd say.'

Finally the doors slid closed and the lift descended a floor. With an accompanying chime the doors slid open to reveal two old age pensioners. Looking slightly surprised they shuffled into the lift.

'Good afternoon Ainsley,' the first old lady announced as she entered.

'Hello Mrs. Kirk,' Elliott replied in turn.

'Afternoon Eamon,' the second old lady added as she followed behind.

'Hello Mrs. Laithwaite.'

'Good afternoon ladies,' Hapkido announced, accompanied by a wink. Yes, it really was the great Hapkido Valentine they had seen. Except they hadn't seen him: no one but Elliott had.

A further two floors down the lift halted to allow the old ladies to exit. Elliott stood confounded as they passed Hapkido without a hint of recognition.

For the rest of the elevator's journey to the ground floor both Hapkido and Elliott stood in silence, complemented by a synthesiser version of Yesterday as it descended. Arriving, the doors slid open to reveal a long corridor stretching out before them. Half way down two elderly men were sitting on hard-backed chairs, each one positioned within the door frame of their respective flats. As Elliott and Hapkido walked down the corridor, the elderly, well rounded man to the right who brandished a cigar in his hand, spoke as they passed.

'Greetings, young man.'

'Hello Winston.' Elliott replied.

Looking to his left he decided that it was only polite to also say hello to the man sitting opposite.

'Hello Colin.'

The elderly man on the left had a more drawn stature, his hair slicked down, a square moustache ominously hovering above his top lip. He allowed a brief pause before replying to Elliott in an eruptive, confrontational tone.

'Willst du meine zwiebeln kaufen!' Colin shouted, accompanied with a short upwards motion of the arm.

Elliott didn't speak German. At least that's what he presumed the language was. So like countless times before he chose not to reply. He had no desire to get drawn into a long conversation that he had little chance of understanding.

Reaching the end of corridor, the sunshine shining through the glass panels of the exit, Hapkido felt that it was appropriate to ask.

'Those two old men, they didn't half look like ...'

'Easy mistake to make,' Elliott clarified. 'Winston used to work on the railways and Colin, well something to do with tents. He keeps mentioning Meine Camp or something like that.'

'Fair enough,' Hapkido replied, dismissing the notion.

Both walked out of the door and into the car park, striding onwards towards the local village with a sense of purpose.

*

First stop on Elliott's list was the local corner shop. Due to Simone having taken any semblance of food the previous night, supplies were most definitely required. The bell above the door chimed as Elliott entered, the man stationed behind the counter giving a cursory glance in his direction. After picking up a sandwich, Elliott headed in the direction of the biscuit section. Hapkido meanwhile trailed behind, persistently asking questions. Considering the convoluted conversation he had already had with Mrs. Clarkson, Elliott chose not to answer. People who talk to themselves were usually crazy and corner shops were a prime attraction for such individuals. Hapkido, growing tired of not gaining any response, chose instead to concentrate on studying the biscuits on display.

'Hob Knobs!' Hapkido shouted with disgust. 'What the hell kind of biscuit is that? Filth!'

It was that sort of comment which reassured Elliott that they should keep their conversations to a minimum.

*

In the early afternoon, pubs are miserable affairs. Loyal customers are often typified as alcoholics, the unemployed and those suffering from mental illness. By coincidence, Elliott satisfied at least two of these criteria to the casual observer. As he entered he noticed the group of men drinking heavily at the far end of the bar, conversing loudly on a variety of subjects reminiscent of The Daily Mail editorial column. And judging by their naked upper torsos, clad only in fluorescent yellow waistcoats that rustled with the movement of hand to pint, they were no doubt builders that liked to lunch on the liquid side.

Elliott made his way silently to the bar as Hapkido diverted towards the fruit machine. The glittering array of flashing lights seemed to fascinate him.

'What can I get you?' The barman asked.

'Just a pint of lager please.'

'I'll have a pint if you're getting them in,' Hapkido commanded as he crouched down, peering intently at the tops of the reels as if he had nudges in play.

'And a ...' Elliott wavered, not sure why he was ordering a pint for a dead man.

'I'll have a pint of stout,' Hapkido relayed.

'And a pint of stout.' Elliott concluded, sighing as he did so.

'Bit thirsty are you mate?' The barman asked.

Making his way over to the pump he proceeded to deliver a full bodied pint for the least bodied person present.

'Something like that,' Elliott replied, casting a glance towards Hapkido who was now busy adjusting himself down below through his costume.

Less than a minute later the barman had placed the drinks on the bar. As Elliott paid Hapkido wandered over and looked down at his pint.

'Can you carry that for me?' Hapkido requested.

'Any reason?' Elliott asked, sarcastically. Aware the barman had gone to the other end of the bar to serve the raucous builders he was confident he wouldn't be heard.

'Just, well you know…' Hapkido spluttered, gesturing with his hands wildly in the hope that it would explain.

'Because you're a ghost perhaps?' Elliott enquired with a raising of the eyebrows.

'A ghost? Don't be stupid, just an old wrestling injury,' Hapkido snorted, shaking his wrist as if it had suddenly begun hurting that very instant.

'Fair enough,' Elliott answered, taking both pints and moving away to the furthest table from anyone else. If he was going to have a conversation with someone that evidently no one else could see, he should at least do it in privacy. The table he finally sat down at backed onto a set of patio doors that led onto the car park outside.

'So what are you going to do for money now that you've lost your job and your missus has left you?' Hapkido enquired bluntly as he sat down opposite Elliott on a heavily varnished wooden chair that was already askew from the table. His question had all the subtlety of a monkey crash landing the space shuttle into someone's front room and then asking for a banana.

'Thanks for reminding me pal. Just to be clear, why is it exactly you are still following me around?'

'We are linked somehow. You losing your job, your girlfriend leaving you. This coupled with my sudden appearance leads me to suspect that there is a greater purpose for the both of us.'

'Of course,' Elliott responded, rolling his eyes.

Elliott couldn't fail to notice the pint of stout that remained untouched on the other side of the table. Instead of drinking it the wrestler reached around to where his back superficially met the chair and with a grunt pulled out a packet of tobacco. Where this had been concealed was a question for which Elliott did not need an answer.

'You going outside?' Elliott asked, desperately hoping that Hapkido would get lost whilst out there.

'Outside. Why?'

'You can't smoke that in here.'

'I don't see anyone complaining, do you? Hapkido replied, rolling up a cigarette and lighting it. As the smoke drifted from his nostrils, Elliott took a moment to look around. Unsurprisingly no one seemed to be taking a blind bit of notice.

'So anyway,' Hapkido resumed, 'until we work out *how* we are linked, I think it is only fair that I help you out with your current financial situation. I have, after all, spent many years learning the ancient samurai codes which could be hugely beneficial to someone in your situation.'

'How exactly?' Elliott asked despondently.

'Well, you are without a job and judging by the poor excuse I saw for wrestling on television this morning, the world is crying out for someone like me. Well, *you*, to be precise.'

'You want me to become a wrestler?' Elliott asked,

incredulously.

'I admit you are perhaps not a classic type for the sport,' Hapkido commented before leaning in and whispering. 'One of the most important skills in martial arts is to use your enemy's strength against him.'

'Wax on, wax off, right?'

'Not with you. Listen, just think about it. With my teaching you could become the next Hapkido Valentine.'

'I'm going to pass if you don't mind. I'll tell you why. For starters, I don't think the world is ready for a wrestler who has learnt his trade from a ghost.'

'Time traveller!' Hapkido corrected.

'Secondly, I have no desire to have my face bashed in for the sake of entertainment.'

'You soon get used to it.'

'Thirdly, wrestling in this country hasn't been shown on television for years now.'

'All the more reason for you to lead by example,' Hapkido persisted.

'Listen,' Elliott spoke forcefully, a little louder than he would have liked. 'I am not, I repeat, not going to become a wrestler because the ghost, sorry time traveller, Hapkido Valentine told me to do so.'

'I really do think this is a golden opportunity for you.'

'I said no!'

'The ancient art of the samurai comes in handy in a number of other circumstances also.' Hapkido suggested.

'Like when exactly?' Elliott enquired.

'Like now.'

Hapkido's eyes darted to the left, signalling someone approaching from behind. Elliott's gaze was drawn over his shoulder and saw one of the builders approaching, Elliott's raised voice obviously having attracted him.

'Oi mate! You do realise you're talking to yourself don't yer?' The builder slurred as he approached.

'Bad habit. Just thinking a few things over,' Elliott replied, hoping this would convince him to return to his side of the pub.

'You're one of those nutters aren't yer?'

'No, no. Just trying to work a few things out.'

'Bloody nutters, ruining my lunchtime drink you are.'

'Looks like he wants a fight,' Hapkido unhelpfully contributed.

'Look, I don't want any trouble. I just came in for a drink,' Elliott appealed.

Suddenly the drunkenness in his face drained as the builder's barely concealed fighting instinct came to the fore, such is the wont with arseholes. His face became hard and unforgiving in an instant.

'Did you say I stink?' The builder roared, advancing menacingly.

'No, I said drink. It's just bad luck that you thought you heard me say ....'

'Did you just call me a fuck?'

'You can take him,' Hapkido advocated. 'Remember, use his strength against him.'

'I'm not fighting him,' Elliott blurted out in frustration. It was then he realised that speaking into a seemingly empty space was the last thing he should be doing.

'You want a fight? If that's the way you want it!'

Before Elliott could think of anything further, alarmingly he found himself being pulled from the chair by his jumper, his feet moving, failing to find the floor.

'Leave this to me,' Hapkido commented, raising himself from his chair opposite with a sure-fire confidence.

Elliott's initial reaction was of a sense of relief. Hapkido had come to the rescue, somehow. This thought quickly dissipated as the wrestler seemed to fade as he stood. Well that was absolutely no help at all, Elliott thought. As the builder pushed Elliott backwards he stumbled over the table, knocking over the chair yet managing to stay on his feet.

'You fucking little shit!' The builder shouted, little arcs of saliva flying through the air.

Managing to stabilise himself Elliott looked back up. Wretchedly the first thing he saw was the builder drawing back his arm and forming a fist.

Then something strange happened.

All of a sudden he could hear a distant hum. A warmth seemed to spread through his body, an energy snapping at his synapses, an electricity charging his being. To describe it would have been difficult; to identify it, impossible. Strange thoughts raced through his mind, trying to find something to latch onto. They were thoughts that didn't seem to belong.

The teachings of the samurai are the one true path to spiritual enlightenment.

A persistent image of an old lady sitting in a chair in a house he recognised. Yet he knew he had never been there.

The flash of a golden jumpsuit.

The images flicked in front of his mind before fading, replaced by a sudden sense of purpose.

There was nothing to fear.

He could beat anyone!

Within a fraction of a second he moved his head instinctively to the left, the builder's fist flying wildly to the right. Instantly he knew his method of counter-attack.

Elliott Rose fixed the builder with a stare.

It was a stare of staggering proportions: determined, intimidating … and pointless. The builder threw another punch, catching Elliott on the cheek and sending him sprawling over the table and down to the floor. Through a sense of shock Elliott could sense others approaching. Luckily, through hazy vision, the builder's mates who were neither as drunk, nor such arseholes, were restraining him. A chorus of *'come on, he's not worth it,'* followed before they led him away reluctantly.

Elliott lay crumpled on the floor, rubbing his tender cheek as the form of Hapkido Valentine materialised above him.

'Okay, so maybe wrestling's not for you,' Hapkido remarked.

Chapter 9

The Brotherhood of Jam

As the lift door slid open at Elliott's floor he could hear a multitude of voices up ahead. There was obviously some sort of gathering behind one of the doors, probably Mrs. Clarkson and her gang discussing inconvenient Post Office opening times. Elliott however hardly registered it, fuming as he was as to what had occurred in the pub. His main objective was to get to his flat where he could open the packet of biscuits in the carrier bag he was holding. That might make things a bit better.

'Don't do that again!' Elliott reiterated for the fourth time as he and Hapkido left the confines of the elevator.

'Do what again?' Hapkido asked.

'The whole possession thing! I got punched in the face because of you,' Elliott replied angrily, touching the side of his face tenderly. His cheekbone throbbed incessantly and now sported a deep purple bruise.

'I was merely trying to help. If you had given yourself to my will completely we could have taken him easily. I am, after all, one of the greatest wrestlers in Britain.'

'Jesus! How many times do I have to tell you? You *were* one of the greatest, now you're simply a ghost, obsessed with some crazy-arse hypnotism shit.'

Elliott took his key out as he got to the door, his lips pursed in barely concealed rage.

'If I can make one correction,' Hapkido suggested, 'when you say ghost, I presume you actually mean time traveller?'

'Ghost, time traveller, I don't care,' Elliott replied forcefully. 'Look, I'm not best pleased so I would be grateful if you could leave me alone for a while.'

'I understand,' Hapkido replied with a nod of the head.

'Good,' Elliott asserted, pushing the door and making his way into the flat. As he turned and closed the door behind him, he kept his eyes on Hapkido who remained outside, looking dejected and confused.

'At last,' Elliott muttered as the door closed. Turning he made his way into the living room.

'So, what's the plan now then?' Hapkido boomed, standing in the middle of the living room with his hands on his hips.

'Oh for fuck's sake!' Elliott exclaimed loudly. The bag containing the biscuits fell to the floor.

'Careful, I was hoping for some of those,' Hapkido admitted.

'What are you doing here? Do you not remember what I asked less than ten seconds ago?'

'I've already told you haven't I? We need to find out what links the two of us.'

Elliott made his way over to the sofa and collapsed into it. He was starting to suspect that the only thing that linked the two of them was that Hapkido Valentine was the most persistent ghost in history and he was clearly the unluckiest man alive.

'I don't suppose if I asked again, you would just leave me alone forever?' Elliott asked, sighing.

'Now what about one of those biscuits?' Hapkido countered.

Regardless of what Elliott had done to deserve this, he was quickly coming to an inevitable conclusion. Hapkido seemed destined to stay for a while. And that meant the whole bizarre, crazy situation was far from over. Elliott stood up from the sofa and proceeded to the kitchen where he found the one plate that Simone had left in a moment of unbridled generosity. Returning to the front room he picked up the biscuits from where he had let them drop and after opening them, let them slide onto the plate, each one resting at an angle against the next. Yet before Elliott could pick one up or Hapkido could even begin the pretence of actually eating one, the doorbell rang. In response Elliott and Hapkido exchanged a glance.

'Who's that?' Elliott asked.

'I have no idea.'

'Great. So you can talk to Mrs. Clarkson's dead husband but you can't tell me who is at the door? Hey, maybe it's Gentleman Jim back from the dead as well?' Elliott replied, making his way towards the door and opening it.

'Hello Elliott,' Carol spoke, leaning against the doorframe in the most seductive pose she could muster. Her voice was so gravelly she could have come straight from losing the regional finals of Miss Lambert & Butler, mature division.

'Carol,' Elliott replied, surprised yet attempting formality.

'Well, aren't you going to invite me in?' Carol asked.

Without waiting for actual permission she sauntered in, letting her hand lightly trail across Elliott's chest as she brushed past him.

Elliott simply threw his hands into the air. Didn't anyone actually ever ask to enter someone's flat nowadays? Following Carol into the living room he was pretty sure that she would be the last person who would notice Hapkido Valentine standing there. Despite being UK television's prime ghost hunter she had seen fewer ghosts than he, and he had only managed the one, albeit reluctantly. As he followed he couldn't help but notice the purposeful sway of her hips, the slow, sensual walk. She was after something for sure and the approach she would be taking was fairly evident. It wouldn't have been the first time she'd tried to seduce him. For years she had been persistently unwilling to acknowledge the boundary between employer and employee, a situation Elliott had no desire to encourage. More importantly, until recently he'd been in a relationship with Simone, a woman intent on amassing a plethora of expensive household items for future theft.

'We need to talk,' Carol declared, walking to the far side of the room and past the ghost of Hapkido Valentine without a flicker of recognition. As she leant with her back up against the wall, her pose was more Mrs. Slocombe from Are You Being Served than the intended Mrs. Robinson from The Graduate.

'What about?' Elliott asked, hardly failing to notice Hapkido Valentine eyeing her up with a vengeance.

'Look Elliott, we may all have been a bit hasty last night. Maybe we can sort things out?'

'Sort what out?' Elliott enquired angrily. 'A redundancy package to stop me going to the papers about what your show is really like?'

Suddenly the air of casualness in the room dissipated in an

instant. Carol came forward, going up on her tiptoes and whispering in Elliott's ear.

'If a single word gets out to the papers about any of our production methods,' Carol muttered, 'I will make sure that you never work again.'

As she finished she gave a quick downwards glance at Elliott's body. He assumed she was either looking at his crotch or further down to his knees and their suitability for having a bar smashed across them. Either way it was a serious threat.

'Feisty, I like it,' Hapkido commented, his words reaching Elliott's ears only.

'Okay, I won't go to the papers,' Elliott replied flustered. 'It's just lot of things have happened since last night.'

'I wouldn't tell her if I were you,' Hapkido suggested, stating the obvious.

'Elliott, Elliott…' Carol spoke slowly with intent, 'I'm sure we can work something out. After all, neither of us wants you to be out of a job.'

Elliott recognised that there was a chance here that he could actually get his job back if he played it just right.

'I just wanted you to know Carol, last night, my failure to … heighten production values was not exactly my fault.'

'Elliott, I know what natural impulses are like,' Carol replied.

'Absolutely,' Elliott replied, trying to give the impression of naivety.

'I admit I was somewhat hasty to sack you on the spot like that. But I was mad and sometimes you act on natural impulse without thinking. You do understand don't you?' Carol replied, letting the tip of her tongue play against the corner of her mouth.

'Dirty girl, I like it!' Hapkido contributed.

'Sometimes we have to act on those impulses wouldn't you say? Sometimes when leaving a job, and then deciding that you need it back we have to make certain concessions,' Carol suggested, running her hand through her hair above the right ear.

'I agree,' Elliott replied timidly.

The words tumbled from his mouth regardless of their effect. He was flustered but he needed time to think. He needed the job,

Christ he needed a whole lot more than that, but a job was as good a place as any to start. Yet, it was obvious what Carol was implying. Could he really bring himself to sleep with her to just get his job back? Was he really that shallow? Yet, he was single now and she wasn't that unattractive was she? He had to make a decision. Carol winked one of her heavily mascaraed eyes suggestively like a panda taking a trip to an ophthalmologist. Elliott opened his mouth to reply.

DING DONG!

The sound of the doorbell reverberated throughout the flat. Elliott had been so overwrought with inner turmoil that he said the first thing that came to mind.

'Thank fuck for that!'

'What?' Carol replied indignantly, her body previously coiled in attempted seduction now at odds with the situation.

'The door bell, I was expecting a....' Elliott replied, flummoxed, desperate for something to come to mind.

'Just get the door, Elliott,' Carol ordered, maddened.

'Of course,' Elliott replied and flew down the hall like a flash. As he approached the door he quietly whispered to himself. 'If I'm lucky it's another dead wrestler, if not it's Carol's twin sister.'

'Hello Endsley,' Mrs. Clarkson announced as he opened the door.

His next door neighbour's presence wasn't surprising in itself. What was more surprising however was the accumulation of old women crowded behind her.

'Hello Mrs. Clarkson, I'm a bit busy at the moment.'

'Don't worry dear, this won't take a moment,' she replied, slipping into the flat with the utmost stealth and the least most invitation.

Once Mrs. Clarkson had entered there was no stopping the rest of them, the collection of old women filing into his flat hurriedly. Before he could close the door behind them he was taken aback by Mrs. Clarkson appearing a mere six inches from his face.

'Any talk of baths and electric heaters sunshine and I'll have your fucking balls in a meat grinder, you understand me?' She conveyed menacingly.

'Yes, Mrs. Clarkson,' Elliott replied, instantly submissive when confronted with such aggression.

Almost as if her previous statement had never happened she flitted off to the front room to join the half of Croydon that had already congregated there. Elliott followed, arriving to find the group of women standing four deep around the plate of biscuits. Hands darted in and out, grabbing the biscuits like hyenas gathered around a freshly killed carcass in the Serengeti. The only difference here was that in the amount of time it took the biscuits to disappear a hyena would only just be starting to think *'Raw flesh, just the sort of thing to brighten up my day.'*

'This is Endsley, girls. He's the one I told you about,' Mrs. Clarkson announced.

Elliott racked his brain. Was he in trouble? What could he possibly have done to have upset half of Croydon's Elite Bridge Club? Before he could contemplate further, one of the women to the side of Mrs. Clarkson stepped forward and spoke.

'You know things don't you?' She declared, her voice taking the tone of an old crone. In truth, the speaker, Mrs. Winterbottom, had quite a normal voice but she thought it fitting to speak as if she were born in a cave in the sixteenth century for some reason known only to herself.

'I'm sorry, I don't know what you're talking about.'

'Don't mess us around sunshine,' Mrs. Clarkson interrupted with a glint in her eye. The glint conveyed a thousand words but the most important ones were, *'I've killed one husband already and I don't need a wedding ceremony to make you the second.'*

'I'm sorry ladies, I really don't know what you mean,' Elliott replied.

As Elliott spoke he scanned the faces of the old women. With every word he dared to utter they were getting more and more agitated. He also caught Carol watching the scene from the sofa with a touch of suspicion and a hell of a lot of confusion. Hapkido in turn was sat next to Carol, looking relentlessly at her ample bosom.

'Look sonny,' one of the women piped up, Dorothy tells us you can communicate with the dead. She told us you managed to speak to her Ronald. The last time she spoke to him was just before he died saving that child from drowning in the river.'

Elliott was going to say something but words deserted him. He simply imagined that the only diving into a river Ronald had done was when Mrs. Clarkson had dumped his body from a wheelbarrow.

'Look, either you can talk to the dead or you can't,' Mrs. Clarkson questioned. 'We can wait here all day if that's what it takes.'

Elliott was confronted with a simple choice. He either started talking to the dead or a gang of angry old women remained in his flat. They had already helped themselves to one of the other packets of biscuits. Eventually they would run out and that could well lead to violence. He needed help. Elliott coughed loudly, hoping to gain the attention of Hapkido.

'What?' Hapkido answered, looking up reluctantly from Carol's cleavage.

Elliott coughed again, attempting to convey that Hapkido was needed, desperately.

'Oh right, you want me to talk to those in the void again, okay, no problem.'

'So,' Elliott spoke, addressing the crowd with his palms facing them. 'You want me to speak to those who have passed over.'

Hapkido filed over, giving Carol an unseen wink as he went and stood behind Elliott. The wrestler was a good foot taller and several stone heavier.

'Well, don't keep us waiting,' Mrs. Winterbottom demanded. 'Can you talk to my Bert or not?'

Elliott stood with his eyes closed to give the impression that he was actually doing something. As he did so Hapkido emitted a low hum, for some reason an integral part of communicating with the deceased. It seemed to go on for an eternity, certainly not helped when Elliott recognised the poorly concealed theme tune to Crossroads at one point.

'I'm getting someone coming forward from the void. Just repeat what I say,' Hapkido declared. Elliott in turn relayed the information to the waiting crowd.

'Yes I have a Bert,' Elliott spoke. 'He says he misses Deborah very much. Can I call you Deborah, Mrs. Winterbottom?'

'No you can't.'

'Bert says he misses you very much,' Elliott added, too busy attempting to repeat the words of Hapkido than be offended. He was expecting the revelation from her loving husband to maybe bring on a few tears.

'Just ask him where the fucking money is sonny!' Mrs. Winterbottom replied, angrily.

'Under the third step on the staircase,' Hapkido added immediately.

'Under the third step on the staircase,' Elliott repeated without thinking.

Mrs. Winterbottom, obviously not one for thanks or for that matter pleasantries, made her way down the hall and through the door without a moment's hesitation. Elliott in turn looked at the crowd, expecting them to be shocked at what they had heard. Instead all he saw were faces filled with anticipation.

'Me next,' Mrs. Levison announced, stepping out from the mass, her weight in stone roughly equivalent to her age. Her uncanny resemblance to a six foot by eight foot brick wall with a crew cut was enough to spur Elliott onwards.

And so on it went. For each old woman who presented herself, Hapkido spoke to the other side. Elliott successively passed on the information. As he did so there didn't seem a lot of love in the room but whatever the message was, they seemed happy enough. One by one the crowd thinned until finally the only people remaining were Elliott, Mrs. Clarkson, Hapkido and Carol. The latter had spent the entire time watching with interest.

'You did well Endsley,' Mrs. Clarkson stated as she prepared to leave.

'Thank you Mrs. Clarkson,' Elliott replied, completely knackered from the endeavour.

'Oh, and one last thing,' she added as she began walking down the hall. 'I've arranged the Women's Institute to convene tomorrow at one o'clock at the local community centre. I trust you can make it.'

Elliott was dumbfounded. He had only gone along with the whole thing to get some peace and now it looked like he was being asked to perform in front of a crowd.

'You see the thing is Mrs. Clarkson, I'm not actually a...' Elliott stuttered, trying desperately to find the words. It would have been a lot easier if it weren't for the fact that Hapkido Valentine was now leaning over his shoulder and making an electrical buzzing sound. Elliott didn't know what sound an electrical heater made when it was plunged into a bath but he was guessing that Hapkido's impression wasn't a hundred miles off.

'Oh don't worry dear; you'll get paid for it,' Mrs. Clarkson confirmed, walking out the door.

Now there were three. It was Carol's turn now, rising from the sofa, no doubt intent on continuing their previous conversation. Elliott's thoughts came back to her proposition moments before. He needed a job but could he really bring himself to do what she was so obviously implying? Just for a job? Something Mrs. Clarkson said suddenly offered an avenue of escape. She had mentioned being paid hadn't she?

'Very impressive,' Carol announced, clapping her hands as she approached.

It all became apparent to Elliott in an instant. Even if he passed on a message from Jack the Ripper saying that he had Carol's home address, nothing would quench the sexual appetite of the country's foremost paranormal investigator. If he said no, there would be no job. And if there was one thing Elliott hated, it was being manipulated. Could he really make enough money out of a bunch of biscuit-stealing old women whose collective blue rinses could act as a warning beacon for light aircraft?

'Well, have you made a decision?' Carol enquired.

'Yes I have,' Elliott replied with determination. 'You can stick your job. I've got bigger plans.'

'What?' Carol answered, her face slipping from seductive temptress to disjointed scowl.

'You heard me,' Elliott replied.

'You're making a big mistake,' Carol responded curtly.

'That's my final answer,' Elliott concluded.

Carol wasn't a person who got turned down. She was angry and she wasn't afraid to show it.

'Let me tell you something. No one turns down Carol Swanson, no one! You'll live to regret this, you hear me?'

Elliott didn't get a chance to respond. Carol stormed out of the flat, slamming the door behind her. Proceeding over to the sofa Elliott collapsed into it, blowing out his cheeks as he did so. It was over and it felt good.

'You're a bloody idiot!' Hapkido declared, sitting down beside Elliott.

'What?'

'I can't believe you turned her down. You only get one chance with a woman like that.'

'Oh well,' Elliott replied with a smile.

'And you let all those old women in and they stole our biscuits.'

'Never mind that,' Elliott declared, sitting upright with a sense of enthusiasm. 'With your powers and my ability to actually be seen by others, we *could* make a lot of money here.'

'I was wondering how long it would take for you to work that out.'

'Well, what do you say?' Elliott asked.

'Okay. But there are things I will need you to do as we embark on this journey,' Hapkido countered.

'What things?'

'That, my friend, is part of the journey itself. Now if you're feeling generous I'd kill for a sausage sandwich.'

Chapter 10

Today strawberry preserve, tomorrow the world

Elliott was having a lovely dream, until things became somewhat odd. Somewhere between the states of dreaming and wakefulness, Elliott's fleeting thoughts became supplemented by a warm fuzzy feeling that rose and fell in accompaniment. As he tried to grasp these thoughts they slipped away, obscured by a sense of ambiguity. Were they even thoughts? Elliott wondered as he became more aware. Was it not more a sensation? Of wearing something perhaps, close to the skin. Lycra maybe? He could feel the texture, between his hand and genitals. That wasn't that unusual was it, the cupping action? But the Lycra, that didn't seem to make sense. The sense of being asleep was dissipating quickly.

Hand.

Lycra.

Genitals!

Elliott's eyes opened with a jolt! Instantly the thoughts that were paramount in the dream only moments before raced away. Almost as if they were the flashes of another's mind.

It subsequently took less than ten seconds for Elliott to fall out of bed, scramble across to his trousers and force them on before racing out of the bedroom and into the front room. Hapkido Valentine, sitting on the sofa, looked up to observe Elliott's frantic arrival.

'You were doing that possession thing again weren't you?' Elliott shouted, standing above the wrestler in anger and distaste.

'No,' Hapkido responded with such exaggeration it instantly betrayed his guilt. A nun lost in a cave system for twenty years wouldn't have believed him.

'You were, you bastard. Don't deny it.'

'Oh okay, yes I was. But I was just trying something new.'

'What? Touching another man's bits? I told you that you weren't to do that possession thing again. Last time I got smacked in the face.'

'If you must know,' Hapkido replied, 'I was trying to communicate telepathically.'

'Via my penis?'

'I didn't say I'd got it quite right yet. The art of telepathy was attained by a few select samurai *but* only after many attempts.'

'Hang on,' Elliott interrupted as a brilliant thought extinguished the anger. 'Telepathy. Can you actually do that? You know what this means don't you?'

'No need to use the phone?' Hapkido asked.

'No you idiot. If we could do this then I wouldn't have to talk to you out loud so that others in the room think I'm a lunatic.'

The seeds of Elliott's brilliant plan had actually formed the night before. As he'd lain awake in bed, trying not to notice the snoring of Hapkido Valentine that permeated the adjoining wall, his thoughts had wandered. For years he had witnessed Jeremy Flashman make a small fortune out of talking to the dead and he was just making it up. Elliott, on the other hand, actually had a ghost who could do it for real. Granted, he was a ghost who didn't respect personal boundaries, but a ghost he most definitely was. If, for whatever reason, Elliott was stuck with him then at least he could make some money out of the situation.

'Try again,' Elliott exclaimed enthusiastically.

'You sure?'

'Absolutely. You try and speak to me telepathically and I'll see if I get anything.'

Hapkido turned and stared in Elliott's direction. Elliott in turn tried to clear his mind.

'KyzbzytuSa4xkiUsa1ge7xw'

The words, if you could describe them as such, came racing into Elliott's mind. What did they mean? He had no idea. It didn't seem to make any sense. Despite this he did know that it wasn't him thinking them.

'Try again.' Elliott announced.

'*KtzvSan5ndl5q9xWi2ch.*'

'And again.'

'*Mt$qqrPle5asjee.*'

On the third attempt Elliott was starting to become frustrated. Just this once it would've been nice if this one thing had worked. Resignedly, Elliott closed his eyes and sighed.

'*Any chance of a sausage sandwich?*'

The words burst into his mind, complete with a Midlands accent.

'It worked!' Elliott declared excitedly. 'It bloody worked.'

'Well of course it did.'

'It bloody worked. Go on say something else.'

'*I really do fancy a sausage sandwich.*'

'I don't believe it, it bloody worked.'

'Of course, although technically speaking, if we are going to speak telepathically then you need to speak back.'

'Absolutely, let's give it a whirl,' Elliott replied, enthused, feeling anything was possible.

Elliott scrunched his eyes up with an immense concentration as Hapkido Valentine sat upright on the sofa. Tilting his head to one side, he started to receive Elliott's thoughts in return.

'*Can you hear me?*'

Hapkido nodded his head.

'*Okay. I'm going to send you an important message. Tell me if you get it.*'

'Okay, I'll make my own sausage sandwich. There's no need to be rude about it,' Hapkido replied, reverting to the more traditional way of speaking.

'This is amazing!' Elliott announced eagerly. 'We can actually communicate telepathically.'

'So we can.'

Hapkido's reply made its way clearly into Elliott's perception. It was so unexpected and seemingly easy to accomplish it took a few seconds for Elliott to realise he should continue the telepathic conversation. Such a momentous occasion demanded a fitting response.

'Fuck a duck!'

'I'd rather not. You know what this means don't you.'

'What?'

'It means that you no longer have to talk into thin air when addressing me.'

'That would be handy, what with you being an invisible time traveller and all.'

Elliott was so impressed that sarcasm seemed to travel along the telepathic pathway just as easily, he inadvertently let his concentration slip. As he did so the connection between them began to fade. Before he could re-establish it, Hapkido spoke, pouring forth the words into the real world.

'As interesting as this is, you do realise that it's now twelve thirty? In case you'd forgotten we have an appointment with the local Women's Institute at one o'clock to demonstrate your *amazing* powers,' Hapkido declared with his own hefty dose of sarcasm, waving his hands about in a mocking fashion.

Elliott looked at his watch. Hapkido was right. For this great plan for fame and fortune to work he couldn't miss his big moment. And if this wasn't enough of a reason to get to the leisure centre forthwith, then the fact that the television flickered on and off at that point was. It could have been a simple power surge. There could even have been something supernatural about it, given Elliott's current house guest. More likely it was a fluctuation in the buildings electricity supply as an electrical heater was thrown into a bath-tub, Mrs. Clarkson no doubt practicing in case he didn't show. Elliott was dressed and out of the door in less than two minutes with Hapkido trailing quickly behind.

*

As Elliott and Hapkido walked into the room it was already approaching capacity. Those already present had a combined age to rival the birth of the Universe and some may have even been there to witness it. A constant nattering emanated from the various groups, no doubt discussing how stamps had been much cheaper when the first stars were forming.

'Elliott my boy!' Boomed a confident voice.

Appearing from behind a proximal cluster of old women, Jeremy Flashman weaved his way through the knotted groups and walked up to Elliott. His crocodile skin shoes shone with a luminance that could rob the sight of a blind man for a second time. His beige trousers came with a crease so severe that with one false move Elliott could have lost an arm. The shirt was fairly normal - normal that is for forty years ago. Expertly unbuttoned to the bottom of his chest it revealed the golden medallion that nestled snugly in the dense forest of hair.

'Hello Jeremy,' Elliott replied despondently.

'I thought I'd find you here. Carol asked if I could come and have a chat.'

'Any reason?' Elliott sighed disconsolately, aware of exactly the type of chat he meant.

'It seems you've been making quite an impression on our local community,' Flashman replied, signalling with a nod of the head towards the growing number of old women. 'Carol mentioned something about you demonstrating your psychic powers. The minute I heard about it, I just knew that I should come for a chat. After all I've been through exactly the same thing.'

'I'm sure you have.' Elliott replied, fully aware of Jeremy

Flashman's past. It was all in his autobiography - My *Spirited* Journey, which Jeremy had handed out liberally the day of its publication. Elliott hadn't meant to read it but devoid of reading material on the toilet one day he couldn't help himself.

'I know Carol can be...' Flashman paused, '...a little forward at times. But that's just her way. I wouldn't read too much into it. What I do know is that she's very keen on getting you back onboard Ghostbusters UK. So much so, she asked me to talk to you.'

Elliott suspected he was not being told the whole truth. It couldn't be that hard to employ someone else to throw stones at them, could it? Elliott assumed that what Carol had observed yesterday had had quite an effect on her. If Elliott could see the financial rewards in his relationship with Hapkido Valentine then so perhaps could she. Even if she had no idea of how he was actually doing it. Maybe he didn't need them? Maybe he could be the new Jeremy Flashman? All he needed was Hapkido Valentine who was (as always) by his side.

'Who's this bloke?'

'This my friend is Jeremy Flashman, television's most famous psychic.'

'Psychic? Well I'm not getting anything off him. Not that I would of course, being a time traveller and not a ghost. I will say one thing though, that is some terrific taste in clothes.'

Elliott tried to reach out into the connection between them to see if Hapkido was being sarcastic. Worryingly he seemed to be sincere.

'I think he's waiting for you to say something.'

Elliott looked at Jeremy to see a face patiently waiting for a reply.

'I don't think I'll be coming back to the show Jeremy, I have something new now,' Elliott explained.

'This?' Flashman replied, gesturing around the room. 'Let me tell you something. This ability is a curse! You'd be better off learning your trade from someone who's been there and done it.'

'Like you?'

'Exactly. Carol and I only have your best interests at heart.'

'He may be one well-dressed fella, but he's only interested in exploiting our arrangement for himself. This guy knows a threat when he sees it. Carol, well she's one foxy minx but she can't be trusted either.'

'I totally agree with you. Except the parts about Flashman being well dressed and Carol being a ... foxy minx.'

'Sorry Jeremy, I've moved on from Ghostbusters UK now,' Elliott replied.

'Learn how to control this ability Elliott and you can have everything, just like me. You can be famous, wealthy, people just begging for your autograph.'

At this point an old lady who had been throwing glances for some time at the two of them decided that she would make her way over. Jeremy, seeing her approach, couldn't have asked for better timing.

'Is it an autograph you're after my love?' Flashman asked.

'What?' The old lady replied.

'An autograph,' Flashman continued, pulling out a copy of his autobiography from seemingly nowhere and starting to sign the inside cover.

'I don't know what you're talking about. Aren't you the disc jockey from Pensioner Party on a Wednesday afternoon?'

'No love,' Flashman corrected with a condescending smile. 'I'm Jeremy Flashman, world renowned psychic and ...'

'I don't care who you are. I'm here for this young man,' she interrupted.

Jeremy Flashman's jaw dropped. Elliott, who was starting to get the hang of this, decided to exploit the moment for all its worth. Out the corner of his eye he could see Jeremy's autobiography beating a hasty retreat back into the depths of his jacket.

'Hello,' Elliott replied, turning to the old woman.

'I'm Mrs. Ramsey, chairwoman of Croydon's Women's Institute, I believe you know Mrs. Clarkson?' Mrs. Ramsey responded, gesturing to the approaching Mrs. Clarkson.

'Endsley,' Mrs. Clarkson acknowledged nonchalantly.

'Mrs. Clarkson,' Elliott replied, catching from the corner of his eye Flashman reaching into his jacket to produce his autobiography again.

'Lovely of you to turn up. Now shall we get started?' Mrs. Clarkson asked.

'Of course Mrs. Clarkson, but if we can first discuss my fee?' Elliott enquired.

Perhaps this wasn't the most subtle way of raising the matter. Elliott knew that he needed the money and without a job this had to be sooner rather than later, but there was a more pressing matter at hand. The book in Flashman's hands was making its way across the space between them. The last thing Elliott needed was another psychic usurping the moment.

'Oh don't worry about that,' Mrs. Clarkson replied, one hand directing Elliott to the front of the room whilst the other dismissed the approach of the oncoming book. 'Do put that away, you silly man,' Mrs. Clarkson added.

The walk to the stage seemed to take an eternity, countless stares falling upon Elliott, magnified tenfold by numerous sets of bi-focal glasses. Arriving at the front he turned, his left leg shaking uncontrollably with nerves.

'Welcome ladies and .... umm ladies,' Elliott began. 'My name is Elliott Rose and I hope to ...'

'Get on with it,' came a shout from the middle of the assembled crowd. Obviously impatient, the clacking of knitting needles could be heard to begin.

'I hope to get in contact with some of your loved ones,' Elliott continued before sending a thought in Hapkido's direction that this was his cue.

'Do you think there's a cafe nearby? I could really do with a sausage sandwich.'

'He's rubbish!' Shouted another woman towards the back.

Elliott looked towards where the voice had come from but could only see Jeremy Flashman displaying a broad smile, wide enough to fit a sausage roll in sideways. At this precise moment a stray bolt of light raced through the window behind him and hit the medallion of Flashman. Bouncing straight back into Elliott's eyes it was more than enough to make him lose concentration.

'I .... er ....,' Elliott stammered.

Hapkido Valentine, perhaps realising that it wasn't going well, stopped adjusting himself through his embroidered dragon costume and decided to contribute.

'Oh right, sorry. You'll probably want to start with Alfred John Peterson.'

'Does anyone know an Alfred John Peterson?' Elliott asked, his confidence returning slightly.

'That's me!' Came an excited shout three rows from the back as an old lady jumped to her feet with the enthusiasm of an unparalleled bingo win. As she leapt her knitting needles flew from her lap with the force of a sidewinder missile, just missing Flashman who lurked nearby.

And so it was that as Elliott Rose continued he became a talking point for the Croydon Women's Institute for years to come.

*

'Brilliant,' Mrs. Clarkson declared as Elliott made his way from the front.

The room was already beginning to empty with the end of the show. This was in part because he'd been able to deliver messages to the majority of the crowd but also because the local supermarket was having a special deal on tinned fruits at the same time. As Elliott scanned the room he could find no sign of Flashman. Neither could he locate Hapkido who had also disappeared. No doubt he was now wandering the local neighbourhood looking for a cafe with mismatched cutlery and without any specific policy on the service of spectral beings. Still, the job had been done and Hapkido's information had been 100% accurate. He could handle the living on his own.

'That was the best presentation since Line Dancing for Zimmer Frames back in July,' Mrs. Clarkson continued.

'That's very kind. I'm sorry to bring this up but you did say there would be a fee involved didn't you?' Elliott asked.

Elliott felt uncomfortable asking but he also knew he had to. Taking money from pensioners was perhaps not the noblest action on his part but necessity had far outweighed charity after recent events.

'Oh yes, of course dear, it's over there,' Mrs. Clarkson replied, pointing in the direction of a table in the corner.

He was surprised he hadn't noticed the table before, conspicuous as it was by a tea towel draped over an object in the centre. Was that the money underneath, Elliott ventured, if it was then it must be a sizeable amount. He hadn't expected an actual pile of money. Maybe he shouldn't take it all? They were old ladies after all. Still, there was no harm in looking was there?

'Well that's very kind but perhaps I shouldn't be taking all of it,' Elliott flustered.

'Don't be silly, come with me,' Mrs. Clarkson replied, grabbing him by the wrist with such force that Hapkido himself would have struggled.

Arriving at the table, the size of the concealed object certainly hadn't diminished. Elliott looked at its shape, there must be piles of cash under there. He couldn't help but feel a sense of excitement and anticipation.

'We collected it for you dear,' Mrs. Clarkson replied with a glint in her eye. Some might have construed the glint as humble generosity. Others, namely Elliott, might have interpreted it as an offer he couldn't, and shouldn't, turn down.

'Perhaps I could take just a little,' Elliott replied, finally giving in to the side of him that demanded curtains for his flat.

Mrs. Clarkson released her vice like grip and whipped the tea towel from the table. She did so with the skill and drama of a holiday camp magician.

Elliott's face didn't conceal his surprise very well. Here he was, worrying about taking their money and the sight before him was that of countless jars of jam. Sticky gelatinous jam. Their payment to him was to ensure that he wouldn't have any teeth left by the end of the week.

Chapter 11

A Midlands mindset

Elliott walked into the flat on his fifth journey carrying the last of the jam, placing it down on the table. Slightly out of breath from the numerous treks down to the car and back he took in the sight of the rows of jars in front of him.

'What the hell are we going to do with all of this?'

'Well don't look at me. Can't stand the stuff!' Hapkido replied as he sat slouched on the sofa. Elliott wasn't quite sure why Hapkido seemed to need a rest as he hadn't done any of the carrying.

'Well you better start liking it,' Elliott added, 'we've seventy two jars and it's the only food in the flat.'

'I'm more of a ...'

'Don't say it!' Elliott interrupted urgently.

'Say what?'

'You know what.'

'I have no idea what you're talking about.'

'Good, let's keep it that way. We have more important things to discuss,' Elliott replied, taking the one remaining dining chair and sitting on it.

'Asides from the jam, it actually went quite well,' Elliott suggested, feeling both conspicuous and uncomfortable on the chair.

'I wanted to talk to you about that,' Hapkido replied casually, studying his fingernails nonchalantly.

'I'm thinking a few local gigs first, get the word out. Then in a couple of months we can do some concert halls before finally a big stadium tour perhaps. I'm thinking we could call it Elliott Rose and the world beyond.'

'Well I do have some contacts in that sort of field, after all I was one of the top wrestlers in my day,' Hapkido replied.

Elliott did wonder if any of these supposed contacts were still alive. If they were would they really appreciate a visit from someone who claimed he could channel the spirit of someone who'd died quite resoundingly many years previously?

'Okay,' Elliott answered hesitantly, drawing out the words as he thought. 'You give me some names and I'll see if I can round them up.'

'Before we do, you do recall our agreement don't you?'

'Go on, what do you want this time?' Elliott enquired, worried that Hapkido was about to ask for something besides a sausage sandwich. When Hapkido asked for something it never seemed to work out well, especially for Elliott.

'I said at the beginning there are a few things I, or more applicably we, need to achieve if this is going to be a success.'

'And they are?' Elliott asked fearfully.

'We shall discuss each one when they become relevant. However it is time for the first.'

'Oh nuts,' Elliott answered. 'It's not another possession thing is it? You're not going to make me wear a stupid costume like yours are you?'

'For your information this costume was the work of one of China's finest tailors.'

'Did this fine Chinese tailor also happen to work in a takeaway?' Elliott asked.

Hapkido took a few moments to let the comment pass, probably because it was true.

'I need you to drive me somewhere. I need to visit someone.'

'Okay, no problem. I didn't realise these requests of yours would be so easy. Who are we going to see?'

'Her name is Mrs. Vivian Cole and she lives in Derby.'

'Derby!' Elliott exclaimed.

'Is it a problem?'

'No,' Elliott sighed. 'Although I do have one condition.'

'And that is?'

'That you don't mention sausage sandwiches for the entire trip!'

'Now there's a thought,' Hapkido replied.

Elliott, conscious of saying anything further for fear of digging a deeper hole for himself, got up to get his car keys. Derby it was then.

*

One hundred and twenty miles later Hapkido Valentine and
Elliott Rose were getting close. The trip would have been quicker
had they not had to stop at various roadside cafes to buy sausage
sandwiches at the bequest of Hapkido. The routine was always
the same. Elliott would buy the sandwich, Hapkido would look
at it before conveniently talking about something else. Under
examination by the adjudicating eyes of various fast food
vendors Elliott would therefore have to eat the sandwich himself.
After the fifth sandwich he was starting to feel slightly queasy.
After that Elliott had refused to stop again, leading to Hapkido
sulking between the junctions for Northampton and Nuneaton.
For Elliott the silence would have been preferable were it not for
the fact that Hapkido had also insisted that the radio be tuned to
a classic hits station all the way. It was Wham as they went
round the M25, Spandau Ballet up the M1 and by the time Duran
Duran began their musical marathon Elliott was fully prepared
to exit the motorway in a fiery ball of death somewhere around
Leicester.

'So who is this Vivian Cole then?' Elliott asked, hoping he
could distract Hapkido long enough to do a sly radio change.

'Just someone I used to know.'

'It's not your wife is it?'

'No it is not!' Hapkido replied angrily.

'Okay, just checking. But you should know that if this Cole
woman can see you then you are very likely going to scare the
living shit out of her. After all you've been dead for over twenty
years.'

'I think you mean time travelled.'

'Absolutely,' Elliott replied, letting his eyes slide in the other
direction.

'I am fully aware that I've been absent in your time line for a
number of years. However regardless of the circumstances, she
will no doubt be pleased to see me.'

'Whatever you say,' Elliott replied and a silence fell between them.

In the solitude Hapkido let the memories return. A smile crept across his lips as the anticipation grew in his heart.

Twenty minutes later they were taking the Derby exit from the motorway and Hapkido was beginning to feel anxious.

*

Elliott allowed the car to trundle to a stop, the engine idling as they took in the scene before them. One side of the street was dominated by a string of terraced houses, their exteriors identical apart from an occasional foray into the world of cladding. Green wheelie bins lined the road, protruding onto the pavements with a sense of abject menace. On the other side of the street, a large brick factory stretched the length of the road, its entrance marked by black iron gates and faded signs that pointed in the direction of the reception area.

'Are you sure it was 32 Arundel Street?' Elliott asked.

'I think I know my own...' Hapkido stalled, 'Mrs. Cole's house.'

'I think it's safe to say Mrs. Cole doesn't live in a factory though.'

'Are you sure you have the right address?' Hapkido asked.

'Quite sure. You're the one who knows the area, you tell me, is this the right place?'

Hapkido looked up and down the road, taking in the view. From his perspective he'd only left Derby a few days ago yet the memories seemed distant, faded almost. He might be struggling to recall the details of his life here but instinct told him this was the right place. There was the fish and chip shop at one end of the terrace, at the other end a pub.

'Yes,' Hapkido answered, dejected. 'This is the street. However it would seem 32 has now been replaced by this factory.'

'So who was this Mrs. Cole then?' Elliott asked.

'No one.'

'Come on, you can tell me,' Elliott persisted, recognising that Hapkido wasn't telling him everything.

'I said no one!' Hapkido shouted, his anger coming to the fore unexpectedly.

'Okay, okay.'

'Forget it. Let's go home,' Hapkido demanded.

'You can't give in that easily,' Elliott suggested. 'Haven't you got another address or something?'

'No,' Hapkido replied, his head dropping, his voice trailing off.

'Anyone who might know where she could have moved to?'

'No one,' Hapkido answered, the words barely spoken.

'Well my friend,' Elliott continued, refusing to let Hapkido's morose demeanour infect him, 'in many respects you are well and truly screwed. However, I've driven all this way and I for one don't intend to give up so easily.'

Elliott shifted in his seat and turned the engine off, taking the keys from the ignition.

'What are you going to do?' Hapkido asked, a glimmer of hope sparking back to life.

'I'm going to go and ask someone inside the factory. They might know what happened to the people who lived here before.'

Suddenly Hapkido felt galvanised by Elliott's words. Had he been this much of a defeatist when he faced Gentlemen Jim fighting for the championship all those years ago? No! Had he used his powers to travel through time just to give in so easily now? Absolutely not.

'You're right,' Hapkido announced. 'Let's go.'

With that, both Hapkido and Elliott got out of the car, Elliott alone using the door in its traditional sense. Hapkido looked up at the sky. It was overcast with the sun concealed behind low heavy clouds, dark at their base as if a storm were coming.

The road felt familiar underfoot. He could feel her here, her life imprinted upon the very cobbles of the street. She had stood in this very spot, calling for Gordon to come in for fish fingers and chips as he played football with his friends. She had looked out from a window somewhere above them to spy on Gordon when he had parked up with Sonya James, only a few months after passing his driving test. She had walked up this very street carrying bags of shopping with the ingredients for his favourite dinner, expecting Gordon home from work, wishing they didn't make him work such strange hours. Hapkido came to a conclusion as he reminisced. Surely when they built the factory they would have bought the house from her at a tidy sum. She probably used the money to buy a nice bungalow in the suburbs. Elliott was right. He was a fool to give in so easily. She was nearby, he could sense it.

Elliott pushed the white plastic door, its base sweeping roughly over the bristled mat on the inside. A blue functional sofa sat to one side with a reception area up ahead. The receptionist was an older woman, complete with crazy perm and oversized spectacles. She sat behind a counter with a light blue plastic façade on the front displaying the name of her employer.

'Hello,' Elliott said as he approached.

With some reluctance the receptionist looked up, drawing herself away from her eighteenth game of solitaire of the day.

'Welcome to Derby Designer Knitwear, how may I help you?'

'I wondered if you could answer some questions,' Elliott asked.

'Depends on what sort, darling?' Crazy-permed receptionist woman asked.

Elliott took a moment to ponder whether 'darling' was just the northern way. Or perhaps he was one of the unfortunate souls that walk the Earth attracting the attention of females of a certain maturity.

'I was after some information.' Elliott stated, casting a glance to the side. Hapkido had made his way over to the sofa where he was now studying the front cover of one the women's magazines available to read.

'Information costs, darling,' the receptionist replied with a sly wink.

'I don't know how you do it but you certainly have a way with the older ladies.'

'I do not have a way with the older ladies.'

'First Carol, now some woman with a microphone on top of her head. You son, have the gift.'

'Shut up and let me do the talking.'

'I was trying to contact a woman who used to live round here,'

Elliott asked.

'As I say darling, information costs.'

'And what would the cost be?' Elliott asked, quieting his voice. He sincerely hoped it wasn't what he suspected.

'Well, that's the age old question, wouldn't you say?'

'I have ten pounds in the car,' Elliott suggested.

'Now darling, what would I want with ten pounds? You see I get very lonely ...'

'Ten pounds and a packet of mints!' Elliott interrupted urgently.

'Oh, it's a tempting offer but I think I'll go with my original idea,' the receptionist concluded, looking at Elliott suggestively over the top of her glasses.

'Come on. We haven't got all day. Just do what the nice lady with the insane hair asks.'

'If I do, do you promise not to mention sausage sandwiches for the entire trip back?'

'Of course.'

'Okay,' Elliott sighed, addressing the receptionist. 'What is it I can do for you?'

*

Elliott had arranged to meet the receptionist outside the factory at five o'clock. Hapkido had already disappeared, claiming to have more pressing matters to attend to. Perhaps he'd sensed the sort of evening Elliott had in store and wanted no part of it. Ironically it was probably the one time where his presence might have been a welcome distraction.

At exactly five she appeared outside the factory as he waited, leaning casually against the car. She was accompanied by a throng of middle aged women who watched her intently as she sauntered over. It didn't take a genius to work out she'd been telling the story to all of them since he'd agreed to take her out - a young man had entered the reception area that afternoon and really taken a shine to the more mature lady, or to give her her proper name, Doris. At her recommendation nay insistence they were going to the early evening showing at the cinema. After that, Elliott wasn't sure, but Doris certainly had plans. And she certainly wasn't shy about greeting him, rising up on her toes to plant a kiss on his cheek. The other women continued to watch intently, no doubt envisaging the start of a magical evening. Elliott was pretty sure this far exceeded what was required to keep Hapkido Valentine happy. All he needed to know was what had happened to Mrs. Cole who had lived in one of the houses that had made way for the factory. It was a long shot but Doris was the only hope he had. She made her way to the passenger side and got into the car. At least he was safe whilst they were driving, surely.

As Elliott took a left turn into the cinema car park he removed Doris's vice like grip from his leg for the seventh time. When it came to unwelcome sexual advances she certainly seemed to possess an incredible strength. Elliott did wonder if her perm gave her Samson-like qualities. Once parked they walked across the car park and through the double doors of the cinema. Doris, who fully embraced the notion that the man pays for everything, made a beeline for the pick and mix, stocking up with enough flying saucers to launch an alien invasion. Then with a sense of immense dread, Elliott walked into the darkened cinema screen leading a woman about to unleash the full power of hormone replacement therapy. Worryingly there were only a few people in the room, dotted here and there. Doris sat next to him, entwining her arm with his. It didn't take long for her hand to drop to his lap and trace small sensual circles on the inside of his thigh.

'Wow, she's not wasting any time is she?'

'Sweet Jesus!' Elliott blurted out in horror, shuddering as Hapkido manifested in the empty seat next to him. A few people turned to look and tut.

'You like that do you?' Doris whispered, thinking the

exclamation was for her, moving her hand to the upper regions of his inner thigh.

'What the hell are you doing here? I thought you said you had something more important to do.'

'Turns out it wasn't important. Besides I fancied watching the film. Is this the one with Burt Reynolds?'

'No it's not a bloody Burt Reynolds film! What the hell am I going to do? Every time I move her hand away it just comes back with a vengeance.'

'What can I say? We all have to make small sacrifices. You promised we would find Vivian Cole at any cost.'

'Small sacrifices. She's about to fondle me like she's loading up a washing machine.'

'I'm sure it's not that bad. All she wants is a nice romantic evening with Elliott Rose, world famous romancer of the elderly.'

Elliott removed her hand from his upper thigh and placed it back onto her lap, again.

'Well there is a plus side.'

'What the hell is the plus side?'

'The film is only one hour and forty two minutes long.'

Exactly one hour and forty-two minutes later, Elliott was escorting Derby's answer to Casanova on the Sex Offenders Register, back towards the car. He needed to get her home as soon as possible. To his dying day he would never mention what had happened in the cinema. Doris on the other hand, mistook speed for intent. Come the morning she would have a story to share as is genetically inherent to all receptionists the world over. Once at the car, both Doris and Elliott sat in the front whilst Hapkido flitted though the back door, filling the rear view mirror with a wide smile. An awkward silence descended, Doris awaiting the question, Elliott prepared to fend off yet another advance.

'So where do you live?' Elliott asked reluctantly. He couldn't just leave her here. He needed the information she claimed to have and she'd made it blatantly obvious she wasn't sharing until the evening was over.

'29 Arundel Street darling, opposite the factory where you picked me up,' Doris replied with a knowing wink.

'You live in Arundel Street?' Elliott asked, not quite believing. Hapkido in turn sat up straight, his eyes widening behind the mask.

'Of course dear, how else would I know about Viv?'

'So you know where she is?'

'Why yes, but first things first …' Doris replied, letting her hand run up the outside of her leg, her middle finger sensually hooking her thin skirt and letting it drift up to reveal a pale white leg, possibly wooden.

Elliott didn't push the line of questioning any further. He fired up the engine and the car leapt forward towards Arundel Street, breaking all known scientific theorems on the universal laws of velocity. Again, Doris was probably getting the wrong idea Elliott thought, but at least if his eyes were on the road he didn't have to see what she was doing. Her planned sexual assault on him would have to wait for the time being. After ten minutes of driving they were getting near her house. Elliott, occupied with worry, failed to notice the graveyard they found themselves driving past.

'She's in there, darling,' Doris announced, suddenly pointing to the side of the road.

'Eh?' Elliott replied, not quite listening.

'You wanted to know what happened to Vivian Cole don't you? She's passed on, lover boy.'

'What? You mean she's dead?' Elliott asked surprised.

'1985 it was. I went to her funeral. Of course I was only a young girl back then.'

Elliott glanced in the rear-view mirror, concerned as to what effect this startling news had had on Hapkido. Hapkido's massive body was flexed as if trying to control a rage. His lips had become thin and pursed.

'I'm sorry,' Elliott exclaimed, keeping his eyes fixed in the mirror so Hapkido recognised the sincerity.

'It's okay dear.' Doris replied, thinking the comment was for her. 'It was over twenty years ago now. They say she died of a broken heart.'

'I don't understand,' Elliott asked, directing his attention back to Doris.

'Surely you know why?' Doris enquired. 'They say she never got over her son Gordon dying.'

'Sorry, who's that?' Elliott asked, confused.

'Surely you must know who Gordon was? It all came out after his death. He was a professional wrestler called Hapkido Valentine and it turned out our Viv never knew. I presumed you knew all this seeing as you were asking about her.'

Suddenly it all made sense. The need to drive up here, the reluctance to talk about it. Elliott had become so embroiled with his plans that he had completely forgotten that Hapkido Valentine was once a man. To Elliott, ever since they had first met, Hapkido Valentine had just been a ghost, a long dead wrestler. But he was also a man, and he had a name: Gordon Cole. It was all too obvious who Vivian Cole was. A deep sense of sorrow flooded Elliott's heart. He couldn't believe he had been so stupid and now that Hapkido needed him, he was stuck in a car with a sexually frustrated nut job and couldn't say a thing. Except of course, he could. Elliott let his mind focus, reaching out to Hapkido yet all he could sense was an absence. He let his eyes glance in the mirror and was shocked to see only the empty rear seat. No Hapkido, no Gordon Cole. Nothing.

'It's this left here, darling,' Doris interrupted.

As if on automatic, Elliott turned the car into Arundel Street.

'Okay, here you go,' Elliott announced, pulling up outside the factory, his mind elsewhere.

'So,' Doris started, her hand finding its way to Elliott's ear and beginning to stroke it.

'Please don't.'

'So, do you fancy coming in?' Doris asked, her fingers now brushing Elliott's cheek sensually.

'No.'

'What do you mean no?' Doris replied, suddenly agitated. 'You do know what I meant don't you?'

'Yes I know perfectly well what you meant,' Elliott replied, starting to grow impatient.

'You can always call it a night inside you know.'

Suddenly his resolve broke. All Elliott wanted was to speak to Hapkido, to help him somehow. Instead all he got was a woman in her forties (if he was being generous) yet again crossing the boundaries of acceptable conduct. He didn't mean to get angry, he just did.

'Will you get out of the fucking car!' Elliott shouted, taking Doris by surprise, her hand immediately withdrawing.

'What?' Doris replied at an incredible volume. It was possible that her microphone shaped hairdo was amplifying the volume of her rage.

'I'm very sorry, it's been a lovely evening,' Elliott answered softly, trying to regain his composure. 'But will you please just get out of the fucking car!'

'You know what sunshine, you've blown your chance!' Doris continued, her hand wrenching the door open.

Elliott did feel a little guilty as she marched across the road to her front door. He let his open hand run from his forehead to his chin, the fingers splayed over closed eyes. When he opened them again he had absolutely no idea what to do next.

*

Derby is a small city, containing only a limited number of places that the ghost of a wrestler might reside, or so Elliott thought. Sandwich shops, dodgy pubs, dubious hot food vans at the side of the road: they all failed to contain Hapkido Valentine. One minute he had been sitting in the back of the car, the next he was nowhere to be seen. It was now five in the morning and Elliott was fast running out of places to look. Finding someone in a city can be hard, when that person doesn't really exist in the first place, nigh on impossible. Parked up, Elliott took one last look at the town square, dominated by an oversized fountain that cascaded water from its peak. Seeing no other choice Elliott began the drive home.

By the time Elliott was making his way to the lift that would take him to his flat, his fellow neighbours were starting to rise. Winston and German Colin had already taken up their early morning positions across the corridor from one other. Perhaps recognising the heavy heart that passed, they sat with their heads bowed. A minute later Elliott was at his front door, positioning the key in the lock before pausing. The one hope that had accompanied him on the journey back from Derby was that Hapkido would be waiting for him inside. Breathing in he turned the key and entered. After looking in the bedroom, kitchen and bathroom he made his way into the empty living room. Hapkido was nowhere to be found. All that was left of their time together was the countless jars of jam that sat menacingly on the table. As Elliott stood in front of them, sorrow engulfed him. If he were the crying type then he probably would have done so.

'Poor bastard,' Elliott announced towards the jam. Jam being jam, it didn't have the decency to reply.

'I leave you for five minutes and you start talking to preserves.' The voice boomed from behind him.

'Hapkido!' Elliott cried, swinging round on his heels with a broad smile on his face.

'You took your time getting back here.'

'How did you get back here? Where did you go?' Elliott asked frantically, wanting to hug the wrestler but realising that if he did so he would probably fall flat on his face.

'How do any of us move?' Hapkido questioned. 'Yet one thing is apparent. We have started something, the two of us.'

'Look, I'm really sorry for what happened. Is there anything I can do?' Elliott asked.

'I searched for her in the void. I looked for so long, but I couldn't hear her. But rest assured…' Hapkido announced, standing up straight and looking off into the middle distance, 'I won't stop until we've finished what we've begun. I can sense that if we see this through to the end then I can say goodbye properly.'

'How does it end?' Elliott asked, confused.

'Now *that* is the tricky bit,' Hapkido replied.

Chapter 12

Flashman, the medallion chronicles

There are streets in London that seem at odds with their surroundings. They are rarely seen by those who live within the city itself, pre-occupied as they are with their proximity to transport links that require the selling of a kidney in exchange for a toilet bowl two feet from where they sleep. Neither are they visited by tourists who alternatively opt to stand around famous landmarks, staring with wonder at a history heavily concealed beneath a thick veneer of pigeon crap. Streets such as these contain businesses that would prefer not to draw attention to themselves. A few streets, through manipulation of local council loopholes, even manage not to be included on maps of the capital. For reasons which are not entirely clear, if you drive down such a street against the express orders of your satellite navigation system you will arrive home to find you've inadvertently purchased online a pair of size fifteen women's shoes and the entire back catalogue of Barry Manilow.

Jeremy Flashman got out of the back of the taxi at the end of the street, *accidently* leaving a copy of his autobiography on the back seat. The ancient oak trees that lined the road on either side swayed in the wind. The sound of the taxi's engine faded as it drove away, quickly disappearing into the low hum of the traffic nearby. Jeremy passed a number of buildings as he walked, painted white with black railings. Casting a casual glance at the brass plaque of one of the buildings as he passed, he wondered what exactly the Sudanese Ski Authority actually did? Five houses later he halted at the bottom of some red tiled steps and looked up. The steps led to a polished black door with another brass plaque to one side. He didn't need to read this one to know he was in the right place. He had been here before. Previously he had not always been welcome, this being the headquarters of an organisation simply known as The Society. They had looked down on him for many years, steadfastly refusing to acknowledge his status as the nation's premier psychic. To them it didn't matter how famous he had become, he had still yet to demonstrate the level of mediumship required to be allowed to join. Their continued disregard had always irritated Jeremy but over the years he had tried desperately to pay it no heed. That was until two days ago. Jeremy Flashman knew he had witnessed something remarkable back in Croydon. It was more than mere showmanship by Elliott Rose: he had been too accurate, too precise. If Jeremy Flashman could use this to his advantage then all the better for both him and The Society. But mainly for him.

Flashman began to climb the steps, running his hand along the brass railing that had been worn down to a dull shine, atom by atom, by the countless hands that had come before. At the door he rapped three times, letting the knocker fall on the last with a clatter against its base. As Jeremy waited, he rubbed his alligator skin shoes against the back of his trousers. Eventually the door slowly opened, gliding effortlessly on pristine hinges. A small elderly man stood there taking in the sight of the visitor before him. Jeremy Flashman recognised him instantly: Mr. Stirling, the Scottish caretaker of advanced years, looking no older than when Jeremy had last met him.

'Good morning,' Jeremy Flashman announced. 'I am Jer...'

'Good morning Mr. Flashman,' Mr. Stirling interrupted with a soft Scottish accent.

'Excellent,' Flashman continued. 'I'm here to see...'

'We were expecting you. Mr. Falkirk will meet you in the library,' Mr. Stirling replied, his arm lifting slowly from his side to point towards a red doorway at the far end of the corridor beyond. Flashman eased himself past the caretaker and followed the finger. As he did so he felt it only fair that the service afforded be suitably rewarded.

'I thought you might like this,' Flashman speculated, his hand reaching into his jacket pocket and sliding out a copy of his autobiography.

'Thank you sir,' Mr. Stirling responded contemptuously, his hand already in place to await the book.

'Don't worry,' Flashman whispered. 'I've left out the bit about this place.'

'Naturally Sir,' Mr. Stirling replied, closing the door behind him.

Flashman moved down the corridor and past the arrangement of black and white framed photographs on the wall to his left. They seemed to portray a number of gentlemen dressed in suits that illustrated the era in which each photograph was taken. The last one showed the man he was here to see. The door swung open effortlessly as Jeremy pushed, revealing a room beyond of polished walnut parquet floors and exquisite bookcases that lined the walls. To his left windows ran from waist height to the ceiling, the light outside muted by wooden Venetian blinds. Flashman's shoes fell heavily on the floor as he entered, his Cuban heels at odds with the floor they walked on. The bookcases themselves were filled with countless leather bound books arranged in an ordered fashion. In the middle of the room sat two green chesterfield sofas, separated by a nineteenth century table. This in turn resided on a Turkish carpet of intricate detail and breathtaking beauty. Yet the decorum and finesse failed to elicit any sense of wonder from Flashman, he was more a chrome and mirrored ceiling kind of chap. Arriving at one of the sofas he allowed himself to sit on its arm, the leather creaking as he did so. Somewhere nearby the rhythmic heart of a grandfather clock ticked as he waited.

'Hello Jeremy,' announced an elderly man who entered from a door at the other end of the room.

'Good afternoon Mr. Falkirk,' Flashman replied, letting his eyes scan the elderly gentleman. He was wearing tartan slippers long past their best and a beige cardigan with a chevron design across the shoulders and back. Resting precariously on his nose was a pair of half-moon spectacles which Mr. Falkirk peered over.

'Well Jeremy, it has been a while, what brings you here?' Mr. Falkirk asked, the tone of his voice modulated to indicate his relative unease as to the visit.

'The first thing is, I couldn't help but notice that you are a fine collector of books,' Flashman proclaimed, gesturing with an elaborate arm movement towards the bookcases.

'We don't want your autobiography thank you,' Mr. Falkirk declared, his glare intensifying over the half-moon spectacles. 'Was that all?'

'Well,' Jeremy stuttered, 'I do have something else, something I think you'll find very interesting. You see I have some news regarding our thing.'

'Our thing?' Mr. Falkirk replied incuriously. 'As far as I'm aware you are not part of *our thing*.'

'If it's about my subscription fees I can assure you that...'

'Mr. Flashman, you have had no subscription fees to pay because you have been barred from joining the society on no fewer than fifteen occasions. If I recall, this is mainly due to the fact that you have repeatedly scored 0% on every aptitude test you have ever undertaken.'

'Now, listen here,' Flashman replied, becoming frustrated. 'I may not have passed your aptitude tests but none the less I am regarded as this nation's leading psychic.'

'Mr. Flashman, success does not necessarily equate to competence.'

'As far as I can tell,' Jeremy contested angrily, 'you may have all the books and the history, but that doesn't lessen the fact that your society is outdated when it comes to the modern world of psychic investigation. I don't need your self-assured ratification to know that I'm out there, getting results.'

Mr. Falkirk delicately removed his glasses, placing them in a case which he had removed from the pocket of his cardigan. When his gaze returned he was in no mood to discuss their differing methods.

'You are a charlatan Mr. Flashman! You prey on the vulnerability of the general public to exploit them for your own financial gain. You may well convince certain people with your crass brand of showmanship but we know who you really are. This society was built on the great work of those who preceded us, who learnt the art of communicating with the deceased via careful examination and application of their gift.'

'Well if that's the case,' Jeremy declared, offended. 'You won't be interested in my information then?'

Mr. Falkirk stared intently at his visitor. If there was one thing he couldn't abide it was those who claimed to practice the arts without being blessed with the gift. The rather inconvenient truth however was that Mr. Falkirk, despite spending the last fifty years attempting to learn, also failed to possess it. He propagated an air of wisdom and competence because he knew the illusion of power was often as good as the real thing. Perhaps he and Jeremy Flashman weren't so different, but he would show him what true showmanship really was.

'Mr. Flashman. I knew you would come here. I am also aware of the information you speak of, but if it makes you feel better, please do share.'

'You expect me to tell you now? Even though you claim to know? After all I'm just a charlatan aren't I? Why don't you tell me?' Jeremy asked, buoyed by the suspicion that he wasn't the only one here making it up.

'I'm not in the habit of ...'

'Please don't let me stop you,' Flashman challenged.

'Very well,' Mr. Falkirk replied. 'Is it in regards to a woman called Agnes?'

'No,' Flashman bluntly replied, letting a smile creep across his lips.

'I meant Andrew.'

'Still wrong,' Flashman retorted.

'I sense... ' Mr. Falkirk mused, 'it has something to do with a broken clock?'

'Shall I just tell you?'

'If you must Mr. Flashman but let it be known I was of course mere moments away from discerning the facts of the matter.'

'Of course you were,' Jeremy nodded sarcastically.

'Are you going to tell me or not?' Mr. Falkirk demanded angrily.

Jeremy Flashman snorted a laugh before speaking.

'Look,' Jeremy began, 'we all know that the reputation of the society has been in decline for over a hundred years now. Actual powers of communicating with those who have passed on have long since been lost to us. You yourself, the actual head of the society demonstrated it in your desperate groping for information. The simple fact is you and I are no different, we both attempt to convey the power of the gift by misdirection.'

Mr. Falkirk frowned but remained quiet.

'A century ago,' Jeremy continued, 'the number of those who possessed the gift in this society numbered in the hundreds. Now you are down to what? Under twenty? The only history of how to actually use the gift is located in these books which you study and guard religiously. Yet, despite all of this information, despite fifty years of attempting to do so, you are still like me.'

'Are you here to give a history lesson Mr. Flashman or do you actually have something to tell me?'

'Seeing as you asked,' Jeremy announced, raising himself from the arm of the chair and standing proud. 'It just so happens I have found someone who is undoubtedly the real deal. I've seen it with my own eyes. He has the gift.'

'Mr. Flashman, seeing as we are being so candid here, I would suggest you're speaking absolute rubbish. No true practitioner has been born in over a hundred years. You have been fooled I'm afraid to say.'

'Are you forgetting who you are talking to?' Jeremy grumbled. 'I know all the tricks in the book. I would have spotted it.'

'And what is his name Mr. Flashman, so we can check out this absurd claim of yours?'

'Now that's the tricky bit. You see, you don't get anything for free in this life,' Jeremy asserted, letting his hands casually slide into his pockets before beginning an insouciant walk around the room.

'What is it you want?' Mr. Falkirk asked, sighing.

'I want a look at the book,' Flashman replied, coming to a halt with his back facing one of the windows which faced out onto the street.

'The book!' Mr. Falkirk gasped. 'The book can only be read by the chief member of the society and then only with good reason. What you have asked is insulting!'

'No book, no name,' Jeremy reiterated, his gaze dancing around the ceiling.

'Mr. Flashman. Are you actually suggesting that we let someone like you view the book in exchange for just a name? A name of someone whom you simply *claim* has true power? As well you know, the book contains information that could tear the very fabric of reality apart. And you think we should just let *you* read it?'

'That's about the sum of it,' Jeremy replied, leaning back up against the window.

'You are even crazier than I remember,' Mr. Falkirk declared, flabbergasted. 'I would be grateful if you could just leave now before I say something I regret.'

'If that's your wish,' Flashman replied, positioning his hand on the frame of the window to push himself level. As he nonchalantly made his way back through the door he turned and spoke again.

'I'm telling you he's real.'

'Good day Mr. Flashman,' Mr. Falkirk replied, turning his back on him and moving over to a bookcase so that his face didn't betray his fury.

In many respects things hadn't quite gone as Jeremy had wished. Yet in other ways it had gone exactly as expected. He knew they would never let him see the book. They certainly would never have let him borrow it. For what he had in mind he needed to study it, for it to be at hand. Whilst Mr. Falkirk was ranting about sanctity and ordering him to leave, Jeremy had flicked the catch whilst leaning against the window. He would have to visit again, he reasoned, maybe when it was a little quieter.

Chapter 13

Stand by for The Subiaco Love Train

Elliott awoke, his eyes blinking against the onslaught of bright sunshine. Reluctantly he was beginning to get used to waking up to the sun and it was oddly refreshing as he lay on his side facing the window. Truth was, he was getting used to a whole lot more nowadays. He had come to terms with the fact that Simone was no longer around. He had even conceded that Hapkido Valentine seemed to be part of his life now. He didn't know when, or for that matter how, it would end between them, but Hapkido didn't seem to be going away any time soon. Therefore he was prepared for the odd surprise. Today, Elliott asserted, I will not lose control of my bodily functions. He could walk out of his bedroom now and find the ghost of the wrestler complaining about something or other in the living room and it would seem relatively normal. With this confidence in place he shifted his position to lay in the other direction, away from the light streaming through the window and towards the door.

'Morning,' Hapkido announced as he lay alongside Elliott, previously unnoticed.

Elliott screamed.

'I didn't want to wake you.'

'What the hell are you doing in my bed?' Elliott protested, jumping clear of the bed in an instant.

'You don't expect me to sleep on the sofa do you?'

'But it's my bed you crazy bastard. Besides, you're a ghost, why do you even need sleep?'

'Time traveller!' Hapkido corrected.

'Okay, time traveller, whatever. Jesus, just stop scaring the crap out of me and stay the hell out of my bed,' Elliott complained.

'Okay suit yourself. Now listen, we have a big day ahead so I need you to get ready,' Hapkido instructed.

'Okay, okay,' Elliott replied, going over to a pile of clothes on the floor to look for a fresh pair of boxers to replace the ones he'd slept in. After retrieving a pair he picked up his trousers and t-shirt that he'd left draped over the end bed post the night before.

There were a few moments of silence as Hapkido looked on, making no attempt to avert his gaze.

'Do you mind?' Elliott enquired, his palms angled outwards to signal disbelief.

'Don't worry about me,' Hapkido replied, his glare not wavering for an instant.

'Get out!' Elliott shouted, positioning the t-shirt crudely over his near naked torso.

'Oh, alright. I'll be waiting in the lounge,' Hapkido replied, trudging through the door reluctantly.

*

Within the hour Elliott found himself sitting in a deserted café with Hapkido sitting opposite. The wrestler was staring at his sausage sandwich forlornly whilst Elliott sipped from a mug of milky coffee.

'Not having your sandwich?' Elliott asked.

'I'm not really hungry.'

'Of course,' Elliott replied, annoyed that on one hand that he'd been made to buy it, on the other, mildly amused as to how long Hapkido was willing to keep up the charade. They could have spoken to each other telepathically but it was quite a personal experience allowing another access to his thoughts. Elliott had had quite enough of personal intrusion from Hapkido this morning already and was willing to risk the disdain from the one other person present for the relative privacy.

It was a café like any other. The cutlery failed to match the crockery, the wallpaper failed to match the decade. A heavy smell of cooking fat and fried meat was ingrained into the very fabric of space/time within the four walls that surrounded them. A woman, aged somewhere in her one hundred and thirties stood behind the counter eyeing Elliott suspiciously. She couldn't fail to notice him speaking to himself but had no inclination to ask him to leave. If she did that to every customer who had one-way conversations in the café then she would have been out of business by the end of the week.

'So,' Hapkido started, 'we are at a crossroads wouldn't you say? You are technically unemployed with the only material items to your name seventy two jars of assorted jam. I on the other hand am still trying to understand how to make the full transition to this world. I had been trying to work out what connects us when suddenly it came to me whilst I was watching you sleep last night.'

'When you were what?' Elliott reacted, still struggling to come to terms with this morning's episode.

'Look, that's not important,' Hapkido replied. 'What is important is what I would term our mutual concern. To fully make the transition to this world I feel I must learn from the void through which I passed. You on the other hand need a new career. Therefore both our requirements have resulted in us forming this alliance.'

'I wouldn't have needed a new career if you hadn't appeared in the first place,' Elliott sighed, failing once again to fully understand the wrestler's logic.

'Regardless,' Hapkido continued, shrugging of the suggestion, 'it would seem we can satisfy both needs if we connect with the void on a regular basis.'

'I don't want any more fricking jam,' Elliott commanded.

'Not jam, I'm talking about proper money.'

'And how do we do that?' Elliott asked, his interest heightening. It was an undisputable fact that he needed to buy curtains, and probably a lock for the bedroom door as well.

'Don't forget, you're talking to one of the main highlights of Saturday afternoon television. I know people, important people. Now go ask the woman behind the counter if she has a phone book.'

'To look for whom?' Elliott asked.

'We'll start with S, S for Subiaco.'

*

Three hours later, Elliott pulled the car up in a suburban

housing estate on the other side of London. On more than one occasion he'd gotten lost in the numerous cul-de-sacs along the way, mainly due to Hapkido's insistence that he navigate. A row of near identical red brick houses stretched out on either side of the street, only interrupted occasionally by a potential mugging hot-spot.

'So you are sure this is the place?' Elliott asked.

'Only one Subiaco in the book,' Hapkido replied from the passenger seat.

'Okay, let's go,' Elliott announced, stepping from the car.

At the front door it took a persistent ringing of the doorbell before it was finally opened.

'What!' A dumpy, ferocious looking woman asked as she opened the door. She spoke with a heavy Russian accent, her hair a shocking red colour unknown to nature. Her dress was a floral design not seen since the moon landings, her fingernails terrifyingly long and sharp enough to have clawed the ring of power from Sauron's grasp as he lay whimpering in the corner.

'Hello,' Elliott stuttered, genuinely scared. 'We, I mean I, was looking for a Bernard Subiaco.'

'Da, what you want with useless husband?' The mad Russian woman asked.

'Your husband?' Elliott replied, suddenly feeling a deep empathy. 'I think I might have some business for him. Could I possibly see him?'

'Da, he at back of house. I take you there, you give him job,' she replied, grabbing Elliott by the sleeve and dragging him into the house by force.

'Older woman. You'd better watch yourself there, given your form,' Hapkido suggested, following behind.

Within seconds Elliott found himself being thrust into the conservatory, confronted by an older man, reclining in a cane armchair, the pattern of the cushions long since faded. The man in front of him, Bernie Subiaco it was to be presumed, was small and wiry with a tan that wouldn't have looked out of place on a garden fence. His gaunt face betrayed a lifetime of cigarettes and cheap whisky, the Hawaiian shirt he was wearing at odds with the immediate impression of the man.

'This man, he give you job, useless husband. You listen to him,' Bernie's wife announced before leaving the room, possibly to conduct a conference call with Satan himself.

'Well, what's this about a job?' Bernie Subiaco asked, trying to appear relaxed.

'Hello,' Elliott replied, checking to see if a) Hapkido was behind him (he was) and b) Bernie's wife had left (she had). 'It's not so much a job, more an arrangement.'

'If you're offering money for my wife, I'll take whatever you've got,' Bernie laughed, looking up with just a faint glimmer of hope.

'No, God no!' Elliott cried. 'Actually, it was about something else. I understand that you were one of Britain's great event organisers back in the day.'

'I was, not that it did me much good. Look what happened eh?' Bernie replied, nodding towards the wall to indicate his wife was on the other side listening with an upturned glass in one hand and a scythe in the other.

'I sympathise,' Elliott replied, feeling not quite at ease with discussing Bernie's personal circumstances. 'It's just that I might need something arranged, something big.'

'Look son, you're speaking to the wrong man. I used to arrange wrestling events back in the day but that died on its arse years ago.'

'I wonder why?' Hapkido suggested with more than a hint of sarcasm, even if Bernie didn't hear.

'Those days are long gone,' Bernie reminisced. 'Those guys are either dead or in old people's homes.'

'Or time travelled!' Hapkido advocated with a wag of the finger.

'It's not wrestling,' Elliott interrupted. 'It's a psychic event, you see I'm a medium.'

'A what? You mean talking with the dead and all that?' Bernie asked. 'I don't know anything about that sunshine. Besides, I'm out of the game, haven't arranged an event for years.'

'I understand, it's just your name was given to me by...,' Elliott paused, '... by a friend.'

'Look son, I don't know how you heard about me. I can't help you,' Bernie replied, lighting up a roll-up.

'Tell him he has to help you or you'll tell his wife about Watford, 1982 and a certain Miss Stokes,' Hapkido advised.

'I don't mean to force the issue Mr. Subiaco. Your help would be greatly appreciated. I wouldn't...,' Elliott cringed, '... want to mention Miss Stokes to your wife.'

As Elliott spoke he felt ever more uncomfortable with the situation. Threatening people wasn't really in his nature, yet here he was, doing exactly that. For this whole thing to work things had to be arranged, even if that meant by coercion. Bernie was apparently the answer to that.

'How did you know about that?' Bernie exclaimed, shocked and angry.

'I really don't want to,' Elliott replied, hoping to illustrate his reluctance.

'You wouldn't!' Bernie replied, furling his eyebrows and flicking some ash from the roll-up into an ashtray to the side. As he did so Elliott couldn't help but notice the slight trembling of his fingers.

'I'm afraid I would,' Elliott replied, nodding to the wall and the room beyond.

There was a look between the two of them and when Bernie looked away first it was apparent who had won.

'You bastard! Okay, listen, I might be able to help out but I want 40% and not a word of you know what to my wife.'

'20%,' Elliott countered, 'and your secret is safe with me.'

'30% and that's my final offer,' Bernie offered in return.

'Mrs. Subiaco!' Elliott shouted.

'Okay, 20%, you bastard!' Bernie conceded urgently, alerted by the sound of the demon rising from the underworld and making her through the house.

'Excellent.'

'I'll arrange for you to meet with my niece Charlotte. She handles the business nowadays. Not a word, remember!'

The door flung open and the ex-SMERSH operative stormed into the room.

'You give useless husband job, da?' Rosa Klebb asked as she entered.

'Yes, we're organising an event, just like the old days,' Elliott explained.

'You speak to Charlotte. He no good any more. She run business nowadays.'

'Yes Mrs. Subiaco. That's the plan,' Elliott replied before adding with a wink in Bernie's direction.

As they left, Hapkido started a conversation that only he and Elliott could hear.

'Why are we leaving so soon? I had questions I needed to ask.'

'At the risk of talking to that woman again?'

'God no! Get that bloody door open and let's get the hell out of here.'

Chapter 14

Back seat persuader

Jeremy Flashman pulled up fifty metres from the front door of The Society, parking under the shadows of an aged oak tree. As the engine idled he flicked off the CD player that had been playing a Barry Manilow album that he'd mysteriously received through the post the morning prior. Turning off the engine, the headlights faded and the street returned to darkness. The only things visible through the gloom were the forms of the buildings and silhouettes of trees overhanging the road menacingly. There were certainly no people around. Deserted, just as he'd hoped, a road cloaked in secrecy, hidden by the night. The silence allowed Jeremy a few moments to collect his thoughts.

Had it really got that bad that he was actually considering breaking into the sacred library to steal a book? But it wasn't just any book was it; it was the greatest book of all, one that could change the world.

Why was he was doing this? Partly to get back at the society itself. For over twenty years they'd excluded him, humiliated him. Yet in that time he'd learnt a great number of the secrets that they'd tried so diligently to hide from him. And the most important secret of all was the book. He knew what it could do.

But was he doing it just to punish The Society? Far from it. There was another aspect to Jeremy's reasoning. He had long denied it, but seeing Elliott up on that stage, he recognised the danger it presented. Elliott Rose was the personification of the next generation coming through and showbusiness was an unforgiving mistress. It was only a matter of time before the public demanded someone new, someone younger, someone who wasn't Jeremy Flashman. And there he was, Elliott Rose, talking to the dead like he was born to do it. How long would it be before Elliott was regarded as a renowned psychic? How long until the general public turned their back on Jeremy Flashman as yesterday's news? Pretty damn quick, that's how long. Jeremy really only had one option. He couldn't continue to peddle the same tired lines, the same guesses wrapped up as sincere statements. He needed to have the actual abilities himself. And for that he needed the book.

*

The wooden Venetian blinds allowed a small amount of moonlight to filter through from the cloudless night sky and into the library. Cast onto the walnut floor they formed diffuse linear rectangles of silvery grey, providing a small amount of illumination to the room. A quietness prevailed throughout the building, punctuated by the rhythmic ticking of a clock from the hallway outside and the scraping of a window being carefully slid open. Slowly the rectangles of light became broader, fractured as one of the blinds was raised from behind. Jeremy Flashman entered through the unlocked window and gently stepped into the room. Careful to conceal his entrance from anyone passing by outside he carefully slid the window back into place and let the blind settle back to its normal position. His elongated shadow stretched out before him, lengthened across the width of the library and onto the lowest shelf of books of the opposing wall. Flicking on a small torch to show the way he made his way over to the bookcases, tracing the beam across the shelves before finding the F section. It was the perfect opportunity he thought, if not a little reckless. Reaching into his bag he took out a copy of his autobiography and slipped it onto the shelves before giving himself a congratulatory smile. Now all he had to do was find the other book. The light from the torch played across the various shelves. Suddenly, accentuated by the quietness, Jeremy heard footsteps in the hallway outside. With the upmost stealth he flicked off the torch and moved quickly to one of the corners, allowing the darkness to envelop him.

The door to the great library opened, revealing the silhouette of a man cast against the illuminated hallway beyond. Jeremy who lay hidden to the right of the open door stood stock still, watching the figure as it entered. The light of the hallway unmistakably showed it to be Mr. Falkirk, carrying a heavy, leather bound book under his arm, its edges gilded in ornate gold. Jeremy meanwhile took the opportunity to move behind the door, all but obscuring him from view.

Mr. Falkirk walked the short distance to the middle of the room and gently placed the book down on the table between the two chesterfield sofas. He then lit a candle that sat in the centre of the table, providing light to his immediate area but nowhere near enough to reveal the presence of the intruder.

'It's okay,' Mr. Falkirk whispered to himself, oblivious to the presence of Jeremy Flashman. 'I'm doing this for the society.'

The light from the candle flickered as Mr. Falkirk opened the book, turning each page delicately until he found what he was looking for.

'I call upon the spirits to make themselves known!' Mr. Falkirk spoke in a grandiose tone. 'Let the great spirit of Eldermon, grand leader of the fifth council of wizards show them the way. I give you this gift so that you may know the path.'

Mr. Falkirk waited. Jeremy Flashman meanwhile raised an eyebrow.

Mr. Falkirk waited further. In fact he waited for a further five minutes before he reluctantly conceded that absolutely nothing of any note had occurred or would likely occur. Closing the book he sighed.

'Why can't it work just this once?' He muttered despondently before standing and making his way over to a large picture of an old man on the wall.

Placing his fingers behind the frame Mr. Falkirk swung the picture away from the wall to reveal an embedded safe. Retrieving a key from his waistcoat pocket he opened the safe and placed the book on top of some yellow parchments bound by a red ribbon. After locking the safe and swinging the portrait back into place, Mr. Falkirk moved back to the centre of the room. Reaching underneath the table he flicked a hidden catch that ejected a secret drawer from the far end. Placing the key inside and closing the drawer he failed to notice the darkened outline of a head peering from around the door, watching.

'Bloody book,' Mr. Falkirk grumbled, blowing out the candle, a small wisp of smoke dancing in the moonlight.

Making his way back over to the doorway he turned and gave one last look at the library before raising his middle finger insultingly at the man in the painting. Mr. Falkirk closed the door behind him and the room returned to darkness.

Jeremy waited until the sound of footsteps had disappeared before emerging from his hiding place. He breathed in deeply, unsure of how long it had been since he had last done so. Tentatively he made his way over to the table, reaching underneath to flick the switch, elated as the secret drawer opened. Delicately taking the key out, he turned it between his fingers for a few seconds, smiling as he did so before eventually moving over to the painting. The man in the picture was elderly, sporting a long grey beard with unwelcome hair curling from his ears and nose. He was dressed in a smart but old fashioned suit, possibly from the Victorian era.

'Mr. Eldermon I presume,' Jeremy whispered as he swung the picture outwards.

Taking the key he delicately placed it in the lock and turned it until he heard a satisfying click, the safe door opening. And there it was, the book that would make him the greatest medium the world had ever seen. Overcome with eagerness he grasped it, embracing it against his chest.

It would have been too easy, too tempting to make his escape straight away. Jeremy had to be cleverer than that. If they found out the book was missing, he would surely be a prime suspect. After all, he had only just been asking about it. Relocking the safe he made his way back across to the table and returned the key to the secret drawer, sliding it closed. Then from a jacket pocket he retrieved some hair clips, an absolute necessity for a man of his notorious hair styling. Moving back to the safe, he proceeded to jam the hair clips into the keyhole as deeply as possible. Jeremy wasn't an expert at safes but he did know The Society pretty well. Penny-pinching tightwads that they were, it would take them an eternity to get round to fixing it, happy in the knowledge that the book remained safely inside. And by the time they did find out what had caused the jam it would be much too late. He swung the picture back into place and made his way back to the window, sliding it open before clambering onto the grass outside. Before leaving he gave one last look back at the library. It was a job well done.

Jeremy Flashman got back into his car, placing the book onto the passenger seat. Now that it was his, Jeremy felt a sense of achievement mixed with guilt. The latter wasn't a feeling he frequently experienced, but when he did so he reverted to a nervous child-like twirling of his hair with his index finger.

'Get a grip!' Flashman muttered, bringing his hand down to his side and forming a fist to control himself. Why should he regret what he had done? More importantly why would he mess up his hair for the sake of it?

Jeremy swivelled the rear-view mirror and leaned over to inspect the damage he'd done to his beloved hair. Well, it wasn't too bad, a bit of extra hair spray and ….

Shit! Fuck! Jesus!

Staring back at him from the rear seat was a figure in the darkness, a mass of curly hair silhouetted in the moonlight.

'Good evening Jeremy,' Carol announced, leaning forward menacingly.

'What the hell are you doing in my car?' Jeremy screamed, recognising the intruder. 'You scared the crap out of me!'

'Well if you will leave your car open whilst breaking and entering strange houses,' Carol declared.

'How the hell did you know I was here?' Jeremy replied, the beating of his heart falling to a less life threatening speed.

'I know a lot of things, especially when it affects my television show.'

'What are you talking about?' Jeremy asked, trying to maintain a sense of innocence.

'The book, Jeremy. I know what you think it contains and it doesn't take a genius to work out what you plan to do with it. You see, whether I like it or not, people only watch Ghostbusters UK to see you make things up. Can you imagine if you actually had the gift? Actually getting things right? It would be a disaster.'

'If that were true,' Jeremy suggested, not quite sure how Carol knew about the book, 'we could still make it work. It would be better surely?'

'Tell me. What if you suddenly had these abilities? You'd drop the show in an instant the minute a global tour came along.'

'And so what if I did? You can't stop me,' Jeremy announced, angry that she was pressuring him.

'Maybe, maybe not,' Carol replied. 'But that's not why I'm here. I believe we have more pressing concerns at the moment wouldn't you say?'

'And they are?' Jeremy asked.

'Elliott Rose.'

'What about him?'

'You saw what he could do, and if we don't do something soon, he could ruin us both. I know you've thought about it. Someone like that, young, convincing. How long until he takes over from you? For me, what's to stop him revealing the secret about Ghostbusters UK?'

'So do something about it,' Jeremy demanded. 'I thought you had him nailed down to a contract.'

'Don't treat me like an idiot, Jeremy!' Carol barked. 'Of course he has a contract. I could sue him to hell and back but that's no use to us once the information is out there. All it takes is for him to go to one of the national rags and it's over for us. We're his competition now. Whilst he was a bum we could have re-employed him but now look. I know you saw his performance at the leisure centre, and he didn't need a book, did he? I even hear from certain sources that's he's trying to arrange an event.'

'So have you tried giving him money to keep him quiet?' Jeremy asked.

'What would be the point? We can't afford to keep him quiet forever and what happens if his career takes off? He would have no need to keep our secret then would he? Remember Jeremy, we are the competition now,' Carol stressed, tapping a condescending finger against her temple repeatedly to illustrate that it was obvious to everyone but Flashman.

'Have you tried sleeping with him?' Jeremy replied in retribution.

'Don't be crude Jeremy!'

'So what do you propose we do?' Jeremy conceded. 'I admit, even with the book, I wouldn't want our little charade revealed. It would ruin me, power or no power.'

'Well then, that's the question isn't it,' Carol announced, relaxing back into the seat. 'We have two options as far as I can see. The first is simple. You confront him and convince him he doesn't have the gift. Maybe show him some of your fancy book spells just to prove what a real medium can do. If that works, and it's a big if, you get him believing that he shouldn't mess with things he doesn't understand, we can turn him back into a bum in an instant. And you know what that means? It means he'll be desperate for any job that comes along. I've been to his flat, he's got nothing. Suddenly his old job becomes available, forgive and forget and all that and we can manage him however we like.'

'And the second option?' Jeremy probed.

'The second option,' Carol paused. 'The second option, well that's something completely different.'

Five minutes later after Carol had explained all, the headlights to the car came on, lighting up the street with the occupants inside having made their decision.

Chapter 15

And the crowd at the back say Bidi-Bidi-Bidi

The Apollo Rooms had survived two world wars and one Max Bygraves concert since its inception. Inside, countless rows of seats upholstered in a blood red velour stretched from the stage at the front to the back, fifty metres distant. The borders of the ceiling were sculpted into a featured landscape of swirls that encompassed the great apple-white plane that loomed over the audience. The Apollo Rooms maintained a touch of grandiose decorum not seen in the more modern builds of today. Good on it, progress can be a right bastard when it comes down to it.

Elliott tried the front door. Locked. He checked his watch to confirm. She had said twelve o'clock hadn't she? He peered through the glass, hoping to catch sight of her. Truth was he had no idea what she looked like even if he did see someone. He hoped desperately that she didn't take after her Russian Auntie, he couldn't live his life constantly looking down, wary of a blade being ejected from the toe of her shoe. It was ten minutes past now and he was definitely at the Apollo Rooms. And he was not alone.

Standing behind Elliott was Hapkido, who had insisted on coming. Apparently, as well as being a wrestler, samurai and time traveller he was well versed in advanced negotiation and business practice. Elliott sincerely doubted that Hapkido was any of these things. Back at the flat he had expertly waited for Hapkido to visit the toilet, for God knows what reason. Elliott seized the opportunity, ran to his car, and sped away. It took two streets before Hapkido appeared inclined on the back seat, oblivious that Elliott was contemplating finding the nearest available tree at 60 mph.

'How do we get in?' Elliott asked, rattling the door as a light rain drizzled from an unenthusiastic grey sky.

'Well if I know Charlotte Subiaco,' Hapkido speculated.

'But you don't,' Elliott interjected. 'There's probably a back door.'

'Yes there is, and with my knowledge of the void I can tell us exactly where it is.'

'Is it round the back?' Elliott asked, sarcastically.

'It is!' Hapkido replied enthusiastically. 'I'm starting to see why we are linked together. Perhaps you too are able to read the void?'

'Come on you moron,' Elliott ordered, trudging round the curved front of the building and finding a side alley decorated with industrial bins.

'It's down there,' Hapkido stated with confidence.

There was only one door down the alleyway, a heavy metallic double door painted in a thick orange gloss. It took a few knocks before they heard the sound of someone unlocking it from the other side.

'I told you it was this one,' Hapkido commented.

Elliott would have attempted a witty retort if he wasn't for the fact he was suddenly distracted by the sight before him. The woman who opened the door was about five foot seven, mid-twenties and with loose blonde curls, the colour of honey. Her eyes were an exquisite aquamarine tint that could have been taken from an exotic tropical sea. Elliott's eyes in the interim were involuntarily drawn down from her delicate face to her cleavage that presented itself tantalizingly from a white cotton blouse. A tight grey skirt to just above the knee finished the look, hugging the curves of her hips and falling in at the waist.

'Elliott Rose I presume?' Charlotte Subiaco enquired.

'Umm yeah,' Elliott stammered, lost for words.

'It's a pleasure,' Charlotte declared, holding out her hand.

'One moment please,' Elliott interrupted clumsily, pulling his phone from his pocket and raising it to his ear as if he'd just received a call. The lack of ringing was a bit unusual but he hadn't thought that far ahead. He did know one thing though: she was beautiful, he was captivated, and Hapkido was an absolute liability. Handy at wrestling, granted. Talking to the dead, not too shabby. Successful with the ladies? Elliott seriously doubted it.

He began to walk down the alleyway, pretending to talk to the imaginary caller, hoping that Hapkido would follow.

'Listen,' Elliott whispered once he was out of range of Charlotte and Hapkido had trotted up next to him.

'Who are you on the phone to? And how is it working without a wire?' Hapkido asked.

'I'm not on the phone to anyone,' Elliott sighed. 'I'm pretending so I can come over here and talk to you.'

'Clever. But why didn't you use our special link?'

'Well obviously I didn't think of that did I? I got a bit, you know, flustered.'

'So what's the problem?' Hapkido asked.

'Well, in case you hadn't noticed, she's beautiful. I was thinking that maybe I could ask her out.'

'Well why don't you? Is it because she's about fifty years too young?'

'Sod off!' Elliott replied deliberately through gritted teeth. 'It's just, how can I put it? When you're around it doesn't always go well for me.'

'Like when?' Hapkido asked, seemingly offended.

'How about the pub and getting punched in the face? I was hoping, just this once, I could make a good impression. Do you get what I mean?'

'Absolutely.'

'Okay, good,' Elliott replied, turning back towards Charlotte, the phone still clamped to his ear.

'Maybe I can possess you and together we can impress her with some wrestling moves!' Hapkido suggested.

Elliott came to a sudden halt, closed his eyes and wondered for a brief second if it were possible that it was he who had died. Maybe this was some kind of reincarnation where he was being punished a thousand times over by an annoying ghost. Perhaps he had been some evil warlord in a previous life? Hang on, that's wasn't such a bad idea.

'Genghis Khan!' Elliott muttered under his breath.

'What?'

'Genghis Khan!' Elliott repeated. 'I've just seen him at the end of the alleyway.'

'I think you may have been mistaken.'

'No, it was definitely him. Now what would he be doing here?' Elliott asked suggestively.

'Well if it was him….'

'It was definitely him,' Elliott reinforced.

'Perhaps he's a time traveller too? Perhaps he has sought me out as a fellow of the Far East?' Hapkido proposed, his focus quickly diverted.

'You should go and ask him,' Elliott suggested.

'I have to!' Hapkido replied with gusto. 'Look, I'm sorry I'm leaving you in the lurch here with this Charlotte girl but I have to talk to him.'

'I understand,' Elliott replied, feigning a sense of disappointment.

Without further ado Hapkido ventured off down the alleyway hurriedly. With any luck, Elliott thought, that would be the last he would see of him for a good half hour. With the coast clear he dropped the phone from his ear and walked back towards Charlotte.

'I'm so sorry about that,' Elliott announced as he drew near.

'That's okay, was it something important?' Charlotte asked.

'It was my …' Elliott hesitated. Should he claim it was his stock broker, perhaps the local Porsche dealership, or maybe go full out MI6? He was concentrating so much on formulating a believable lie that he forgot to speak for a disproportionate period of time.

'You okay?' Charlotte enquired, wondering if Elliott had entered a catatonic state during the extended pause in conversation.

'It was…' Elliott flustered. Damn, the only thought that kept flashing into his mind was walking in on Hapkido in the shower.

'Do you need some time?'

'It was my plumber. My new shower has arrived. It's the E3000 with dual nozzle attachment,' Elliott rambled in panic.

'Okay,' Charlotte replied, drawing out the reply that indicated the strong suspicion of moron in proximity.

Elliott, realising that his first impression lacked refinement, decided to move on, and quickly.

'I'm here about the show. Your uncle sent me,' Elliott announced.

'Of course, follow me. I'll show you the venue and we can talk details along the way,' Charlotte replied, heading back into the building.

Elliott promptly followed. Maybe he should have shown her some wrestling moves after all, it certainly couldn't have been any worse.

If you were to ask Elliott what they had actually talked about in the ten minutes it took to walk around the Apollo Rooms he would have had no idea. Whilst she was talking gate receipts, he was becoming an expert on the captivating sway of her body. When she talked about local regulations his eyesight was drawn towards her cleavage as if a tractor beam were installed there.

When Elliott finally snapped out of his daze he found himself standing on the stage with Charlotte facing him, acutely aware of the thousands of empty seats to his right. Although they were unoccupied if felt as if the eyes of an invisible audience were upon him.

'So that's the date sorted and you know what you have to do,' Charlotte detailed. 'I'll handle the advertising, ticketing and management, you just turn up and do your thing. I just hope my uncle wasn't wrong about you, there are a lot of seats here to fill.'

'No problem,' Elliott replied nervously, feeling the presence of the empty theatre now more than ever. He'd got so carried away with managing Hapkido that he hadn't really considered standing in front of a thousand complete strangers hanging on to his every word.

'Charlotte,' Elliott asked. 'Do you mind if I have a few moments alone so I can get a feel for the place please?'

'Of course, I have to go see the manager anyway. Will you be able to find your way out when you're done?'

'Absolutely.'

'I'll pop round to your flat tomorrow at eleven with my uncle to discuss things further,' Charlotte replied before making her way from the stage with her heels providing a seductive beat.

Elliott couldn't actually remember agreeing to her coming

round to his flat but then there were large portions of the conversation he hadn't really been concentrating on.

When he was sure he was finally alone he turned to face the rows of seats. They seemed to stretch on forever before becoming lost in the darkness towards the back. How many people would be here, each and every one of them watching him intently? Would he really be the showman they all expected? Would Hapkido stop banging on about sausage sandwiches for five minutes and actually be of any help? To those questions, Elliott truly didn't know the answers. As he continued to ponder his fears he heard footsteps approaching. She had obviously come back, this time he wouldn't cock up his first impression.

'I was thinking maybe we could discuss some of the finer points over coffee,' Elliott began before stalling when he noticed it certainly wasn't Charlotte Subiaco who was approaching.

Elliott had expected to see a vision of perfection. Instead he was met with the disconcerting sight of a golden medallion nestled in a forest of chest hair. Jeremy Flashman came to a halt ten feet away.

'Hello Elliott. I'll skip the coffee if you don't mind.'

'What the hell are you doing here?' Elliott asked, confusion merged with anger.

'I'm putting things right,' Flashman replied, reaching into the inside of his jacket and pulling out a book.

'Oh Christ, not your autobiography again?'

'I'll show you who the real medium is here,' Flashman heralded, letting the book fall open in his hands and studying it intently.

'What are you doing?' Elliott asked, bewildered.

'I call upon the spirits to make themselves known,' Flashman began. 'Let the great spirit of Eldermon, grand leader of the fifth council of wizards show me the way.'

Flashman waited a few seconds, expecting a wind to pick up from somewhere. When it became apparent that the Apollo Rooms were devoid of any supernatural occurrence he began again, louder and with more authority.

'I call upon the spirits to make…'

'Jeremy,' Elliott interrupted, 'are you having another one of your episodes?'

'Be quiet!' Flashman snarled. 'Let the great spirit of Eldermon, grand leader of the fifth council of wizards show me the way.'

'What exactly are you trying to do?'

'I call upon the spirits … Look, shut up! You're putting me off here!'

'Putting you off what?'

'If you must know,' Flashman protested. 'I am attempting to raise the spirits onto this plane of existence so I can show you what it's like to be a real medium. Once you see that these powers aren't to be meddled with then you'll realise that this calling is not for the likes of you.'

Elliott took a few moments to look around the empty theatre.

'How's that working out?' He asked sarcastically.

'Look, you wouldn't understand. I just need to say it the right way,' Flashman complained, scanning the page to see if he was missing something.

When Elliott had worked on Ghostbusters UK he could just about tolerate Flashman. But seeing he was no longer paid by them, he felt no such obligation. He was on a different path now and the mere presence of Jeremy Flashman vanquished his doubts in an instant.

'Good luck with that,' Elliott declared as he made his way from the stage. He didn't have time for idiots like Flashman anymore, standing in the middle of a theatre speaking a load of nonsense to no one.

In reality, Elliott wasn't quite right. There was at least one other person present and despite Flashman's best efforts, she hadn't been raised from the dead. Hiding in the shadows at the back, Carol watched the scene unfold in front of her.

'What is that moron doing?' Carol whispered to herself. 'Well, I suppose if you want something done, you have to do it yourself. I was so hoping it wouldn't have to come to this.'

Chapter 16

The cubicle paradox

Whilst Elliott stood brushing his teeth in t-shirt and boxers, staring into the bathroom mirror, his mind considered the events of the day before. Had Jeremy Flashman really tried to raise the dead? What the hell was he actually trying to achieve? It would have been useful to have Hapkido's opinion on the matter but he still hadn't returned from stalking Genghis Khan across the great expanse of time and mortality. Elliott was sure that when Hapkido did finally realise that the 13th century leader of the Mongol empire hadn't been mooching around the back end of London he'd surely be back. Besides Elliott had enjoyed the break and he had more pressing concerns. As if on cue the doorbell rang.

Elliott stifled a yawn as he opened the door, he'd only been up half an hour but the least he could do would be to appear interested when he saw her. He'd messed up their first meeting, he was adamant he wouldn't ruin their second.

Bernie Subiaco and Charlotte stood in front of him. She had forsaken the business ensemble and gone for a more casual attire today of tight blue stonewashed jeans and a purple and black horizontally striped jumper. Did it do anything to lessen her beauty? Certainly not in Elliott's eyes.

'Morning,' Bernie proclaimed with a sly grin.

Elliott took a second to reply as he could see Charlotte scanning him, hopefully experiencing a feeling of sudden attraction.

'Hi,' Elliott commented, delighted she might feel the same.

'Ahem,' Charlotte unsubtly coughed, nodding towards his bottom half.

Elliott had been so preoccupied with thinking about the previous day he had quite forgotten that he was wearing just boxer shorts when he'd answered the door. As an opening to the greatest romance ever it lacked a certain level of refinement.

'Come in,' Elliott replied nervously, darting back along the hall and into his bedroom. As he attempted to pull on a pair of trousers, it became the most complex action ever attempted in the history of mankind. A new definition of hopelessness came into existence as he frantically hopped around the room with one leg in, the other leg steadfastly refusing to comply. When he did finally manage it, he tucked himself in, drew the zip and rushed hurriedly into the front room.

'I'm really sorry about that. I didn't realise what the time was,' Elliott apologised.

'Perhaps we can get down to business?' Bernie impatiently asked.

'Sure,' Elliott replied, resolute to keep his mind on the job. She looked lovely though, and he couldn't help but stare.

Unexpectedly the doorbell rang again. After apologising once more for the interruption he made his way back towards the front door, planning on getting rid of whoever it was as soon as possible.

'Hello dearie,' announced Mrs. Clarkson.

'Hello,' Elliott replied, exasperated. He didn't have much time to think anything else as she slipped past him and down the hallway without a word of explanation.

'I heard you had visitors so I thought they might like to buy some raffle tickets to the W.I fete next Tuesday?' Mrs. Clarkson enquired as she entered the front room.

It was easy to surmise that her mission was less fund raising and more nosiness. An absence of raffle tickets about her person did little to disprove the hypothesis. A ray of light streamed through the window and illuminated Mrs. Clarkson from behind, prompting a look of utter infatuation on the face of Bernie Subiaco.

'Well, hello,' Bernie announced as suggestively as Terry Thomas's entire career.

'And you are?' Mrs. Clarkson asked, holding out her hand enticingly.

'The name's Bernard Subiaco and the pleasure is all mine,' he replied, taking her hand in his and kissing it gently. It would have been a scene deserving of a Jane Austin novel were it not for the fact that Elliott felt a small lump of vomit come up at the back of his throat.

'So, business?' Charlotte suggested, obviously bewildered by the situation and hoping to get back on track.

'This is certainly not the time for business,' Bernie interrupted with an evocative wink in Mrs. Clarkson's direction.

'Perhaps we can talk somewhere else other than Ernest's flat?' Mrs. Clarkson asked mischievously.

'Elliott,' Elliott corrected.

'I'm sure we can find a more pleasant place to become more acquainted,' Bernie affirmed. 'Lunch perhaps? There's a small place just down the road from here. Ernest and I have some things we need to discuss but we can soon sort that out and get onto more important things.'

'Elliott,' Elliott corrected again.

'That would be most agreeable,' Mrs. Clarkson replied, fidgeting with the buttons of her lilac cardigan.

All that was left was for Charlotte and Elliott to exchange a look of mutual understanding. It had been a lot less awkward when Elliott didn't have any trousers on.

*

Ten minutes later the four of them found themselves standing outside a local café with an assortment of baguettes displayed in the front window. Beyond that could be seen the counter that ran lengthwise along the shop and further back, an arrangement of half occupied tables.

'Is this alright?' Bernie asked Mrs. Clarkson. She nodded in return and judging by her face, Bernie's method of wining and dining a lady met with her approval.

'I'm sorry, I've got a phone call,' Charlotte suddenly announced, pulling a phone from her handbag and raising it to her ear.

In an instant Elliott knew what was going on. There was no phone ring, no vibration as if on silent. She too was obviously playing the old fake phone call trick. She had no intention of being a part of this, and Elliott was annoyed that he hadn't thought of it first. He couldn't go in there with just Bernie and Mrs. Clarkson. If Charlotte came then at least it would seem like a double date, albeit an extremely weird one. Elliott shuffled stealthily over to where Charlotte was having her pretend conversation.

'Yes, okay, immediately you say,' Charlotte announced loudly to her made up caller.

'I know you aren't talking to anyone,' Elliott whispered.

'Shut up, they don't know that,' Charlotte whispered back.

'Come on. Don't leave me alone with them. You're not really going to use the fake phone call trick are you?'

'Why not, you did yesterday,' Charlotte replied quietly.

Elliott was dumbstruck. How had she known the truth? Had it really been that obvious? With any riposte struck from his mind his only response was to allow his mouth to fall open. Appearing recently lobotomised was certainly not a look that would convince her to stay.

'I'm really sorry,' Charlotte announced to all present, moving the phone away from her ear. 'I can't join you. Something has come up with the venue.'

'Of course. You do what you have to do,' Bernie replied, not overly concerned.

With that Bernie and Mrs. Clarkson proceeded to walk into the café and Elliott, having absolutely no excuse besides the Universe hating him, trudged in resignedly behind them.

*

Elliott found himself sitting next to Bernie Subiaco at a plastic table, convinced that Charlotte's uncle and Mrs. Clarkson were playing footsie under the table. Any attempts he'd made to start a conversation had been completely ignored. With little other option Elliott instead decided to remain quiet and wait longingly for the chicken and bacon baguette he'd ordered. He might be stuck here but at least he'd get something to eat that wasn't jam. Elliott slouched back onto the chair, crossing his arms and staring at the ceiling tiles. Listening to the sounds of the cafe around him he could hear the steam from the coffee machine hissing, the sound of the bell attached to the top of the door ringing as someone entered. This was followed by the clacking of stiletto heels on the tile floor as someone walked nearby. Elliott finally started paying attention when the sound of footsteps was replaced startlingly with that of someone shouting.

'Da, you useless man! I know you up to no good this morning. I follow you. I find you with whore!'

Elliott looked up with a start. The shocking red hair, the fingernails fashioned in the style of Mola Ram, it could only be one person.

'But, you misunderstand,' Bernie stuttered, taken aback by his wife's sudden arrival.

'You bad man. You with this whore now!' Mrs. Subiaco snarled.

'I'm here on business,' Bernie protested.

'You in whore business now? You pimp to this thing?'

'Now listen here,' Mrs. Clarkson complained. 'This is a business meeting and I don't care who you are but you can't come in here and start calling me a whore.'

'I'm his wife, whore!' Bernie's wife replied, her fingers flexing, eager to grasp a still beating heart.

'Don't you dare speak to me like that!' Mrs. Clarkson shouted back.

'Look, this has all been a big misunderstanding,' Bernie proposed, unconvincingly.

'No mistake. You bad man. You with this whore now!'

'Look I understand what this might look like,' Elliott interrupted, not actually quite sure why he was getting involved.

'You get this boy to speak for you? You no good man, you not stand up for yourself.'

That was enough for Elliott. He could handle being woken up every morning by a wrestler for whom the wheel was spinning but the hamster was dead. He could handle making a terrible first impression on one of the most beautiful women he'd ever met. At a push he could even handle the unpleasant circumstances of being forced to go for lunch with two old age pensioners who were attempting to jump each other's bones. But he absolutely drew the line at being involved in a domestic argument that was quickly escalating to culpable homicide. To add insult to injury, where the hell was his baguette? He slid the chair back subtly and made his way over to a door at the back, hoping to escape unseen. The last thing Elliott saw as he slipped through was Mrs. Clarkson wielding a bottle of brown sauce and waving it menacingly in the face of Bernie Subiaco's wife.

As the door closed behind him, it was obvious that this wasn't a back door but the men's toilets. Still, the argument from the restaurant seemed to be getting louder and this was as good a place as any to hide. Yet he wasn't entirely convinced that he was safe in here either. Any moment now a full-blown fight between those of bus pass eligibility could spill into the men's toilets. Just to be sure he made his way over to the far cubicle and locked the door behind him. It might not be the most glamorous hiding place but it was safe, for the time being. The only downside, Elliott quickly discovered was that the cubicle next to him was also busy, its occupant not shy about making his presence known via the medium of his arse. Despite not trying to listen, it sounded like Elliott's neighbour was having the mother of all dumps, somewhere between a plane crash and Hiroshima. Oh for God's sake, Elliott thought, this is turning into a total disaster.

'Disaster, I'll tell you about disaster. Fourteen hours I spent trying to track down Genghis Khan and not a sign!' A voice announced from the next cubicle.

'Hapkido?' Elliott enquired timidly.

'I'll tell you what. I think you might have been mistaken about seeing him.'

'Hapkido, it's you, thank God!'

'Of course it's me. Who else would it be?'

'You have no idea of the morning I've had,' Elliott explained.

'You mean the fact that Mrs. Clarkson currently has Bernie Subiaco's wife in a headlock?'

'Something like that.'

The sound of scuffling could be heard against the main door, the fight now going full pelt. The combined age of the combatants may well have been into three figures but one of them was a suspected husband killer and the other possessed fingernails that would intimidate Wolverine. All Elliott wanted to do was to get out of here but leaving by the front door could result in him losing an arm.

'Hap. Let's get out of here. Any suggestions?'

'There's always the window,' Hapkido advocated.

Elliott turned to see an open window high above him. If he climbed onto the cistern and pulled himself up it might just be wide enough for him to slide through.

'Hapkido, you're a star. I'll see you back at the flat okay?'

'My pleasure,' Hapkido replied before proceeding with phase two of his bowel movement.

Were the fight outside not enough to convince Elliott, the thunderous sounds of Hapkido on the toilet certainly was. With haste he clambered onto the cistern, levering himself out of the window and dropping to the floor of the alleyway outside. Safe, for the time being.

Chapter 17

Sandwich spread and a sawn-off shotgun to boot

The taxi pulled up at the entrance of Reading train station but the passenger had no intention of boarding a train. Carol Swanson had a more sinister purpose. Stepping from the car she made her way to the entrance of the station, past a gathering of smokers that stood outside a neighbouring pub that specialised in a multitude of sports channels. The smokers would have been hard pressed to recognise her, the expensive sunglasses expertly obscuring her identity from anyone who might cast a glance in her direction.

Entering the foyer Carol looked around for the sign for platform thirteen. This was where she'd been told to meet him at noon and if she were being honest, she found the anticipation oddly thrilling, flirting on the wrong side of danger. To negotiate the barriers she brought a ticket to Twyford, wherever the hell that was, and made her way over the bridge. After passing the coffee stand she descended the final set of stairs that led down onto the platform. It was around midday, a weekday and the next train wasn't due until one o'clock. Her contact had obviously planned this in advance, the place was deserted.

Looking up and down the platform Carol had no idea what her contact would look like. She imagined a rough-hewn face with piercing lonely eyes that had seen far too many lives slipping away in front of it. His was no doubt a tortured soul, pressured into committing crime by a society that demanded his services yet refused to acknowledge them. The more she considered it, the more likely that he would be the type of man who took the pleasure of a woman to distract him from his own tormented thoughts. Luckily Carol was just that type of woman. She would soon find out: at the far end of the platform there stood just one other person. Carol walked purposely along, the distant figure getting ever nearer. Not only had he chosen the perfect time but also the perfect spot, far away from prying eyes. She was now within twelve feet of the man, his back turned to her so that she couldn't make anything out except a beige jacket, dark trousers and mousy brown hair at the back. Hearing her approach the stranger began to turn around.

'Well hello,' the stranger announced in a nasal tone. 'Did you know that the 12:15 from Exeter St David's is due through at any moment? The A1450 carriage is of course equipped to run on a number of gauges but is perfectly suited to the current gauge on the South-East network.'

The figure that had turned displayed none of Carol's expected traits. There was neither a scar running the length of his face nor an inner turmoil forged from the atrocities he'd witnessed. Instead, she was confronted by a man in his mid-forties wearing elasticated trousers and a checked shirt, half untucked at the waistband. His eyes were magnified ten-fold by the large-framed glasses which did nothing to distract from a complexion you could mountain bike over.

'I'm so sorry, I think I've got the wrong person,' Carol replied, backing away in horror.

'Carol, right?' The stranger asked.

'What?'

'Carol. It's me. You came here to see me,' he announced, letting loose a snigger which would have made a normal person run for the nearest figure of authority.

'This is a joke right?' Carol enquired.

'I don't know why you would think that,' the stranger replied, seemingly hurt. 'You asked for someone to sort out a problem for you. It was arranged that we meet here. I don't see the problem.'

'But you're, you know…'

'A ruthless assassin?'

'No a…'

'A crack hitman?'

'No a trainspotter!'

'Yes, so? Don't you think professional hitmen are allowed hobbies?' He replied, taking off his glasses and cleaning the lenses on the untucked tail of his shirt.

'It's hardly the image you imagine though is it?' Carol replied, her hands on her hips. 'Look, I'm sorry but there has obviously been some sort of mistake.'

'I don't think so. Either you want me to take on the job or not.'

'Well of course I don't want you to take the job. I was looking for a professional hitman and somehow I got put in contact with you. I was looking for someone to do a job, not someone to tell me when the next train to Maidenhead is due. How the hell would you even think you could do a job like this?'

All of a sudden steely look came over his eyes, his irksome smile paling to insignificance.

'Questions about my hobby are one thing, questioning my competence, that's inexcusable.'

'Well I'm sorry,' Carol retorted. 'But I don't believe a trainspotting hitman is what I'm really after.'

'Really? Well perhaps I can change your mind.'

The trainspotter slid the small notepad he was carrying in his right hand into the front pocket of his shirt. Crouching down he opened up the Thomas the Tank Engine lunchbox at his feet.

'My mum makes these,' he stated, taking the cling-filmed sandwiches out and resting them on the inside of the lid. Revealed underneath was a sleek black gun with silencer attached.

'Is that real?' Carol asked, a little excited, perhaps sexually so.

'Of course.'

'That's all very well but can you actually use it?' Carol enquired, her hand moving from her hip to play with some coiled hair near her ear.

The train spotter raised his eyebrows in return. Turning towards a clump of tress jutting out over a side cutting and away from the main hub of the station, he raised the gun and closed his left eye, taking aim. A few seconds later, startled by an approaching train, a bird lifted into the air from one of the branches. In an instant the hitman let a single round fly and the bird fell like a stone towards the ground. Immediately the muffled sound of the shot was drowned out by the sound of the train rushing through the station, as the hitman stashed the gun within the confines of his jacket. Both he and Carol stood in silence until the train had thundered through.

'Did you see?' The hitman asked.

'Oh I saw,' Carol replied, panting.

'That was the 12.10 from Hereford.'

'No, not that,' Carol replied. 'What you did to that bird.'

'Oh that. I hate birds! Always crapping on the trains!'

All the excitement of seeing the gun and the shot being fired was enough to get Carol more than a little excited. She had never seen someone fire a gun before. She knew she liked it.

'Do it again!' She demanded in a seductive purr.

'You wanted proof, you got proof. The next shot costs you.'

'You're hired,' Carol declared. 'What do I call you?'

'They call me the Lunchbox Killer. The hit will be forty thousand, twenty up front, twenty on completion. Now who's the target?'

'Rose, his name's Elliott Rose.'

Chapter 18

You built a time machine, out of a Renault Clio?

Elliott let the door to the flat swing open, checking for anyone that might be waiting on the other side. Elliott wasn't totally convinced that Bernie's estranged wife didn't hold him personally responsible for having introduced her husband to Mrs. Clarkson. Was it possible that she'd raced ahead to lie in wait for him? Would entering his flat be like Bilbo Baggins entering the lair of Smaug?

'Get in there you tart!' Hapkido announced, pushing Elliott from behind. Quite how he had managed to exert force from arms not of this world was a mystery.

'Okay, okay,' Elliott replied, stumbling into the hallway.

After checking every room in the flat, Elliott finally reassured himself that it was only himself and Hapkido present. He slumped onto the sofa in the front room with Hapkido standing above him.

'Well, that was rather disagreeable,' Elliott declared, casting a glance out of the window that looked over the park.

'So what do you fancy doing now? May I suggest after all the excitement, we do something more mundane?' Hapkido suggested, sitting down beside him.

'By normal I'm presuming you're classifying sitting on a sofa with the ghost of a wrestler a natural occurrence?'

'Ghost of a wrestler? I think you are taking this whole psychic thing a little too seriously. As you know ....'

'Don't say it!' Elliott interrupted.

'.... that I am ...'

'I asked you not to mention it,' Elliott reiterated

Hapkido didn't respond as such, more coughed the poorly concealed words *time traveller*.

'TV then,' Elliott replied, more than keen to change the subject.

'I agree, but as long as it's not that American wrestling I saw the other day.' Hapkido entreated. 'I'll tell you something, with my skills I would be champion within a week.'

'Of course,' Elliott sighed, flicking on the television to find the film Back to the Future being shown.

'What's this?' Hapkido asked, his interest piqued.

'This? You'll probably like it, it's about time travel.'

'Is it a documentary?'

'Yeah, why not,' Elliott replied, half in resignation, half mischievously.

The next hour was probably the quietest Hapkido had ever been. From the very first minute the wrestler had sat forward eagerly, smiling with a childlike wonder as the plot unfurled in front of his eyes. Elliott happily sat watching too, until finally he could no longer ignore the growing desire to urinate. With exaggerated effort he extracted himself from the comforting embrace of the sofa and made his way along the hallway towards the bathroom. It was only then that he noticed something amiss. Looking down at his feet they no longer felt as if they were his own, obediently following instructions that didn't seem to come from him. He continued to walk, past the bathroom and onwards towards the front door. His hand moved upwards as if it were the most natural thing for it to do, too light to hold down anymore. His fingers, numb at the tips, grasped the catch and turned it. Finally a milky cloud descended like a veil in front of his eyes and Elliott felt his thoughts withdraw inside him.

*

It was a suggestion of a name at first. A whisper in the darkness, a word carried on the wind, fading to distance. Then came warmth, reminiscent of the sun on bare skin on a winter's day. The warmth came from the light, growing in the darkness. A thin grey smoke emanated from an infinite point and became the form, finding life. Along tiny filaments within the smoke the light raced, stretching and rushing along. The form welcomed the light, allowing it to define it. The definition was life and the life was familiar, knowing it had existed before. It had breathed the same air before, drawing it down into its welcoming lungs. But the mouth could do more than merely breathe, it knew how to produce shapes that allowed words to come.

'What the fuck!' Elliott screamed as the haze lifted in front of him, suddenly finding himself behind the steering wheel of his Renault Clio.

'How's it going?' Hapkido asked, materialising in the passenger seat beside him.

'What … what the hell is happening!' Elliott screamed, his head swinging wildly from side to side.

'Keep your hair on, you're driving a car after all.'

'I'm driving a frigging car at …' Elliott exclaimed, looking down at the speedometer. 'Jesus Christ, 89 mph. The last thing I remember was being in the flat.'

Realising that he was solely responsible for the car he released the pressure from the accelerator, allowing the speed to drop.

'It's okay. You can slow down now anyway, the experiment didn't work.'

'What are you talking about?' Elliott enquired before it finally dawned on him. 'You bloody possessed me again didn't you? You absolute cretin! Didn't I tell you never to do that again?'

'I apologise, but it was necessary given the new information I received from the documentary.'

'What documentary?'

'The one on television, just before I possessed you.'

'You weren't watching a documentary you idiot, you were watching Back to the Future. Oh for fuck's sake, please don't tell me you were trying to drive this heap of crap at 88 mph to travel back in time?'

'Well,' Hapkido mused, 'as it happens I was, but may I suggest you have a more pressing concern to deal with first.'

'Well whatever it is, I'll sort it out by myself,' Elliott suggested, his anger failing to subside.

'Very well, but I do suggest you look in your rear-view mirror first.'

Elliott flicked his eyes towards the mirror and was instantly confronted by an alarming sight. Following behind, its lights swirling in astute anger was a police car. It was only then that the sound of the siren - the rather loud and noticeable siren - came to his attention. How had he missed it? The fact he had been technically elsewhere up until a minute ago was probably a good enough reason but he concluded the Crown Prosecution Service probably wouldn't be so understanding.

'What the hell do I do?' Elliott asked, glancing over to the passenger seat, only to find it devoid of Hapkido Valentine.

'Well that's just great,' Elliott proclaimed and with no other choice, he steered the car across the lanes and onto the hard shoulder, slowing the car to a stop.

Once stationary Elliott glanced in his mirror as the police car pulled up behind. A full minute passed before the door opened and the policeman approached, dressed in the standard black uniform with aviator sunglasses, slicked back hair and turning a toothpick over in his mouth. Elliott wasn't sure whether he was still dreaming as he wound down the window.

'Going pretty fast back there boy,' the officer announced with a drawl somewhere between Louisiana and Romford.

'I'm sorry officer, I guess I just didn't notice.'

'Do you know exactly how fast you were going?'

'I'm guessing around 88 mph.'

'Damn right boy. Now let's see your driver license.'

Elliott reached over to the glove compartment and opened it. As he did so he caught sight of the police officer moving his hand to his belt, ready to draw a non-existent weapon. He needn't have worried, the only things contained within the glove box was a Now 13 compilation tape, a half-eaten packet of Werther's Originals and another map of Belgium. Elliott's driving license was absent which came as no surprise as he normally kept it in his wallet. A wallet he had left back at the flat. A flat he hadn't actually intended to leave.

'I'm really sorry. I seem to have left it at home,' Elliott confessed.

'Well, how about you start by telling me your name?'

At this moment Elliott started to feel light headed, not quite in control of his actions. What was his name again? Elliott? That sounded familiar. Or was it Gordon? He couldn't quite recall. He was sure of one thing though, the car was registered to a Simone

Phillips. Simone? No, that's a girl's name.

'My name?' Elliott announced suddenly. 'Simon, Simon Phillips.'

'Wait here,' the officer ordered, making his way back to his car. Two minutes later he returned.

'Did you say Simon Phillips?' The police officer enquired.

'Yes, that's my name,' Elliott confirmed, not sure why.

'Not Simone?'

'No it's Simon.'

'And you are male aren't you?'

'Yes,' Elliott replied, suppressing the desire to be offended given the circumstances.

'The car is registered to a Simone Phillips, you know with an e. And our records say you are also female.'

'Well, I don't know what to say about that,' Elliott responded. 'Maybe I ticked the wrong box on the form?'

'Wrong box eh? Maybe you did, maybe you didn't,' the officer replied, obviously finding the story suspicious. 'I'm going to have to take some more details from you.'

The officer placed two fingers into his top pocket to slide his notebook out before they withdrew suddenly.

'What the?' The police officer exclaimed, looking at his fingers to see a thick covering of strawberry jam. Elliott looked up and alternated his gaze between the officer's fingers and the jam starting to bubble up from the top of his pocket.

'Is there a problem?' Elliott enquired.

'No, it's just …' he paused, seemingly confused. 'I was looking for my notebook and …. it doesn't matter, I'm sure I have it here somewhere.'

The officer put his other hand into his trouser pocket, whipping it out seconds later with jam dripping in thick congealed clumps from his fingers. Elliott looked across to see more jam bubbling from his pocket, forming a viscous ooze that was beginning to flow down his trouser leg.

'What the!' The policeman flustered.

'You seem to have some jam on you,' Elliott remarked.

'I know what I've got on my hands!' The police officer replied forcefully.

'You might want to …'

'Shut up!' The police officer replied, flustered.

At this precise moment a globule of jam began to leak out from under his hat and trickled down his forehead. Wiping it away with the back of his hand he looked down and became even more confused. It was all too much to comprehend, what the hell was happening?

'Look,' the police offer muttered, his mind elsewhere. 'Just go.'

'Are you sure?' Elliott enquired.

'Go!' The police officer shouted, desperate to deal with this on his own.

'Okay, will do,' Elliott replied, noticing the hat was now beginning to bulge. He was pretty sure what it contained and didn't want to be around any longer than necessary.

Elliott slipped the car into gear and gradually pulled away, casting a cursory glance in the rear-view mirror. The policeman was now looking in bewilderment at his removed hat with jam slopping over the side. He quickly made his way back to the police car, got in and closed the door with force. What came next can best be described as an explosion of a fruit preservative nature. Where previously the officer could be seen through the front windscreen, all that could now be seen was a thick veneer of jam covering the inside of the car, oozing freely from the partially opened driver's side window. Best keep on going, Elliott reasoned.

Ten minutes later Elliott found himself leaving the motorway again and pulling in at the services. The car came to a halt at the back of the car park, far from any other parked vehicles.

'I presume that was your work then?' Elliott asked into the silence.

In response a form began to materialise next to him, quickly becoming Hapkido Valentine.

'Yes, I admit it,' Hapkido replied.

'But why jam?' Elliott asked.

'You did say you didn't know what we were going to do with the countless jars we'd received. I merely moved it from your flat to someplace it might prove more useful.'

'And I suppose when I gave him a false name, that was you as well. You bloody possessed me again didn't you?' Elliott asked, getting annoyed.

'Not possessed, more a suggestion that you didn't entirely make of your own choice.'

'I told you not to possess me anymore!'

'Why are you complaining? It got you out of trouble didn't it?'

'That you created in the first place!' Elliott fumed. 'God knows what that police officer is going to do when he finally looks back on what just happened.'

'Correct me if I'm wrong,' Hapkido suggested, 'but he is currently looking for a Simon Phillips and that leads to a certain ex-girlfriend who has a surfeit of household fittings.'

Elliott took a few moments to consider this. If the police officer did follow it up, which he might not considering the strange events he had been subject to, Simone would be the one in the firing line. And, as Hapkido had said, she'd left him without a second's hesitation, taking practically everything in the flat with her. Maybe it was only fair she get to share in the ups and downs of knowing Hapkido Valentine. Elliott let a thin smile creep across his lips, fired by a sense of satisfaction and revenge.

'It's imperative that we get one thing straight first,' Elliott demanded. 'No more possessions okay?'

'I wouldn't dream of it,' Hapkido replied.

'Good, now I wonder what food they do in there?' Elliott speculated, pointing towards the service station across the other side of the car park.

'What do you fancy?' Hapkido asked, knowingly.

'I really fancy a sausage sandwich.'

Elliott quickly followed his statement with a quizzed expression, not quite sure why he had said it. Hapkido merely smiled.

Chapter 19

I believe in ghosts and can talk to them, after the break

The train sped through the outskirts of Croydon, allowing only fleeting glimpses of a blurred kaleidoscope of greens and browns. In time the view would become dominated by housing as it travelled onwards towards central London. In the meantime however, Elliott and Hapkido spoke as they sat in their empty train carriage.

'Where are we going again?' The wrestler asked.

'I'm not exactly sure. Charlotte said to meet her at the television studio at eleven.'

'And remind me again. Why are we meeting her there?'

'Did you not listen to a word I said earlier?'

'Not really,' Hapkido confessed. 'You see I was contemplating the dimensional shift of the paradox equation.'

'Really? When you were reading the Daily Star was it?' Elliott enquired sarcastically. 'Okay, I'll tell you again. Charlotte has arranged for us to be interviewed on television as promotion for the show. Therefore I need you to be amazingly helpful with the whole talking to the dead thing, understand? No possessions! No crazy stuff about sausage sandwiches either.'

'I wouldn't dream of it.'

'I mean it!'

'You can trust me,' Hapkido replied and Elliott didn't believe a word of it.

Meanwhile the train hurried on, rushing past streets of terraced houses with small gardens and a distinct lack of privacy from the South-East train network. Onwards towards the city, onwards to an interview that would change everything.

*

Two tube stops later Elliott found himself approaching the television studio, a resplendent array of chrome handles and reflective windows. Yet more attention-grabbing than any of that was the sight which drew his eye. Standing near the front steps, Charlotte wore an emerald green skirt which stopped quite some distance above the knee. She abetted the look with a tightly fitting white top which did little to conceal her striking cleavage. Her hair was severely pulled back into a ponytail. Crikey, Elliott thought, it wasn't quite the look he was expecting.

'Just because she isn't seventy-two, you shouldn't dismiss it,' Hapkido contributed as he shuffled behind.

As Elliott got nearer he was drawn towards those soul-capturing eyes. It was quite an achievement given the more conspicuous attributes on display.

'You're late,' Charlotte announced.

'I'm sorry, had a bit of a problem with the trains,' Elliott replied. The problem was not the trains as such, rather Hapkido's reluctance to pass through the automatic ticket barriers, being as they were the work of Satan, apparently.

'Okay, listen. We're here just in time,' Charlotte directed. 'This is how it will work. I'll go in now and you follow in a couple of minutes and then we'll meet again in a short while. In the meantime they'll take you through to the preparation area and then onwards from there.'

'Why do we go in separately?' Elliott asked, worried that he might have to go on TV without her nearby. Whenever she was around her confidence seemed to rub off on him.

'I'm sorry, I don't have time to explain,' Charlotte replied, hurriedly making her way and leaving Elliott standing bemused on the steps outside.

'Okay, just before you go,' Elliott shouted after her. 'What kind of show is it? Chat show? That sort of thing?'

'Yeah, something like that,' Charlotte replied as the door slid closed behind her.

Two minutes later Elliott approached the reception and was quickly ushered through a door to the side. He was met there by a young female assistant who chastened him for being late, reminding him that the show was going out live. Before he had a chance to consider this he was led on a bewildering journey along countless corridors before being instructed to sit on a sofa alone in a quiet hallway. There he sat awkwardly, staring at the walls as he waited. Hapkido meanwhile, having accompanied Elliott through the corridors, soon became bored with waiting. Dropping to the floor he proceeded to spend the next twenty minutes doing push-ups. By the end he'd claimed to have set a new world record, although Elliott suspected Guinness would probably have insisted that they were completed more than two at a time, and certainly without the considerable rest in-between. Eventually the assistant reappeared and with a well-practiced technique attached a small microphone to the neck of his t-shirt and placed the associated pack into his back pocket. She ushered Elliott towards the door at the far end. It was about to begin.

As Elliott made his way around the perimeter of the set he noticed that the wooden walls facing away from the audience were unpainted and raw. He could hear the crowd beyond, a loud chatter interspersed with the occasional jeer. Elliott speculated that the audience were taking advantage of a lull in recording to chat. Before he knew it he had been guided through a door and found himself walking out onto the main stage.

'And here he is, the man who talks to ghosts at the expense of his own girlfriend,' the host declared angrily.

'Booooooooooooo!' The crowd responded.

Elliott came to an abrupt halt and stood motionless. What the hell was going on? The cameras were pointed solely in his direction, the audience in a state of frenzy. This wasn't a break in recording, it actually *was* the recording. And Elliott had just walked straight out into the middle of it. It didn't take long to work out what the show was either. There, directing an angry and condescending stare in his direction was none other than Dermot Kilgallon himself.

The Dermot Kilgallon show. Akin to Dante's eighth level of hell, broadcast every weekday morning and featuring members of the public raised on lead paint fumes and noodles in a pot. Elliott glanced at the crowd, an assortment of students and housewives that had left their respect for humanity at the door.

Looking at the stage he saw Charlotte sitting in one of the seats, the one next to her empty. She gave him a shrug that was enough to convey the message *I'm sorry, this was the best I could do.*

'So what have you got to say for yourself?' Dermot asked confrontationally.

'I'm here for the interview,' Elliott replied at a barely legible volume.

'Damn right, it's time you started answering some questions. You don't know how lucky you are to have a woman like this in your life. Take a seat and maybe you can start acting like a man for once!'

'I'm sorry,' Elliott apologised as he made his way to the empty chair, not sure what exactly he was apologising for. 'What exactly am I supposed to have done?'

'Typical,' Dermot replied, turning towards the audience. 'You know, I see a lot of people in this job but you really take the biscuit. You still can't see what you've done wrong can you?'

'Did someone say biscuits?' Hapkido asked as he materialised for Elliott's eyes only.

'Sorry, what is this actually about?' Elliott asked, lowering himself into the chair.

'I'll tell you what it's about sunshine. It's about you neglecting your girlfriend Charlize because you think you can talk to ghosts.'

Elliott was just about to ask who Charlize was when it dawned on him. Obviously Charlotte had provided a name to better fit the circumstances and as trashy names went, it wasn't half bad, Elliott grudgingly admitted.

'But I can talk to ghosts,' Elliott replied, despite it immediately becoming obvious this was last thing the crowd wanted to hear.

'Damn right he can,' Hapkido added. 'Where's my chair?'

'Oh really?' Dermot questioned with a disbelieving look. 'Well how about you stop lying? You're just using it as an excuse to deal with your commitment fears. Let's ask a member of the audience what they think?'

Dermot moved over to the front row and gestured for a heavily overweight man to stand. When he finally got to his feet the man readily took the microphone.

'If I had a girlfriend like that I wouldn't be making up lies!' The man exclaimed proudly.

Hapkido who had been looking around the stage for somewhere to sit turned towards the accuser.

'You don't know him!' Hapkido shouted angrily. 'You people should be ashamed of yourself.'

Elliott sensed that despite Hapkido's fervent reply, he should perhaps add something himself, since no one had actually heard the wrestler.

'But I really can talk to ghosts!'

Dermot made his way over to another studio audience member, a tall skinny student-looking girl with long blonde hair.

'So if you can talk to ghosts, why aren't they here?' She asked, stutteringly.

'They are,' Elliott replied. 'There's one right next to me now.'

'Prove it!' A man with two days of stubble growth shouted from the back.

'Don't make me come up there,' Hapkido shouted back.

'Well, it doesn't quite work like that,' Elliott announced, rather more defensively.

The crowd changed in an instant from confrontational to mocking, their laughter ringing unhindered around the studio.

'Let me ask you,' Dermot spoke. 'Why do you continue with this charade at the expense of your own relationship?'

Help, Elliott thought. He was in way over his head.

'Let's show them. Tell that fat geezer in the front row that you've got a message from his grandmother.'

'Excuse me sir.' Elliott announced, hesitantly pointing at the man in question. 'Your grandmother says she's sorry that she fed you all those sweets as a child. She didn't know you'd get an eating disorder as a result.'

'What did you say?' The fat man demanded, jumping from his seat before being quickly held back by a nearby security guard.

'I'm sorry. I didn't mean it to sound harsh but Eleanor wants you to be happy,' Elliott offered.

'You son of a bitch, how dare you talk about my grandmother

like that?'

'Your grandmother was Eleanor wasn't it? She was married to Bill Turner from Hull and she worked as a receptionist for an accountant.'

'How did you know that?' The man stuttered, confused.

'Yes, how did you know that?' Dermot further enquired in a supercilious tone.

'I have a guide. He's my link to the spirit world.'

'And where is he? Is he here now?' Dermot asked, the disdain in his voice showing no signs of relenting.

'Yes, he's right next to me,' Elliott replied. It was a small lie as Hapkido had actually left his side and was now at the back of the room swinging ghostly punches at the man with the stubble.

'Let me come over there,' Dermot added, making his way over to the fat man. 'Can I ask your name Sir?'

'It's Bob.'

'And that was total rubbish wasn't it Bob?'

'Well, no, not really. My grandmother was called Eleanor and she was married to Bill and she did work for an accountant.'

'Well I'd say it was a lucky guess. I put it to you that you're making all this up,' Dermot fumed, turning back towards Elliott.

Hapkido stopped his wild swings and shouted from the back.

'Tell that student bird the following.'

'Caroline, if I may call you that,' Elliott relayed, nodding towards the student. 'I have a message from your dog Toby. He wants you to know that he doesn't bear you any ill feeling after you ran him over with your parent's car.'

'Oh he can communicate with dogs now,' Dermot exclaimed, throwing his arms up into the air in a dramatic gesture. 'Caroline is it? Tell our so called ghost whisperer that he's talking absolute rubbish.'

'Actually I did run over my dog in my parent's car,' the girl confirmed before adding, 'but it was an accident. He ran straight out in front of me. I don't know how he could have known that.'

'Tell us Elliott, how did you know that?' Dermot asked with a terribly false smile.

'I told you, my guide is my connection to the other world.'
'Oh really! Tell me about your guide then.'

'Tell him I'm a Samurai Warrior that can traverse time and space.'

'Oh, he's just an ordinary guy,' Elliott replied.

'Well I think you're full of it,' Dermot argued. 'I know the sort of person you are. You find things out about people and then make them believe your line of crap. There I said it, on daytime television, you're full of crap.'

'But I've never met these people before,' Elliott countered.

'Well sunshine you're far from convincing me.'

'How can I prove it?' Elliott asked.

'Disclose something about me then. Go on, if you're that clever. Tell me something about me that no one else knows.'

'I don't think you want me to,' Elliott replied.

'Why? I've got nothing to hide. I'm going to prove to the audience and everyone at home that you've made all this up,' Dermot answered, not quite thinking through the consequences.

'Okay, if you insist,' replied Elliott. 'On Tuesday you like to dress up as a woman and call yourself Marjorie.'

A dreadful silence fell upon the room, punctuated only by what sounded like the popping of the plastic catches on a lunch box.

'What!' Dermot asked, astounded.

'Or maybe I could tell them about the time you slept with one of your researchers behind your wife's back.'

'This is …' Dermot flummoxed, trying desperately not to appear guilty.

'You did ask,' Elliott expanded.

'Well, I can categorically state that none of those things ever happened.'

'You would say that … Marjorie,' Elliott replied, feeling mischievous. He had grown tired of being attacked by Dermot Kilgallon and had decided to fight back.

'You really are a joker, aren't you son?'

'Okay, why don't you ask some more of your studio audience and I'll show you,' Elliott proposed.

'Good idea,' Dermot replied, eager to move the conversation away from himself. 'What about this lady?'

Dermot moved over to an older lady in a floral dress.

'Claire has two cats called Cliff and Hank,' Elliott stated. 'Her mum was called Angela, she passed on in 1982. Angela says that Claire should stop spending money on hair dye and go back to her natural brown,' Elliott revealed.

'Is that true love?' Dermot asked the woman.

'Yes, it's all true. Amazing,' Claire replied.

'And what about this gentleman?' Dermot enquired, thrusting the microphone in the direction of a middle-aged man sitting in the row behind.

'Derek sells car insurance in Swindon and is married to Bonnie who is currently at home preparing for the Women's Institute jumble sale on Saturday. His father passed on in 1995.'

'And is that true?' Dermot asked.

'That's all true. I don't believe it!' Derek confessed.

'And what can you tell me about this gentleman?' Dermot asked, moving back a couple of rows and gesturing for a man to stand. He was dressed in an anorak and a wide brimmed hat that covered his face in shadow.

Elliott waited for Hapkido to disclose the relevant information.

Only one word came, slamming into his brain with the upmost urgency.

'DUCK!'

What about ducks? Elliott thought.

He almost missed what happened next. The audience member pulled what appeared to be a gun from a plastic lunch box and aimed it in his direction. The muzzle of the gun flared and a tremendous bang echoed around the studio and all the way back again.

Chapter 20

Out goes the new, in comes the old

The residents of Elliott's road had seen nothing like it before. A veritable throng of reporters were currently crowded around the door to Elliott's block of flats, causing endless complaints over breakfast tables up and down the road. How would poor little Tristan get to school now? There was hardly any space to navigate the 4x4 out of the driveway. Tristan meanwhile sat transfixed in front the television, watching the story unfold on the morning news.

'Reporting live from outside Elliott Rose's house, we can now talk to Rebecca McDonald,' announced Felicity Harris, the morning newsreader. A million viewers at home waited eagerly, their spoons suspended over bowls of cornflakes.

> 'Yes, thank you Felicity,' Rebecca confirmed. 'I'm here outside Elliott Rose's flat following yesterday's dramatic turn of events on the Dermot Kilgallon show. What started as a normal recording of the show soon became one of the most shocking scenes ever caught on television. Elliott Rose was being interviewed about his career as a medium when an assassination attempt was made on his life by a member of the audience.'

'Can you tell us anything further about the incident?' Felicity asked back in the studio.

> 'Well it would seem,' Rebecca replied, pausing to brush a few strands of hair away from her face, 'that the shot narrowly missed Mr. Rose. Subsequently the attacker was able to escape from the studio despite the security team present. Witnesses report security appeared transfixed

during the entire incident whilst muttering - *Leave him to me boys. I know karate.*

'Rebecca. What have the police said about the suspect?'

'This morning they have released a statement. It reads that although the suspect was able to escape, they have reviewed the video footage and have a number of leads. As you can see from the pictures, the attacker was white, in his thirties to early forties and wearing a beige anorak and corduroy trousers. Perhaps most distinctive was the fact he was carrying what appears to be a plastic lunchbox with a picture of a train on it. Police are advising the public not to approach him as he is armed and dangerous.'

'And I believe Dermot Kilgallon has released a statement himself?' asked Felicity.

'Yes and it reads as follows:'

I am shocked and appalled that my television show has been witness to such a terrifying attack. In response to those in the media who claim this was a publicity stunt, I categorically state this to be untrue. We at the Dermot Kilgallon show would never lower ourselves to exploitation. Tune in to our three hour special this morning for an in-depth review of events.

'That is a very blunt statement from Marjorie *cough* I mean Dermot Kilgallon,' Felicity commented. 'What can you tell us about the target of this assassination attempt Rebecca?'

'Well it would seem that Mr. Rose is a self-proclaimed medium and claims to be able to communicate with the dead. However we've learnt that many in the psychic community have no knowledge of his previous work up until now. He has a show planned at the Apollo Rooms in Lewisham on the 17th of this month and many are saying that this was all just an elaborate hoax in order to boost ticket sales.'

'An elaborate hoax?' Elliott protested loudly.

Ever since rising from a sleepless night, Elliott had sat dumbfounded as the news reports had started rolling in. In tandem the crowd of reporters grew exponentially outside. Charlotte meanwhile sat on the sofa having arrived earlier that morning, whilst Hapkido demonstrated a stunted version of ju-jitsu in front of her.

'An elaborate hoax?' Elliott repeated. 'That nutcase nearly fricking killed me!'

'Well, they do say there is no such thing as bad publicity,' Charlotte commented, her palm resting on her forehead, her fingers splayed as she sat wearily.

'Why the hell would someone want to kill me?' Elliott asked frantically.

'I have no idea.'

'I know The Dermot Kilgallon Show might not be everyone's cup of tea, but attempted murder, that's crazy.'

'Look I'm as shaken up as you,' Charlotte replied. 'Remember I was sitting right next to you. I truly wasn't expecting any of this.'

'Yes.' Elliott enquired. 'What exactly were you expecting … Charlize?'

'Okay, I admit it was unfair to spring that on you, but ticket sales for your show have been practically non-existent. I had to drum up publicity somehow. I knew that if I'd asked you beforehand you would have said no. The Dermot Kilgallon Show is not exactly high-brow is it? But *it is* watched by a large proportion of your potential audience.'

'Okay, okay. That's all well and good but it does rather ignore the fact that some nut bag tried to shoot me. Not only that but at the last count the BBC, ITN, ABC News, Sky, Al Jazeera and Newsround are currently camped in the street outside. And where the hell is your uncle? You told me he would be coming straight round as he knew how to deal with this sort of thing. That was over two hours ago.'

'He got a little bit held up,' Charlotte replied, failing to disclose the entire truth.

'Well, I wish he would hurry up.'

'You know what I think? It was obviously the Illuminati,' Hapkido suggested before being abruptly interrupted by a loud bang.

Elliott jumped. Charlotte jumped. Hapkido leapt into a karate stance. They all soon relaxed when it became apparent that the source of the bang came not from a gun but the wall which joined Elliott's front room to Mrs. Clarkson's bedroom.

'What the hell is she doing in there?' Elliott asked. 'Hopefully not knocking off another husband.'

'What do you mean?' Charlotte enquired.

'Well ……' Elliott began.

Another bang followed, followed by another shortly afterwards. Elliott waited a few seconds to ensure he could speak uninterrupted.

'Well …..'

Another prolonged period of banging emanated from beyond the wall, stopping Elliott in his tracks as it appeared to reach its crescendo. Charlotte however suspected Mrs. Clarkson was engaged in something a touch more amorous than hanging up a picture hook with a sledgehammer.

'I think I'd better go. I'll try and sort something out about the reporters downstairs,' Charlotte announced, getting to her feet. She had no desire to be present when the source of the banging made his way across the hallway. It did however seem the perfect opportunity for her to talk to the reporters outside. Their presence might seem like a nuisance to Elliott but they were also an opportunity for free publicity.

Elliott broke from his slovenly posture and sat upright.

'When will I see you again?'

'I'll ring,' Charlotte replied, making her way towards the front door. Elliott trailed behind as if he were a lost dog and she smelt of dog food. She didn't, she smelt lovely and Elliott was already missing her by the time she'd closed the door behind her.

'So, you still got a thing for our promoter friend there?' Hapkido asked as Elliott returned to the front room.

'She's lovely isn't she?' Elliott asked. Before Hapkido could reply they were quickly interrupted by the doorbell again.

'Probably another reporter,' Elliott speculated, wearily making his way to the door.

'If it is,' suggested Hapkido. 'Ask them if they want to interview a world-famous wrestler who has mastered the arts of time travel and communication with the dead.'

'Or I could just tell them to piss off!' Elliott replied, opening the door a little too quickly.

Unfortunately the words 'piss off' were the unintended welcome proffered to the visitor.

'Well that's lovely,' Simone replied, standing in front of him.

Elliott's jaw dropped as if the zombie apocalypse had just caught up with its latest victim. Simone stood in front of him, as plain as day. She was wearing jeans with a tight white t-shirt, noticeably enhanced by her massive norks.

'Simone,' Elliott stuttered. His eyes instantly fell to her breasts as the special law of gravity governing men's eyes and women's breasts exerted its influence.

'Can I come in?'

'Er, okay,' Elliott replied, gesturing her in, not sure what else to do.

'What the hell is happening outside your flat?' Simone asked, making her way into the front room.

Elliott would have replied had it not been for Hapkido distracting him.

'Woah, look at those fun bags!'

'How are you Elliott?' Simone asked, turning to face him.

'I'm fine thanks,' Elliott replied. The absence of any furnishings and the proximity of the culprit raised his level of resentment at seeing her.

'I heard you were sacked by Carol. What's more, I also hear you're attempting to set yourself up as a medium. How's that going?' Simone asked, the derision evident in her tone.

'Have you watched the news this morning?' Elliott asked.

'No, should I have?'

'No reason. So what brings you here Simone? I presume it's not to bring back the furniture?'

'It's not about the furniture,' Simone replied coldly. 'So why a medium?'

'Things have just turned out this way I guess. Anyway, what does it matter to you? I thought you stopped caring the minute you left.'

'Elliott,' Simone protested. 'I haven't stopped caring. We just couldn't be together anymore.'

'Why? Was it someone else?'

'No,' Simone replied forcefully. 'Have you met anyone else?'

Elliott pondered the question and considered the two potential answers. On one hand there was Charlotte, but she was a long way from being *someone else*. On the other hand was Hapkido who was currently struggling with his eighth push-up on the floor in front of them. He imagined she wouldn't understand the latter. He wasn't sure he did either.

'No. There's no one else,' Elliott replied, succinctly.

'Look Elliott, I'm sorry it turned out like this but I have something I need to ask you.'

Elliott looked into her eyes. Was she going to ask to get back together? He wasn't sure how he felt about that. What about Charlotte?

'Okay, go ahead, what is it you want?' Elliott asked.

'Why,' Simone began, 'have I had the police round asking about your car? Until yesterday I'd forgotten it was even registered in my name at my parent's address. The officer kept talking about some incident on the M1 motorway.'

'The M1?' Elliott asked, flustered.

'I thought at first you'd been caught speeding. Then the policeman starting talking about jam, making absolutely no sense at all.'

'What exactly did you tell him?' Elliott enquired nervously.

'I told him that although technically the car is in my name, it belongs to you and recently we'd split up. I gave him the address of the flat but out of courtesy I thought I would let you know beforehand.'

Elliott didn't know what to make of this revelation. After their years together, it would have been nice if she'd been less willing to incriminate him so readily. Regardless, pretty soon it looked like he'd be receiving a visit from the police. He would have preferred it if they spent their time trying to find out who was attempting to kill him, not working out how seventy-one jars of jam exploded within the confines of a motorway patrol car. Now not only did the police know where he lived but thanks to the reporters outside everyone else did as well. That included the man who had tried to kill him. He had to get away, to lay low. The absolute last thing he needed at this moment was Simone in his front room after all she had done.

'Simone,' Elliott announced, his patience with everything finally exhausted. 'You are without doubt the most self-centred, obnoxious bitch I have ever met. You did me a huge favour by walking out of my life before. I would be extremely grateful if you could repeat the kindness by leaving now!'

'What did you say?' Simone asked, taken aback, her voice full of surprise.

'Did I leave out obnoxious? No, I think I mentioned that.'

Simone would have said something in reply but she was too preoccupied with storming down the hallway and slamming the door behind her.

'I take it that was Simone then?' Hapkido asked between heavy breaths, bringing his exercise routine to an end.

'Yep, that was her.'

'I take it you won't be getting back together then?'

'I think that's probably a given. More importantly I think she's just inadvertently shown us what we need to do?'

'And that is?' Hapkido asked, getting to his feet and adjusting himself down below.

'To get as far away from here as possible, before matey comes back to finish the job!'

Elliott walked towards the door, taking a black canvas jacket from the coat hook. Stuffing his wallet and phone into one of the side pockets he felt the dryness of paper against his fingers and brought out a twenty pound note.

'Hey, look at that!' Elliott declared, turning the note over in his hand before slipping it into the back pocket of his jeans. 'It could be a good day after all.'

Chapter 21

I get up when I want, except on a Wednesday when I get rudely awoken by the Flashman

The sun was just beginning to rise from behind the rolling hills, extended rays striking through the gaps between the thatched cottages. Jeremy drove along the quaint high street of the village. He was now deep in the heart of the countryside that surrounded London. A milk float emerged from a side road forcing Jeremy to overtake with venom.

'It's still the bloody 1950s down here,' Jeremy complained, weaving back onto the left-hand side of the road.

He was almost right. The village had many of the qualities that one might expect – country pub, local shop, overt mistrust of those born outside its medieval boundaries. What it also had however, lying on its outskirts, was the house of Carol Swanson. The only thing she had in common with the 1950s was her hairstyle.

Jeremy swung his car down a side road, showing no signs of lessening his speed. A trail of dust kicked up by the wheels lifted up into the air. Finally, the house came into view and Jeremy swung the car through the gates and up the paved driveway.

'Time for some answers,' Jeremy muttered to himself as he stopped the car and ascended the marble steps that led to the front door.

The door was eventually opened by Carol, standing at the entrance to her opulent hallway in a burgundy silk dressing gown. The hem resided a lot higher above the knee than was palatable. Her hair, normally a tight perm, had been shifted in her sleep so that it formed a lethal wedge.

'Jeremy, what the hell are you doing here?' Carol asked, stifling a yawn.

'Don't give me that! You know exactly why I'm here!'

'You do know what time it is don't you?'

'Would you rather we discuss this later? And by *this* I think you know what I mean. Perhaps we could reconvene at a time more convenient, maybe somewhere a lot more public, maybe a police station?' Jeremy replied.

Standing to one side she gestured him in. Jeremy slid inside with a glance behind to ensure no one was watching.

'Make it quick Jeremy, will you? Carol asked as she followed him into the dining room. 'I'm a bit busy this morning.'

'Funny, it looks like you've just got out of bed,' Flashman replied, his annoyance as to the situation undiminished.

'Not that sort of busy. Come on Jeremy, use your imagination,' Carol replied as she raised her eyebrows suggestively. The nearby rattling of a coffee cup in the kitchen indicated the sort of busy Jeremy had walked into.

'Oh Christ, Carol,' he replied, 'not another one. Who is it this time?'

'If you must know we are very much in love and the person in question is very mature for his age.'

At this point a man entered the room carrying two coffee cups and wearing an identical version of Carol's silk dressing gown. The belt at the waist was only loosely tied and threatened an inadvertent reveal of the utmost horror. It took Jeremy a few seconds to realise who he was looking at.

'Oh, hi Mr. Flashman,' Sinclair announced.

Jeremy hadn't recognised him at first. Christ, Sinclair the sound guy from Ghostbusters UK.

'Sinclair?' Jeremy enquired distastefully.

'Sinclair, my dear,' Carol spoke. 'Why don't you pop back upstairs and wait for me there sweetheart?'

'Sure thing,' Sinclair replied, making his way from the room.

Jeremy and Carol waited until his footsteps could no longer be heard.

'Look Jeremy, if you're going to say what I think you're going to say, don't worry, everything is under control.'

Flashman turned his back and began to pace agitatedly around the room.

'First thing,' he announced. 'Sinclair. Really?'

'I told you. We are very much in love, but that's not why you are here is it?'

'Of course not! The last time we met I found you lurking in the back of my car. If you remember we discussed the Rose situation.'

'Yes, I remember.'

'And you stated that there were two options. The first was that we try to discredit him, or at least that I try to show him that being psychic is a gift, not something you can fabricate.'

'It's never stopped you.'

Jeremy sighed, putting the insult to one side for the time being.

'Well I kept my end of the bargain. I showed him what could be achieved when you truly have the gift.'

'And how did it go?' Carol asked, fully aware that all Jeremy had managed was to mutter some nonsense in an empty theatre.

'That's not important,' Jeremy answered, turning back to face her. 'What is important is that Elliott didn't listen. He's still prepared to do the show. Do you know what this means? If people start listening to him, actually paying to see him, then we become his competition. It's in his interest to discredit us and if you haven't forgotten he knows everything about us. But then I think you already knew this.'

'Get to the point,' Carol demanded.

'You said there were two options and if my plan didn't work then you would use your alternative.'

'What is it you're suggesting exactly?' Carol asked condescendingly.

'What I'm suggesting Carol is that you've sanctioned the most insane plan anyone, ever, has ever had.'

'Honestly, I have no idea what you are talking about,' Carol replied unconvincingly.

'Have you not seen the news? Elliott was on the Dermot Kilgallon show yesterday when some moron jumped up and tried to shoot him.'

'I do hope you aren't suggesting that I had anything to do with that?'

'Come on Carol, I wasn't born yesterday. You'll do anything to protect your beloved show, even if it means trying to kill someone.'

'*If* I had something to do with this, which I didn't, do you not think I would have hired someone who was a total professional? Someone who couldn't be traced back to us?'

'Us? There's no us! I just wanted to scare him. What you are doing is off the scale!'

'Having someone try and kill you is pretty scary, wouldn't you say? Perhaps the person hired to do the job missed for some reason. Even if it didn't exactly go to plan, being shot at is probably scary enough to stop that person actually doing their show.'

'So you admit it was you then?' Jeremy countered.

'What I'm saying is, if someone was trying to kill our ex-employee then of course I would be very sad, but ultimately it would be to our benefit.'

'Carol. You have to stop this,' Jeremy demanded.

'Stop what? I had nothing to do with it.'

'You know what,' Flashman suggested. 'I hope you lie better to the police than you do to me.'

'And *if* that time ever comes,' Carol quipped, 'then I hope you put on a better performance of innocence than you do of mediumship.'

'How dare you!'

'Now listen very carefully Jeremy. If you go running to the police with your wild story then I may be forced to tell them everything I know.'

'Well that doesn't affect me does it?'

'Are you sure? I might get confused and claim that it was all your idea.'

'Are you threatening me Carol?'

'I wouldn't dream of it.'

'I had nothing to do with this,' Flashman argued, a quiver of panic in his voice.

'I'm sure you told me we had to do something about Elliott Rose.'

'I didn't say you should try and kill him!'

'Oh I think you'll find you said a lot of things you don't remember saying, at least that's what I might finding myself telling the police.'

Jeremy could handle being lied to. He could handle his psychic abilities being questioned. But what Carol was doing was insane and he steadfastly refused to be part of something as desperate as murder. Yet he also knew that if he did go to the police then Carol would have no qualms about implicating him as the main perpetrator. Would they believe her? Would they think that even though he had been the one who told them about it, he wasn't completely innocent? After all, she was Carol Swanson and the public persona was a lot different to the private version. He wasn't sure he could risk it. If he couldn't go to the police and she wouldn't call the hit off, then he would have to do something else about it instead. Jeremy Flashman turned and without a word headed for the door.

'Where are you going?' Carol asked as if addressing a mischievous child before her tone quickly turned to menace. 'Don't do anything stupid!'

There was no stopping Flashman now. Within seconds he left the house, got in his car and raced up the driveway. Carol stood in the doorway watching him go, one hand on her hip so that the dressing gown rode up a little. Carol thought about what Jeremy had said. Yes, it wasn't quite how she'd imagined it. Maybe she should put a stop to it? Then again, all that talk of shooting, she started to feel the same sense of excitement she had experienced at the train station.

'Oh Sinclair dear,' Carol shouted up the stairs. 'It's time for the *extra special* employee benefit scheme.'

Chapter 22

To have or to have not (a sausage sandwich)

Hapkido was the first to walk out into the bright sunshine. The assembled journalists, preoccupied with interviewing one another, unsurprisingly failed to notice his appearance. They did notice Elliott however as he followed behind. The whirl of camera motors accompanied the microphones thrust with an urgency in his direction.

'Elliott! Elliott! Can you tell us your thoughts on yesterday?'

'Elliott! Do you know why someone would try to kill you on national television?'

'I ... I ... I have no idea.' Elliott stuttered.

'Do you disagree with those who say that practicing spiritualism is an invitation for this sort of thing to happen? What do you say to people who claim this was all an elaborate hoax in order to generate sales for your show?'

'Why would I do that? I was nearly killed,' Elliott protested. Hapkido meanwhile darted around the back of the pack, questioning why no one wanted to ask him about his wrestling career.

'Are you really psychic Mr. Rose?'

Elliott sensed there was an opportunity here for him to promote the show. Charlotte would be proud of him. Hapkido, perhaps picking up on the thought nodded his head knowingly in Elliott's direction.

'Excuse me. You at the back. Your Auntie Doris wishes to

tell you that you shouldn't have left your first wife for a flight stewardess.' Elliott expanded. A number of journalists turned towards the reporter whom Elliott had addressed.

'Is that true? Can you confirm Mr. Rose's story?'

'Well yes, it is but it hardly proves his powers. He's probably been hacking my voicemail!'
An awkward silence fell over the journalists. Some stared at their feet, not knowing what to say next, one even started whistling as he averted his gaze towards the sky. Finally, a single reporter broke the silence.

'Mr. Rose, can you demonstrate your powers further?'

'Eddie, it's Eddie right?' Elliott asked, reaching out and gently touching the man's right shoulder. He wasn't sure why he did this but it seemed like the sort of thing a psychic would do.
'Yes my name's Eddie.'
'Eddie. Your Uncle Reg is here. He's worried about your drinking.'
'It's true, my names Eddie and I'm an alcoholic!'
Perhaps carried away by his own showmanship, Elliott felt he should leave on a high. It seems the ideal team to strike.
'My show is on at the Apollo Rooms on the 17th. Tickets £20. Thank you for ...'

*

It was instant pandemonium when the shot rang out. Reporters ran in a chaotic multiplicity of directions, any sense of solidarity readily abandoned in the desire to escape. Elliott meanwhile stood stock still. The first evidence of the shot he felt was something rushing past his left ear. But then came the sound of it, quickly followed by the rapid and desperate dispersal of the reporters. In an instant he knew that it had been a bullet that had narrowly missed him, embedding itself with a burst of wooden shards into the door behind. Elliott went from confused to terrified in a fraction of a second. He knew he had to run but his legs refused to respond.

'Run!' Hapkido screamed into Elliott's face.

'I can't.'

Elliott's head jerked upwards. Across the street he caught sight of the sun glinting off something in a window two floors up in the building opposite. This was surely it, the end, good bye world, never got to go to Belgium.

Suddenly from out of nowhere a car screamed to a halt in front of him, smoke pouring from the back wheels. As the passenger door swung open another shot rang out, shattering one of the rear windows.

'Get in!' Jeremy Flashman shouted.

'Flashman?'

'Can we spare the pleasantries till later!' Jeremy replied, frantically gesturing for Elliott to enter. 'Get in the car before you get yourself shot!'

Elliott didn't need a second invitation. He leapt in, slamming the passenger door closed behind him. As he pulled himself into a cowering ball crammed into the seat-well, he allowed himself a glimpse out of the front window. Hapkido rolled across the bonnet and swung himself into the back seat via the shattered back window as if he were in an episode of a 1970s cop show. Flashman in turn fired the engine and the car jumped forward, the sudden acceleration forcing Elliott into the seat. As Flashman slammed the car around the corner of the road and away from the madness, Elliott found the courage to speak.

'You saved my life!' Elliott exclaimed.

'Don't mention it,' replied Jeremy. 'Look, I know we've had our differences but the last thing I want to see is you killed.'

'I don't know how to thank you,' Elliott replied, gingerly raising himself higher in the seat.

'That's not important right now. What we need to do is get you somewhere safe,' Jeremy replied, taking another corner at speed.

'Just take me anywhere away from here!' Elliott asked

desperately.

'Why don't you take some time to think about it?' Jeremy professed. 'In the meantime, there's a bottle of water in the glove box, you should drink it to keep yourself hydrated. I heard that people in shock need water and you've definitely had a shock, no doubt.'

'Cheers,' Elliott replied, opening the glove box and finding a bottle of water resting on top. He unscrewed the cap and took a large swig, draining half the bottle in one go.

'Um, I'm not sure you should've done that.'

Even as the words filtered into Elliott's brain he knew something was wrong. The world had started to slow, the perimeters of his vision becoming clouded.

'Something's wrong Hap!' Elliott garbled.

'Who are you talking to Elliott?' Flashman enquired, a thin smile creeping across his lips.

Elliott felt himself slipping away. It made so much sense to close his eyes. Before he did he should probably answer the question that the nice man had asked.

'Hapkido,' Elliott slurred. 'Hapkido Valentine.'

Chapter 23

Safety from the Grease MegaMix

Elliott could feel himself waking from a dreamless sleep, coming back to a reality that was proving elusive to grasp. He could sense it, he just had to focus. There were birds nearby. He couldn't see them, his eyes were not willing to participate just yet but his mind was welcoming the sound of their song. Concentrate on the birds, listen!

Elliott could feel the sense of belonging, to a world just beyond the feeling of peremptory grogginess. He was slowly coming round, he just didn't know where. He seemed to be lying on his back somewhere, hard yet soft in equal measure. The moisture laden air seemed to smell of salt and seaweed, reminiscent of childhood trips to the seaside. He had to open his eyes because this no longer felt like a dream.

What the hell?

Elliott was lying in a field. Quickly propping himself up onto his elbows he took in the scene before him. He seemed to be on a hill, high above the sea which was present on all sides. The land stretched away from him, rolling downwards to where it met the sea two hundred metres away. Beyond the sea, clouded in an early morning mist on the horizon, Elliott could just about make out another larger landmass. He was on a bleeding island!

'I'll tell you what,' Hapkido broadcast, coming into being alongside. 'When that Jeremy Flashman said he was going to get you far away from danger he wasn't kidding was he?'

Elliott sighed. It wasn't a great surprise. Wake up in a field near the sea, talk to a dead wrestler. It was much the same thing on the weirdness scale.

'Where are we?' Elliott asked, his voice hoarse.

'Well, if I'm not mistaken we have transported ourselves to the legendary Japanese island of Sushi.'

'Sushi?' Elliott replied, half coughing. 'Is that the best you can come up with?'

'Well if you've got any better ideas I'd love to hear them.'

Elliott took a few moments to consider the circumstances. What was the last thing he remembered? Some idiot had tried to kill him, again! Something happened after that though, didn't it? How did he escape? Flashman! Jeremy bloody Flashman! He had offered him something, what was it? Whatever it was, the memories seemed to fade abruptly after that.

'I was drugged you idiot,' Elliott asserted. 'Why didn't you do something? You know, possess him or something.'

'Strange you should mention that,' Hapkido countered. 'You see, when you fell asleep I found I wasn't my normal self. It was as if I couldn't quite grasp your reality. I needed you fully functional within this realm. Frankly, I'm a little disappointed in you.'

'Oh shut up you plum!' Elliott angrily replied.

'Anyway,' Hapkido continued, 'next thing I know I appear here. I'm chalking this one up as trans-dimensional teleportation.'

Elliott struggled to his feet. From the top of the hill where he was standing he could see the sea in all directions, grey and flecked with white as it rolled and crashed against the immoveable coastline. A path lay off to the left, traversing the hill before descending a few hundred metres to some whitewashed buildings below. There it became a gravel road, tracing its way onwards towards a break in the cliffs, possibly in the direction of a harbour.

'Let's find out where the hell we are,' Elliott commanded, checking his pockets as he started off. Finding his wallet and phone missing he cocked his head towards the sky and shouted furiously. 'Bloody Flashman!'

'Maybe there'll be café down there 'cause I really fancy …'

'Please,' Elliott interrupted, closing his eyes in despair. 'Just five minutes without you talking about sausage sandwiches or mystical Japanese islands, that's all I ask.'

'You have my word as a samurai,' Hapkido replied.

Elliott's first tentative steps suddenly became a full blown stride, intent on maintaining at least ten feet of distance between them on the way down.

As they got closer, Elliott could better discern the buildings as they came into view. Three in all, they were painted in near identical whites. In places the underlying coat had been exposed, where the vicious unrelenting sea air had had its effect. Dark curtains were drawn across the windows, their gardens heavily overgrown.

'Well this is amazing,' Elliott asserted. 'There's absolutely no one here! It's a bloody ghost island.'

'It would appear that I might have been wrong about this being Japan,' Hapkido admitted. He too had come to the same conclusion: whoever had once lived here was now long gone.

'What the hell are we going to do?' Elliott asked, throwing his hands up into the air dramatically. 'The show is in two days and we have no idea where we are or if we can even get off this island.'

Before either of them could say anything more a nearby sound startled them into silence. It sounded like footsteps, slowly treading the gravel of the road. Glancing back and forth the source of the steps was not easily determined but seemed to be emanating from behind one of the cottages. Even if they weren't sure of whence it came, they were sure of one thing: it was getting nearer.

'Zombies, guarantee it!' Hapkido whispered, rather unhelpfully.

Finally a shuffling figure emerged from behind the nearest cottage, silhouetted menacingly against the morning sun.

'When I say run, you run, okay?' Elliott instructed quietly.

Both Hapkido and Elliott waited nervously. Should they run now or wait to see the face of the person who would run them down and scoop out their eyes with a spoon? When they did discover the truth it wasn't quite what they were expecting.

'Well bugger me sideways!' The figure exclaimed in a strong Essex accent. 'We've only gone and got us a new player! Gaz, Baz, get out here, we got us another one!'

The door to the cottage flung open and two men ran out excitedly.

'Well he ain't being the boot, I'm the boot!' Baz (or was it Gaz) claimed as he got nearer.

'Look, Baz,' the other man reassured. 'Ain't no one wants to be the boot apart from you, chill bro.'

'He can be the dog if he wants,' Gaz replied, 'It's about time someone was the bleeding dog!'

It was safe to say that Elliott didn't have a clue about what was going on. The outstretched hand offered by one of the approaching men seemed friendly enough, not classic zombie procedure at least. Elliott relaxed a little, even if he remained completely clueless. All three were dressed near identically, casual trousers and shirts that had long seen their best days.

'Hello. I'm Elliott.'

'Nice to meet you Ellster. I'm Wazzer and this 'ere is Gaz and Baz,' Wazzer replied, shaking Elliott by the hand enthusiastically whilst nodding in the direction of the other two.

'Hi Bazzer.'

'Wazzer,' Wazzer corrected.

'Sorry, Wazzer, of course,' Elliott apologised. 'Can you actually tell me where we are?'

'You sunshine are on Gruinard Island, as far as we can tell,' Wazzer replied as a matter of fact.

'Where's that?' Elliott asked, doing little to conceal the puzzled look on his face.

'It's off the North-West coast of Scotland, numb nuts,' Wazzer replied. 'Ain't no one lived here for years, apart from us three.'

'If you don't mind me asking,' Elliott enquired, casting a glance towards the other two, 'what exactly are you doing here? You don't look the sort to be living on a deserted island.'

Baz took this moment to step forward, declaring as if it were obvious. 'We were on a stag do weren't we.'

'I'm sorry,' Elliott probed. 'You were all on a stag do and you ended up here! How?'

'Not the same stag do!' Wazzer replied, laughing. 'Each of us were the groom weren't we. Our mates got us well wankered and only gone and left us 'ere for a laugh. Turns out there's no way back.'

'I'm sorry, let me get this straight. You were all on your own separate stag do's and your mates left you here and you couldn't make it back. Why didn't they come back for you?'

'You know how it is. What happens on a stag do stays on a stag do. I don't blame 'em, you can't break the code.'

Elliott was totally confused, the whole situation seemed insane to him. That was until he remembered he had the ghost of a long dead wrestler standing next to him.

'How long have you been here?' Elliott asked the three of them.

'I've been 'ere for four years now, Gaz for three and a bit and Baz is the new boy, he only arrived July before last,' Wazzer replied.

'But how have you survived? What did you eat? How have you kept yourself sane?' Elliott asked, not quite sure his last question was entirely valid.

'We found an old military silo. Found loads of food there, you know tins and shit,' Gaz explained. 'And as for keeping sane, you're in luck. We're just about to start again?'

'I'm sorry, start what again?'

'Start what?' Gaz hooted. 'This guy's a joker ain't he.'

Wazzer suddenly reached out and put a firm arm around Elliott's shoulders. Before he knew it he was being guided, under duress, towards the doorway of one of the cottages. It was matey in appearance but menacing in its application. With the other two following closely behind Elliott felt he had no other choice than to comply. As he approached the open door he could just about make out the dimly lit room beyond. In the middle was a small table with four chairs on each side. On the table sat a Monopoly board.

'You ain't being the boot. I'm the boot, alright!' Gaz whispered intimidatingly in Elliott's ear as they entered.

'I'm guessing ...' Elliott suggested with a quiver in his voice, '... that when you talked about staying sane, you do this by playing Monopoly, correct?'

'Listen to this Geezer, talking like it's just a game,' Wazzer asserted. 'This ain't just a game son, and it ain't just Monopoly. This, is Stag Monopoly.'

'What's the difference?' Elliott asked.

'You know, much the same, none of that free parking bullshit though.'

'And you play this a lot?' Elliott enquired.

'Play this a lot?' Baz replied, laughing. 'This is game 4832. You playing?'

'I'm really sorry but I don't have the time,' Elliott replied, worried what effect his reply would have. 'You see, I need to get off this island. I have something very important I need to get to.'

Suddenly the three looked intimidating in the reduced light, naked fury dancing in their wild eyed stares. They'd been here for years, playing this game non-stop, God knows what they were capable of. Elliott quickly concluded that this wasn't a request to be refused. Obediently he sat down at the table, laying his palms flat on the surface and awaited the dread that was to come.

'You can be the iron!' Wazzer declared and they all sat down alongside.

Chapter 24

Calico stag

'Didn't I tell you to let them win!' Hapkido shouted as he ran behind Elliott.

The three stags were fifty feet behind as Elliott raced down the road towards the break in the cliffs.

'I was trying …' Elliott panted, '… but Baz wouldn't trade Trafalgar square and it all got a bit personal after that.'

Elliott and Hapkido rounded the corner first, buying them a few seconds out of sight of the pursuing pack. Hapkido, displaying a turn of speed that was frankly unexpected, overtook Elliott and veered off to the right. Diving into the undergrowth that grew wildly alongside the road, Elliott, not knowing what else to do, followed. His trousers caught on the brambles, thin branches whipping his face as he dived through. Hapkido, already couching down on the other side, showed no after effects of his desperate lunge. Elliott on the other hand hadn't fared so well. The large rip in the fabric of his trousers ran from the knee to the ankle and perfectly exposed the scraped and bleeding skin below.

'Sssshhhh!' Hapkido whispered urgently.

Seconds later Wazzer and Co careered around the corner, failing to notice Elliott's exit and continued to tear down the road. The voice of Gaz could be clearly heard as they raced away.

'If I'd known he was going to win I wouldn't have given him ten pounds for finishing second in that beauty competition.'

When Elliott was finally sure that they had gone he turned to address Hapkido.

'Well that's just great. Not only are we stuck on a deserted island but now we have three nutcases chasing us as well,' Elliott whispered.

'Who said we're stuck. I sense there's a boat nearby,' Hapkido whispered in return.

'You heard what they said. There's no way off the island. If there were then they would have found it already, instead of slowly going insane.'

'It's hidden.'

'And you know this how?' Elliott asked sceptically.

'I'm getting a message from the other side. It's a man. I think he might have been a pirate.'

'A pirate?' Elliott asked disbelievingly. 'I'm not exactly an expert but I don't think pirates sailed round these parts.'

'I'm only telling you what he told me.'

'Okay, where's the boat then?'

'Ah, there might be a problem there. You see, he'll only tell you in person. He wants to communicate via me.'

'You mean you're the one who gets possessed?' Elliott laughed quietly. 'That makes a change. Okay, fire away.'

Hapkido gave a couple of twitches of his head before his left eye closed tightly and his shoulders rose up.

'Arghhh, me hearties!'

'Seriously? That's your best pirate impression is it?' Elliott enquired.

'It not be an impression you salty dog. I be old Jack McGubbins.'

'If you're going to make stuff up, can you at least try to be convincing?' Elliott asked despairingly.

'I don't know what you be saying land lubber. I be old Jack McGubbins, scourge of the seven seas.'

'Okay,' Elliott sighed. 'Jack, can you tell me where your boat is?'

'That I can me lily-livered matey. It be in a cave on the other side of the island, I hid it there when I was looking for me treasure. Argghh, it be left there for many a year now as I never made it off this infernal rock.'

'Okay, where is it then?' Elliott asked, desperate to return to some form of normality.

'I will show thee, arghhh!' Hapkido Jack replied and proceeded to stand.

Making his way from the bushes Hapkido Valentine seemed to be carrying a significant limp.

Forty-five minutes later and with Elliott on the verge of a nervous breakdown, they finally found themselves clambering over some rocks on the other side of the island. Hapkido Jack claimed that nearby lay the entrance to his cave, although he had also been claiming that for around two hours now. The sea rushed in with a violent surge against the shoreline, crashing against the sharp grey rocks, rushing into the many inlets that could hide a cave.

'Sixteen men on a dead man's chest,' Hapkido Jack sang heartily.

'Will you just be quiet!' Elliott demanded.

'I hear thee, I swear to Davy Jones himself I won't sing no shanties no more. Besides, the cave be over there,' Hapkido Jack replied, pointing a contorted finger in the direction of one of the inlets.

Elliott could just about make out a gap which seemed to widen as it twisted its way through the rocky foreground. Where it met the cliff above, a crack just wide enough for a man to slip through, possibly even a boat, was masked by the shadows. With some trepidation Elliott approached, crouching down to peer inside. As dark caves went, it really was up there with the best. Elliott could feel the damp saline air from inside blowing across his face as he squatted, peering desperately in. The absence of any light made it difficult to discern anything at all. There was but one option, Elliott gingerly lowered himself down.

Landing with a splash in a stagnant puddle Elliott quickly recovered, fired by a sense of immediate fear. Raising himself to his full stature Elliott reached out to feel the ceiling of the cave mere inches above his head. Rough and undulating it matched the surface of the floor on which he stood. Slowly, as his eyes became more accustomed to the dark, he began to make out further details of the cave. There, at the back, maybe ten feet away, was something he couldn't quite make out. Elliott moved forward, his hand outstretched, groping hopelessly in the near darkness. His fingertips came into contact with it first. Whatever it was, it was damp and slimy and if this were a boat it certainly didn't feel as expected.

'Arghhh, there be my fine ship!' Hapkido Jack announced, bellowing through the hole as he crouched down outside.

Reassured, Elliott moved his hand along its length. He could feel the curve of the hull, finding the sharp angle where it became square at the stern. His eyes, now fully adjusted to the gloom, permitted a more thorough examination. No obvious gaping holes in the hull, even what looked like oars inside. She might just be seaworthy, Elliott hoped. Strangely it looked relatively modern, certainly not hundreds of years old as you might expect for a pirate boat.

'I don't understand,' Elliott declared, turning back towards the hole. 'It's in good condition. If you were a pirate, surely it would have rotted away by now?'

'Arghhh, well I may not quite be the pirate I made myself out to be.'

'Who are you then?' Elliott sighed, moving back towards the entrance to the cave.

'Well …' Hapkido Jack paused, changing to a middle class English accent. 'Actually my name is Ernest Clutterbuck. I was an insurance salesman from Bedford and I died here in 1997. It is my boat though.'

'Okay,' Elliott replied, clambering back out of the cave. 'But what were you doing here?'

'Well you know how intense insurance gets?'

'Not really, no.'

'Oh it's mad, third-party this, comprehensive that. I just couldn't stand it any longer. So I rowed over here to start a new life, away from the modern world.'

'And you never went back?' Elliott asked.

'No, stashed my boat here and two minutes later I slipped on the rocks. Knocked myself unconscious and got washed out to sea. Bloody unlucky if you ask me.'

'Does sound like a bit of a shitter. But why all the pirate stuff?'

'Oh you know, I've been hanging round here since then, being all ghost-like. Then you and your friend pop along and I find out I can actually speak to someone. Seemed a good opportunity for a laugh. You know what insurance salesmen are like, crazy ain't we.'

Elliott wasn't sure his stereotypical image matched up with that of Ernest's.

'So the boat is okay. I can use it?' Elliott asked.

'Oh yes, it's about a kilometre to the mainland but you can only use it on one condition.'

'And that is?' Elliott enquired.

'You tell my family. They'll probably be wondering what happened to me.'

'Absolutely,' Elliott promised.

'Good man, now hurry. Those three idiots are not far from here.'

'Thanks Ernest. One last thing, can I have Hapkido back?' Elliott asked.

'Sure. Good luck.'

Hapkido started to twitch, halfway between a seizure and a body-pop. Seconds later he returned.

'Interesting sensation,' the wrestler declared, returning to his normal self.

Suddenly Elliott could hear voices. The three *were* near.

'Here, help me get the boat to the sea,' Elliott asked, instantly realising his ridiculous request. 'Never mind, I'll do it myself.'

Elliott moved back into the cave and started to drag the boat across the dank rocky floor. The scraping of the hull across the bottom of the cave combined with Elliott's grunting from the effort, radiated around the small enclosed space. With some considerable determination Elliott lifted the front of the boat until it was supported by the lip of the opening. Making his way back to the stern he then proceeded with great difficulty to lift the entire weight of the boat, grappling and pushing it, so that slowly it began to edge out of the cave. Finally with one last push he managed to release the boat from its hiding place and clambered out after it, heavy with sweat. His heart was racing faster than a rocket full of amphetamine-addled monkeys.

'You know I could have helped you with that,' Hapkido suggested after the fact.

Ignoring him, Elliott began to push the boat down the dip of the rocks, onwards towards the sea. For the last ten feet of the journey he had no control as the boat careered down the incline, slamming into rocks and landing with a triumphant splash into the water. Amazingly the boat was still in one piece and bobbing away happily.

'Come on!' Elliott shouted, scrambling down the rocks and leaping from the shore.

Landing heavily, the boat rocked wildly from side to side, sea water spilling into the boat as it rolled. Hapkido followed suit, the boat failing to register his arrival as he landed. Both men looked back to the shore to see the Monopoly three sprinting over the rocks towards them, looking as friendly as a bear being poked with a shitty stick.

Elliott sat himself down onto the seat and pushed away from the rocks with one of the oars. He then slid the other oar into the water and began to row furiously, quickly putting distance between boat and shoreline.

'You arsehole!' Wazzer cried, coming to a drastic halt at the edge of the rocks. 'All I wanted was a hotel on Mayfair.'

Baz and Gaz arrived shortly afterwards and proceeded to stop Wazzer from jumping into the water after them. Admittedly Elliott felt bad that he was leaving them there, stranded, but it certainly wasn't a good idea to be sharing a boat with them either. He'd get them some help once he was back on the mainland: a rescue first and foremost followed by some psychiatric help for good measure.

'That was close,' Hapkido commented, legs apart, peering off toward the horizon with his hand shielding his eyes. 'To the mainland!'

Chapter 25

The Inspector is waiting for you sir, in the caravan

By the time Elliott made it to the mainland it was now late morning. The boat bobbed disconcertingly as it approached the short stony beach, the hull gently nudging the cobbles underneath. A relieved Elliott jumped from the boat, his feet landing in the water, the sea coming up to his knees. Sloshing and scrabbling the rest of the way, he finally allowed himself to collapse once he had reached dry land and took a look back towards the boat. Hapkido was emerging from the water too, as far removed from Ursula Andress in Dr. No as one could possibly imagine.

'Where's the arcades?' Hapkido asked, coming to a stop and towering over Elliott who lay exhausted below.

Looking up gazed across the scrubland that sat behind the beach. In the distance he could make something out.

'I think there's a road over there, maybe even a railway,' Elliott announced, squinting in the morning sun.

'If we're really lucky it might be one of those bullet trains the Japanese are famous for.'

'This is not bloody Japan!' Elliott pronounced, getting to his feet.

With hope and desperation in equal measure both Hapkido and Elliott walked up the remainder of the beach and across the scrubland, negotiating a low strung barbed wire fence along the way. As they got nearer, Elliott saw that he was right: it was a road, albeit devoid of any actual cars. They had little other choice but to walk, Elliott's wet footprints quickly drying as he began striding with a new-found resolve. It took around half an hour before Elliott heard the welcome drone of an engine from behind. Turning to look he could make out a Winnebago type camper van coming over the hill behind him, travelling at such a speed that it was as likely to break the speed limit as a zombie smoking a reefer. When it finally did get closer Elliott waved his arms frantically, desperately hoping it would stop. As luck would have it, the camper van rolled to a halt, pulling over to the side of the road. The window rolled down and a head emerged.

'What's the problem?' The older man asked. He was quite short, overweight and wore a striking auburn wig which sat askew on his head.

'Hey,' Elliott replied, wiping his sleeve across his forehead to clear the sweat. 'Thanks for stopping. I desperately need a lift.'

'You do know that the police strongly advise against the practice of hitchhiking? I'm not in the habit of picking up strangers, especially not when I'm on holiday.'

'I appreciate that but you see I have to get to London. I have something really important to do tomorrow night and if I don't get there I'll probably lose the one chance I'll ever have with this girl I really like.'

'You do realise that you're a long way from London don't you?'

'Nearer to Tokyo I'd say,' Hapkido interjected.

'I know but I have to at least try,' Elliott replied, ignoring the wrestler. 'You see it's not my fault, I was drugged and left on an island back there by a man who wants to ruin everything. Plus I think someone is trying to kill me.'

'Well if that's the case then son, get in! No one breaks the law whilst Inspector John Polston sits idly by!'

'You're the police?'

'Retired. Now get in!'

Elliott moved around the front of the camper van and opened the passenger door, climbing up into the seat next to the driver. On the dashboard there was photo of a small dog but Elliott didn't ask the significance.

'How far are you going?' asked Elliott.

'I can take you as far as Inverness. After that you're on your own.'

Elliott wasn't quite sure where Inverness was. He was pretty sure that it was still a long way from London though. Still, this seemed his only option.

'Thanks Mr. Polston.'

'It's Inspector Polston son. Now buckle up, this might get a bit hairy.'

The Inspector revved the engine and proceeded to drive up the road at a consistent 28 mph. In response Elliott closed his eyes, trying to block out Hapkido who had made his way into the back of the van and was asking where he could find the frying pan and some sausages.

When they finally arrived in Inverness, Elliott asked to be dropped off at the bus station. Inspector Polston duly obliged before driving the camper van into the early evening sun. The station itself was an uninspiring beige brick building with striking blue window frames. Outside, multiple stands stood empty with a handful of people waiting expectantly under Perspex canopies.

What was he going to do now? Elliott had no idea. Truth be told he hadn't really thought this far ahead. Flashman had taken his wallet, phone and anything of any value worth trading. He sincerely doubted that any employee of the national coach company would be willing to exchange a one way, six-hundred mile journey for the Casio digital watch on his wrist. Suddenly a dormant memory sparked back to life. Just before he had left the flat, he'd found that twenty pound note, hadn't he? He'd completely forgotten about it in the turmoil of being shot at, drugged, kidnapped, left on an island with three monopoly crazed lunatics and an encounter with the ghost of a pirate come insurance salesman. Elliott slipped his outstretched fingers into his back pocket hopefully. Amazingly it was still there.

'Result!' Elliott announced ardently.

As the people waiting in the nearest stand looked around, Hapkido materialised alongside.

'Twenty quid! That will get us a ticket to London?' Hapkido excitedly suggested.

'That's nowhere near enough,' Elliott replied under his breath. 'Again, I have to remind you that this isn't 1983. Things have moved on a bit since then. The ticket office is over there, let's go and find out how far it will get us.'

Elliott and Hapkido trudged across to the ticket office where they found a stout older women with a face that could drive the hope from a person quicker than an enforced viewing of Jaws 4.

'Hello. I need to get to London but I only have twenty pounds,' Elliott announced as he arrived at the counter.

'Can't get to London for that,' The woman replied in a thick Scottish inflection, uninterested.

'Okay. How far south can I get?'

'One moment,' she replied, turning to her computer.

'Twenty pounds on the bus leaving in twenty minutes will get you, via Glasgow, to either Coventry, Sheffield, Nottingham or Derby.

'Go to Derby, go to Derby!'

'One moment please,' Elliott asked the woman behind the counter.

'Look, I appreciate you lived in Derby before you know what.'

'Transported through time and space.'

'Yeah that. But we need to go as far south as possible. I suppose from there we could maybe hitchhike to London.'

'Trust me. If we get to Derby we can get to London easily. When have I ever let you down eh?'

Elliott took a moment to compile the list of failures, losing count somewhere around seventeen. Sadly he couldn't think of any other options and turned his attention back towards the woman behind the counter.

'One ticket to Derby please.'

Emerging with a singular ten pence piece in change and a ticket to some hell-hole in the Midlands, Elliott couldn't help but feel that his chance was slipping away. What would Charlotte think if he didn't make it back in time? Would that end any chance he had before it even began?

Twenty minutes later Elliott found himself on the late-night coach to Glasgow watching the street lamps flash by, signalling the beginning of the longest four hours of his life. Hapkido sat in the empty seat next to him talking about the British Leyland Motor Company and explaining how one day it would be possible to invent a phone so small you could actually carry it around with you. When they finally arrived in Glasgow they found a bus station so depressing that micro-organisms usually found clinging to underwater volcanic chimneys would have refused to live there. More disturbingly it soon became evident that the next bus to Derby wasn't until six in the morning. They were going to be stuck there for the night.

'Cracking!' Elliott exclaimed, watching the other passengers walk out the main door of Dante's Inferno as designed in 1967 by some concrete-obsessed shitbag architect.

'So ....' Hapkido mused, 'that bench over there looks nice.'

'Yeah, looks delightful,' Elliott replied in a tone heavy with sarcasm. 'But before I do, I still have ten pence left. I need to ring Charlotte.'

After eventually finding a phone that actually worked Elliott slotted in the ten pence piece and dialled the number that he had memorised in his fixation.

'Hello?' Charlotte answered.

'Charlotte it's me, Elliott,' Elliott spoke rapidly. 'Just listen, not sure how long my money will last. There's been a problem and I'm currently stuck in Glasgow on my way to London. Is there anything ...'

The phone cut off.

'In 1983 you would have got a lot longer call than that,' Hapkido ruminated.

'Just don't.'

Making his way back to the bench, there was nothing else Elliott could do. They would just have to see what the next day brought, and if today was anything to go by it would probably be a nuclear attack by a rogue state.

Chapter 26

The nature of the beast

The street outside Elliott's flat was quiet, the reporters having long since fled. The police had also departed, leaving but a solitary police car to monitor events. A rigmarole of tedium had dulled the senses of the officer within, so much so that he failed to register Charlotte as she passed.

Charlotte knew Elliott wasn't home. That much was evident from their brief telephone conversation the night before. She had actually come to see her uncle, currently resident at Mrs. Clarkson's flat due to his estranged Russian wife waiting behind the door of his own home with a harpoon gun. Charlotte rang the bell and waited.

'Oh hello dearie, how are you?' Mrs. Clarkson enquired, opening the door with her hair in disarray.

'Fine, thank you. Is Uncle Bernie here?' Charlotte asked, knowing full well he was.

'Oh I would say so. He's in the front room,' replied Mrs. Clarkson, moving to one side to allow Charlotte in.

When Charlotte arrived in the front room, she found her uncle sitting exhausted in an armchair smoking a roll up. He was wearing a string vest underneath braces which held up his beige trousers.

'Uncle Bernie,' Charlotte announced. 'I think we have a problem.'

'I'll tell you what it's not,' Bernie replied attentively. 'It's not ticket sales. Ever since some loony took a dislike to our Elliott the publicity for this thing is huge. The venue told me they've completely sold out. That's a sweet seventy grand in all our pockets.'

'Seventy thousand you say?' Mrs. Clarkson enquired as she shuffled slowly across the room to sit on Bernie's knee.

'I think Elliott went into hiding after the second attack,' Charlotte elaborated.

'So he should. Can't have some nutter killing him before the show,' Bernie confirmed.

'The problem is, I got a phone call from him last night.'

'All raring to go I hope.'

'Well, from what I can tell he's in Glasgow on his way down.'

'Glasgow, what the bleeding 'ell is he doing in Glasgow?' Bernie shouted. 'I hope you rang him back and told him to get his arse down to London for the show.'

'I did, or at least I tried. His mobile just kept being answered by someone trying to sell me his autobiography.'

'Well he better bleeding get back to London on time. We've got a lot at stake with this show. We could be talking extra nights, stadiums, world tours, the whole shebang.'

'Think of all that money, Bernieboops,' Mrs. Clarkson drawled, running her finger sensually amongst the grey chest hairs that protruded from the top of his vest.

'Yes, but it's not just about the money is it?' Charlotte interrupted, casting an evil glare in the direction of the old woman. 'Someone is actually trying to kill Elliott. What happens if we put him on stage and someone actually manages to shoot him? You know what that would mean?'

'Seventy grand split two ways?' Mrs. Clarkson suggested.

'No,' Charlotte protested. 'It means we'd be to blame. I've spoken to the police and they think the previous attempts were publicity stunts. They suggested we hire security but the safest option is surely to cancel the show.'

'What!' Bernie howled, jumping to his feet and toppling Mrs. Clarkson onto the floor. 'This is our one chance of actually making money for a change, if that dipshit actually turns up.'

'He said he would,' Charlotte replied, even though she didn't have the faintest idea of where he actually was.

'Okay, okay,' Bernie replied, gesturing with his hands for calm.

Mrs. Clarkson got to her feet and gave Charlotte a disapproving stare.

'So what are we going to do?' Charlotte asked.

'I promise I'll sort something out with security. Trust me. I don't want him dying either, not when we could be onto something big here. I'll speak to some friends I know and we'll make sure everything goes according to plan.'

'You promise he'll be okay?'

'Absolutely!' Bernie replied persuasively.

'Thank you,' Charlotte responded. 'Now, if you'll excuse me I need to get to the venue. There are a lot of things to get ready.'

'Good girl,' Bernie replied and Mrs. Clarkson escorted her to the door.

Within twenty seconds of Charlotte leaving Mrs. Clarkson and Bernie Subiaco were stumbling towards the bedroom, falling onto the bed in a fit of passion.

'Are you really going to get security for that boy Bernieboops?' Mrs. Clarkson mumbled.

'Nah,' Bernie replied with a laugh. 'He'll be just fine.'

Chapter 27

Now pay attention Elliott Rose, I want you to take good care of this equipment

It had been six long hours since they'd left Glasgow that morning. Hapkido Valentine had spent this time on the coach recounting to Elliott interesting facts such as the history of cotton weaving and Elizabeth the first, Queen of England or time travelling Mick Hucknall?

'What exactly are we going to do in Derby in this great plan of yours?' Elliott whispered, staring at the motorway exit sign that signalled that this stage of their journey was nearly over.

'We need to get to Arundel Street, to where my old house used to be,' Hapkido expounded.

'But haven't we already been there? You do remember don't you? The whole thing with your mum passing on and the crazy lady who tried to seduce me?'

'Yes,' Hapkido answered. 'But there was one thing we didn't do. I'll explain everything to you in good time, it's a fair old walk from the station to my house.'

*

The coach finally pulled up at Derby coach station. Elliott was the first off, and under Hapkido's direction walked away from town and into the depths of the terraced suburbs. Hapkido filled the time that it took to walk by expanding upon his previous life. It seemed that life in 1983 for a well-known professional wrestler came with financial benefits. These didn't stretch to yachts or supermodel girlfriends, more super-sized breakfasts at motorway services and a second car. Hapkido had invested in both. Gordon Cole had loved two things in life: his mum and that second car. As he told it, in his last will and testament it was stipulated that in the event of his death (or as Hapkido corrected:

the misidentification of trans-dimensional transportation) his car should be looked after at all costs. To this effect he had ensured that enough money was available to go towards the car's care. The twenty year old son of one of his neighbours had been recruited to ensure that it was kept in pristine condition and in perfect running order for the price of a small yearly fee. All he had to do was give the car a run every week and then return it to a specified garage nearby which was owned by a certain Japanese sounding gentleman. In addition Gordon Cole had hidden a spare set of keys nearby, just in case of emergencies. Emergencies like this. Elliott was somewhat surprised: this might actually work. Here was the opportunity for him to get back to London, and given the effort Hapkido had put into preserving the car, he would probably have only gone to so much trouble for an automobile classic.

'So, let me get this correct,' Elliott asked as they walked down Arundel Street. 'You drove an Austin Maestro 1.3 whilst you had your dream car locked away in this garage?'

'That's correct,' Hapkido beamed proudly.

'But you continued to drive an Austin Maestro?' Elliott asked unbelievingly.

'Don't dismiss the Austin Maestro young Elliott. It had an electronic engine management system, bumpers that were the same colour as the car and … ' Hapkido paused for dramatic effect, 'a little light that came on when you were towing a caravan.'

'Yeah, sounds sweet. But what car was it that you made sure was looked after so well for all these years?' Elliott asked excitedly.

'All in good time my friend, all in good time. Now, you see that alleyway opposite the factory where my old house used to be? We have to go down there.'

Elliott slipped down the alleyway, after twenty feet it opened up to reveal a row of lock-up garages that backed onto a council estate. The garage doors were an assortment of colours complete with dents and flaking paintwork. In the corner, propped up against the wall, a rusted bicycle was entwined with overgrown weeds, long since lost to nature's advance.

'Look underneath those bricks in the corner,' Hapkido advised.

Elliott made his way over to the other corner and crouched down, moving one brick away at a time. When he was done he was disappointed to find nothing underneath.

'Brilliant,' Elliott exclaimed.

'You have to dig for them,' Hapkido instructed as if it were obvious.

'Jesus, okay,' Elliott replied, beginning to sweep away the dirt with his hands. Several minutes later and at about twenty centimetres down he came upon a sealed Tupperware box. Inside were two keys, a small silver one and a larger black one.

'There you go,' declared Hapkido happily, pointing in the direction of a nearby garage. 'Now let's go check out my princess.'

To Elliott's surprise the small key fitted the silver lock shaped like a handle. Elliott began to turn it before pausing.

'I've seen this in a Bond film. I'm going to open this and find an E-Type Jaguar aren't I?'

'Just open it up and see,' Hapkido directed proudly.

Elliott swung the door up with a grating of metal and a loud clatter. What he found on the other side required contemplation for a good thirty seconds before he said something.

'It's a fricking Austin Maestro.'

'Yes,' Hapkido replied, not quite understanding Elliott's statement.

'You told me you drove an Austin Maestro as your normal car. Now correct me if I'm wrong but is this or this not another Austin Maestro?'

'Of course but as I said my other car was a 1.3. This is a 1.6 Vanden Plas. You get an extra 0.3 with this bad boy!'

'An extra 0.3?' Elliott asked, still struggling to comprehend the exchange.

'Plus a digital speedometer. And not forgetting the caravan light of course.'

'Wouldn't dream of it,' Elliott replied, resigning himself to the fact that he would no longer be cruising down to London in style. He was expecting a classic, what he got was an answer to an automotive question never asked.

'Let's get it fired up!' Hapkido demanded, his hands gripped near his chest in excitement.

Twenty minutes later, after numerous attempts characterised by whining motors and billowing black smoke, the car unexpectedly started, accompanied by a cacophony of knocking from deep within the engine. As Elliott slowly edged the car out of the garage, the car bounced along the uneven slabbed tarmac. Yet by the time they had negotiated the exit from the garages and onto the roads of the council estate, Elliott no longer felt the car was likely to explode at any moment. They were on their way to London.

Chapter 28

A convergence of ends

'Where is he?' Charlotte flustered, pacing up and down the alleyway outside the Apollo Rooms.

'Relax, he'll be here,' assured Bernie Subiaco.

The show was due to begin in half an hour and people were starting to arrive. The hum of their collective voices drifted around to the side of the building where Charlotte and Bernie found themselves waiting.

'And where's the security you promised?' Charlotte demanded.

'Ah, you see there's been a slight problem on that front. Turns out the security firm double booked us and can't make it. What are the chances, eh?''

'Oh, you're truly unbelievable,' Charlotte replied, frustrated and angry, continuing to pace. 'I asked for one thing and you lied to me. I knew I shouldn't have let you talk me into running this firm for you. When you get involved, everything I've worked towards just goes up in smoke.'

'Now look here,' Bernie retorted, not willing to let his young niece over-rule fifty years of experience. 'It's the truth. Besides I don't like being called a liar, not by you, not by anyone!'

'Give it a rest,' Charlotte bellowed. 'I know you too well. You promised security and I trusted you. Yet you chose profit over safety. If someone gets hurt I'm holding you personally responsible.'

'Who exactly is going to get hurt anyway? As far as I can tell we don't even have a performer. If you ran this firm properly then you would've at least ensured your client turned up to do the show!' Bernie countered.

'That's the thing Uncle Bernie. I don't want to run this business anymore. I've had it. You can do it on your own from now on.'

'Now don't do anything hasty.'

'I mean it Uncle Bernie! I'm through. Now where the hell is he?' Charlotte pleaded, glancing back down the alleyway for the umpteenth time.

And so it was that Charlotte and Bernie Subiaco waited by the stage door, their nervousness and dislike for one another escalating by the second.

Miss Carol Swanson

Carol had brought her ticket and was waiting patiently as the line slowly filed through the main doors. In the distance she could hear some kind of argument but paid it no heed, she had other things to think about. Pretty soon this whole charade would fall down and Elliott Rose would be a problem no more. She was rather looking forward to it.

As she waited she thought back to the conversation with Jeremy at her house. Was this really the only way of getting rid of him? Elliott Rose had been a thorn in her side for far too long now and looking around at the excited faces around her, he was no doubt the next big thing. This next big thing had a secret to tell and Carol couldn't allow that to happen. So no, Carol reasoned, there was no other way. If she wanted to protect her show, to protect herself, this was the way it had to be.

Mr. Eric Morris

The Lunchbox Killer navigated his way along the deserted corridors of the theatre, the breezeblock walls painted a colour of charmless beige. Finally at the end of one of them he found the door he was looking for, complete with warning signs as to what lay beyond. The assassin slipped through into the near darkness, closing the door behind him. In the centre of the enclosed walls a ladder stretched upwards, the metal painted an industrial dark grey. With the handle of his lunchbox clenched tightly between his teeth, a thin case strung across his shoulder, Eric Morris began to climb.

Eventually he reached a deserted platform twenty feet above. Normally reserved for lighting technicians, it was the perfect place to set up, affording an unparalleled view of the stage on the other side of the hall. The Lunchbox Killer edged his way along, inching himself carefully around the various parts of scaffold that jotted out at sharp angles. At the middle he crouched, sliding the case from his shoulder and laying it quietly on the floor of the platform. Inside lay the assorted pieces of a rifle he had carefully selected for the job. There could be no further mistakes. His previous two attempts had been complete disasters due to a rather unfortunate affliction. At the Dermot Kilgallon show the target was firmly in his sights, then for no obvious reason he thought about a Class 57 locomotive rolling through Bury St Edmunds. It was just enough to shift his aim. Miss! And then at the target's flat, he had inadvertently thought about the 12:47 due through Swindon just as he pulled the trigger. Miss! He was determined it wouldn't happen this time. This time everything was going to go according to plan.

<u>Mr. Jeremy Flashman, author of *My Spirited Journey*, available at all good book shops and currently marked down due to an excess of stock</u>

Jeremy arrived at the Apollo Rooms, despite knowing that the star attraction was 560 miles away, or so he thought. Finding his seat at the end of the row he gave a smile to the woman sitting next to him. Yes it really was him. She in turn smiled back, checking her bag to ensure she had brought her can of Mace with her.

Twenty minutes after the show was planned to start he could feel the growing frustration of the crowd. It began as a murmuring that rolled across the audience, growing in volume as the minutes ticked by. Eventually an announcement came over the speakers apologising for the delay but this did little to appease them. Well, Jeremy pondered, it looks like the main attraction hasn't shown up, it's lucky they have a replacement at hand. Jeremy Flashman was here to save the day.

The steward, fed up with the constant abuse from approaching members of the audience sent Jeremy towards the manager. The manager, recognising the worth of Jeremy's suggestion sent him in the direction of the stage door. There he found Charlotte and Bernie Subiaco, standing impatiently outside in the alleyway, lit in the darkness by a security light.

'Excuse me,' Jeremy began. 'You probably recognise me. I'm Jeremy Flashman, psychic.' 'Um, hello,' Charlotte replied, not quite paying attention, her mind elsewhere.

'If I'm not mistaken it looks like Mr. Rose hasn't turned up and I'd thought you'd like to know that the crowd are getting restless in there,' Jeremy added, hooking his thumb over his shoulder in the direction of the theatre.

'Thank you, I'm sure he'll be here any second. Why don't you take your seat? It won't be long now.' Charlotte replied, hoping the man would disappear accordingly. She had other things to worry about.

'I don't like to see people disappointed Miss,' Jeremy continued. 'If you like, as a personal favour, I could perform the show for you.'

Charlotte turned, taken aback by the suggestion. Weighing him up with her eyes she finally connected the name to the person, Jeremy Flashman, no less. It was certainly tempting, yet deep down a thought prevailed. She had to give Elliott one last chance.

'No thank you,' Charlotte answered. 'It's a kind offer Mr. Flashman but the audience have paid to see Elliott Rose. I'm sure he'll be here any minute now.'

'Well hang on Charlotte,' Bernie interjected, enthused by the stroke of luck that had befallen them. 'Let's hear Mr. Flashman out, shall we? Elliott isn't here and the audience are on the verge of walking out.'

'We have to give him a few more minutes,' Charlotte beseeched.

'No, Charlotte!' Bernie persisted. 'Like it or not I'm still the managing director of this firm and I make the final decisions. We can't let an opportunity like this slip away.'

And so it was that Bernie Subiaco and his niece argued. Meanwhile Jeremy Flashman waited, wetting the tip of his middle finger and smoothing down one eyebrow as he waited for them to say yes.

Valentine and Rose, righting wrongs, one at a time

The alleyway lit up like the Second Coming, as sponsored by Osram. The source of the light: two rectangular headlights, belonging to a car that raced towards Subiaco, Subiaco and Flashman. The guttural throb of the engine missed something important as it sped, the resulting backfire echoing off the high walls. Charlotte hoped and prayed. Bernie Subiaco dived into a nearby industrial rubbish bin. Jeremy Flashman let out a little bit of wee. Finally the car came to a screeching halt mere feet from them and the driver's side door swung dramatically open. Elliott Rose emerged.

'I'm sorry I'm late,' Elliott apologised as he rushed up to Charlotte, feeling the urge to kiss her.

'Vanden Plas. Yeah!' Hapkido screamed, punching the air.

'Thank God you're here, I thought ....' Charlotte answered, experiencing a similar sense of desire.

Their eyes locked, their hands tentatively reaching out for one another.

'Flashman!' Elliott screamed, finally noticing him to the side. 'You prick. You left me on that island. I'm going to smash .... I'm going to .... I'm ... Why the hell have you got a urine stain on the front of your trousers?'

'Elliott, we don't have time for this,' Charlotte implored. 'You have to get inside and do the show.'

'Yes, you do that,' Flashman added, letting his arm hang over his crotch to cover the stain in a quite unnatural pose.

'I'll deal with you later Flashman!' Elliott threatened as Charlotte led him forcibly inside.

'Oh, yes,' Flashman whispered. 'And do make sure you take Hapkido Valentine with you.'

Bernie Subiaco, busy extracting himself from the bin, just for a second, thought he'd heard a name that sounded awfully familiar.

'Ladies and Gentleman!' The announcer broadcast with a considerable dose of fervour.

The audience sat up in their chairs, their conversations paused as they listened.

'It gives me great pleasure to introduce to you the sensation, Elliott .... Rose!'

On cue a stirring 80's rock anthem blasted out from the speakers. As the guitar solo began to fade away, Elliott Rose, a man who had escaped assassination attempts and desertion on a Scottish island stepped apprehensively onto the stage. The sound of his slow, nervous steps seemed to fill the entire room. The spot lights shone with a ferocity of a supernova, blinding him as a silence prevailed across the audience. Elliott could feel the hundreds, perhaps thousands of eyes that were watching him intently.

'Um, hello.' Elliott muttered uncertainly. He was shocked to hear his voice projected at such volume around the auditorium.

'More showmanship!'

'Okay,' Elliott gabbled, a long way from the self-assured entertainer the audience were expecting. 'I'm getting the name Gladys, three rows back from the front. Are you there Gladys?'

Elliott peered into the gloom. Nothing. Oh my God, he was obviously way out of his depth. Should he run? Would he make it out alive?

Eventually a hand tentatively rose. The spotlight operator, mirroring Elliott's own relief, swung the beam round and illuminated an old lady who shied away from its nuclear glare. Seconds later a stage hand was next to her, handing her a portable microphone.

'Are you Gladys?' Elliott asked optimistically.

'Yes,' came a timid reply.

'Gladys I have a message for you from your husband, Dave.' Elliott stated, his fear beginning to dissipate.

What happened next certainly wasn't part of the plan.

'Stop!'

The voice rang out, sudden and commanding. Surprisingly, it didn't come from the audience but rather from the side. Elliott looked around to see Jeremy Flashman emerge onto the stage.

'This man is a fraud!' Flashman roared, his voice carrying to the far reaches of the room.

'What are you doing?' Elliott asked bewildered, his question broadcast throughout the auditorium.

'Something I should've done a long time ago.' Jeremy avowed quietly. 'You see, I know now why it didn't work before. Foolishly I didn't know who I was actually calling. But now I do.'

'Eh?' Elliott enquired, confused.

The audience had no idea what was going on but their interested was certainly piqued. Jeremy took up position and addressed the crowd.

'Ladies and Gentlemen. If you don't know me, which I'm sure you do,' Flashman smiled, 'I'm Jeremy Flashman and I'm here to show you that this man is a fraud. He has no power, no connection to the spirit world, you have been misled. Whereas I have the real gift, which co-incidentally you can read about in my autobiography. I will show you what a real psychic can do.'

Jeremy Flashman began to chant.

'Let the great spirit of Eldermon, grand leader of the fifth council of wizards show *Hapkido Valentine* the way. I give you this gift so that you may know the path.'

A feeling of electricity filled the air, an uncomfortable and oppressive sensation that made the audience members near to the stage shift in their seats. Halfway between where Jeremy and Elliott were standing, a mist began to form, rising from the stage. It snaked and curled as it rose, dancing in time to an unseen universal pulse. At a height of just over six feet it looped back downwards, weaving itself expertly with the filaments that continued to climb from below. The smoke began to coil, condensing into a form more solid than before. The first structure began to emerge, an arm, muscular and defined. The smoke, remembering the form of a life once lived picked up speed, streaking across the chest and adding definition. Thick, powerful legs coalesced to support the weight of the body. From the hands, fingers became discernible, a hint of colour saturating the fingertips before moving on upwards, spreading throughout. The colour became more vibrant, effervescent reds and golds streaking along the fine detailed stitching of the dragon embroidered mask.

The audience gasped and Jeremy Flashman smiled.

Chapter 29

The cascade of history

Those not already getting out of their seats were instead favouring hysterical screaming at the manifestation of Hapkido Valentine. It was all too obvious that he came from a realm of neither special effects nor stage trickery but from somewhere else entirely. Most of the audience wanted no further part of whatever the hell this was. As they fled, those remaining seated looked at one another before a collective thought prevailed: follow.

Charlotte, not sure as to what was happening, recognised in an instant that the whole show was falling apart at the seams. Whatever Flashman had done, whoever that other person on stage was, the sight of people running for the exits was not how she'd imagined the show would go. What the situation needed, Charlotte reasoned, was calm. In an attempt to dispel the rising panic she made her way over to the lighting control panel and flicked the main lights on in the auditorium. A bright, sudden radiance flooded the room and any remaining members of the audience couldn't help but look back at the stage. Hapkido Valentine stood, visible for the world to see.

'You see!' Flashman shouted. 'Those that have the real gift can bring forth the spirits. Ladies and Gentlemen, I give you the great Hapkido Valentine, killed thirty years ago and returned to us now!'

'What the hell have you done?' Elliott cried in despair.

'I have shown the people that they have no need to fear. Ghosts walk amongst us,' Flashman replied.

Hapkido, his eyes betraying an overwhelming sense of sadness, bowed his head and began to mutter softly. 'They were not meant to see this. This was not their world to see.'

'But see they do,' Flashman announced. 'I, the great Jeremy Flashman have shown that I am the world's greatest psychic. I can raise the spirits; I can cross the divide between this world and the next!'

'No,' Hapkido continued, the desolation in his voice paramount. 'You don't understand what you've done. You've opened the door.'

Somewhere off to the left and towards the back, a scream rang out. Elliott instantly directed his gaze in that direction to observe another figure beginning to form. The smoke began to rise, quickly becoming a complete figure of a man of olive complexion and drooping moustache, dressed head to toe in thick furs.

'Who the hell is that?' Elliott asked.

'Genghis Khan,' Hapkido confirmed.

'What the hell is Genghis Khan doing here?'

'He has opened the door,' Hapkido reiterated. 'Evil has been allowed to enter this world and they've been waiting so long. When you said you thought you saw Genghis Khan before that was why I had to investigate. I had to make sure they weren't able to find a way through.'

'That was a joke,' Elliott corrected. 'You know, so I could spend some time with Charlotte alone.'

'It doesn't matter. He's here now.'

Another scream erupted from the other side of the room. Elliott looked over to see another figure forming, this time a portly man in military uniform and moustache, instantly recognisable.

'Is that Joseph Stalin?' Elliott asked disbelievingly.

'It is,' Hapkido verified.

A shriek now came up in the centre of the room. Another man had now appeared, also dressed in a military uniform. He was noticeably thinner than Stalin, his hair slicked down, a square moustache prominent on his upper lip.

'It's gonna be Hitler isn't it?' Elliott speculated.

'So it would seem,' Hapkido gloomily replied.

'Hapkido,' Elliott asked. 'Why are the most evil people in history appearing? And why do they all have moustaches?'

'Kind of puts the career of Tom Selleck in a new light doesn't it?' Hapkido offered. 'Regardless, we haven't got time to dwell on that, the door is open Elliott, the door is open!'

The audience were now scrambling over one other to get to the exits, panic widespread as yet more ghosts began to appear. The masses brought forth ranged from murderers to estate agents and all in all there were around fifty of them. Their intent was focused on the stage, advancing menacingly.

'Well,' Jeremy Flashman leant over, 'I think I'd better go now.'

As Jeremy ran from the stage Elliott desperately wanted to follow. Yet despite the overwhelming desire to do so his body was resolutely unwilling to move. It was the same feeling he'd experienced outside his flat as he was being shot at. Now here he was, completely immobile as every evil person he could think of moved towards the stage. They were led by a lean muscular man, dressed in a gold jumpsuit and a blonde perm up top.

'You!' Hapkido shouted.

'It's time we finished this!' Stardust Simpson replied, their eyes locking.

'Hap, what are we going to do?' Elliott gasped.

Hapkido breathed out heavily through his nose before bringing his arms out at ninety degrees to his body. With his eyes closed and his head tilted backwards he began to shout.

'Come forth to this world, come forth.'

A deep rumble emanated from the floor, the stage shuddering. The wooden planks on which Elliott and Hapkido stood began to bend and warp, springing free to become an assemblage of buckled planks with gaping holes between. Deep below a light began to shine, warm, golden and with a welcome vivacity. Small yellow orbs, diffuse at their edges began to rise, collectively coming to a halt at around chest height before rays of light began to strike out, reaching out to find a point, defining an edge. The forms started to take shape, melding into figures, around fifty of them, perhaps more. Watching as they came forth, Elliott had but one thought. Holy Crap!

Anyone remaining in the theatre (of which there were precious few) may well have recognised these new arrivals. Elliott certainly did as they became fully realised. There was Disco Dale, a wrestler from the eighties. Over there, more wrestlers: Mike 'Madman' Milligan, Leroy 'Crazy' Jenkins, Dancing Derek Davis. One of the last to form was a man of considerable weight and girth, dressed in a leotard that was far too tight for him.

'Alright there Gordon?' Gentleman Jim enquired.

'Champion, Jim, ruddy marvellous,' Hapkido replied.

'What can we do?' Jim asked.

'Get rid of these evil bastards will you, but not that one, he's mine,' Hapkido replied, singling out Stardust Simpson.

'Pleasure,' Jim acknowledged, launching himself from the stage in a massive belly flop onto the nearest opponent who also happened to be the former German Chancellor.

'Mein Gott!' Hitler screamed as the full weight of Gentleman Jim landed on top of him.

The rest of the long-dead wrestlers needed no further invitation, leaping one by one from the stage. Hapkido leapt too, intending a ninja type landing but touching down like a walrus dropped from the Empire State building. All Elliott could do was stand and watch. Hapkido pulled himself uncomfortably into a standing position before advancing on Stardust Simpson.

'You know what Gordon, funny how...' Simpson declared before being suddenly interrupted by a punch squarely to the face. Reeling backwards and clutching at his bloodied nose he garbled a string of obscenities through his cupped hand.

'Was it that important to you Simpson?' Hapkido asked. 'To actually kill me just to prove a point?'

'You should have stuck to the script. If you had then I wouldn't have needed to,' Stardust lectured, bringing his hand away from his face and looking at the blood smeared across his palm. 'You weren't the only one who suffered. Everyone blamed me and I had my whole career in front of me. No one wanted to employ the man who killed Hapkido Valentine. Did you even think about that? No, of course you didn't. Five years after Hapkido Valentine died in the ring, they found me dead on the floor of some squalid little bedsit on the south coast. Cirrhosis of the liver it was, not a penny to my name.'

'Am I supposed to feel sorry for you?'

'You were supposed to stick to the script. Any other decrepit wrestler would have! But no, you couldn't let it go could you? So don't blame me, you killed yourself.'

Stardust Simpson was remembering his life, memories emerging as he peeled back the aftermath of death. His fury was growing, solely directed towards Hapkido, the wrestler who had taken everything from him. He didn't need to explain himself further, he wanted revenge.

Stardust Simpson launched himself, catching Hapkido with a cross body press that sent both of them heavily to the aisle floor. As they scrabbled around, each trying desperately to gain an advantage, neither of them noticed the small point of light that appeared mid-air behind them. Hovering three feet from the ground it was accompanied by a persistent undulating buzz, the point growing rapidly outwards to form a flat horizontal disk. At its centre, if you could bear to look at it long enough, was a void of the deepest black, its edge ringed by flames that flicked at the air. The space that it intruded upon warped in response, reality itself twisted. Elliott could only watch as the void got bigger. Whatever it was, it didn't look good.

The first person to witness first-hand what lay beyond the darkness was the former Reich Chancellor and all-round general shitbag, Adolf (I spent my honeymoon on fire) Hitler. Moving towards the vortex Gentleman Jim carried the Fuhrer high above his head before propelling him head first into its void. His body quickly slipped below, the surface twisting and spiralling towards a singularity at its centre. The darkness was lit in an instant by a thousand strands of vibrant colour which swirled towards the core in a dazzling maelstrom. Each strand began to thin and elongate, the colour changing rapidly to a translucent milky hue as it was dragged downwards towards infinity. When the last strand was finally pulled inwards, the surface immediately returned to darkness with a series of waves that radiated outwards. It was the same effect that followed shortly afterwards as Joseph Stalin found himself following his WWII adversary. The General Secretary of the Soviet Communist Party disappeared beneath the surface after a convincing impression of spaghetti in a washing machine. With each intake the circle seemed to expand outwards and now measured six feet across. Elliott could quite plainly see it was growing and had no intention of finding out what would happen if it reached him. Fired by purpose, Elliott felt the fear release him and without a moment's hesitation he sprinted towards the side of stage.

Carol wasn't trying to get onto the stage, she was more intent on keeping Elliott there. Elliott on the other hand had failed to notice his former employer emerging from the side. They collided head on, bodies crashing into one another, arms flailing. To Elliott's surprise he found himself falling backwards onto the stage, followed by Carol landing on top of him. The softness and warmth of her body permeated through their clothes. It was certainly awkward, the exchange of looks confirming this as her face hovered dangerously close to his. Elliott was terrified. Carol seemed to quite enjoy the embrace.

'Well this is nice,' declared Carol, 'but I really should be going. You on the other hand should stay exactly where you are. My compatriot has you in his sights and I wouldn't want him to miss a third time.'

Carol rolled off Elliott and began to get to her feet. Seconds later a shot rang out. He jerked his head up, scanning his prostrate body to see where he'd been hit.

'Ah, my tit!' Carol screamed above him.

Elliott looked up. Carol was stumbling about, looking down horrified at one of her rather sizeable breasts. The right side of her blouse was liberally soaked in blood. By a stroke of luck (or rather an ill-timed thought about the Exeter St. David's line) Carol had been hit instead. Judging by the fact she was still standing it appeared that the pure mass of one of her breasts had slowed the bullet to a stop, preventing it from damaging any of her vital organs. Still, it wasn't an experience Elliott wanted to encounter either. Scrambling to his knees he began to crawl desperately towards the side of the stage, casting a glance back towards the fight. Hapkido stood upright and proud, watching Elliott edge towards safety as he held Stardust Simpson in a firm headlock.

'Go! Make sure you're safe. I'll be alright. Trust me. Go!' Hapkido shouted.

Elliott gave a nod. At the same time Stardust Simpson was wrenched from his feet and swung wildly into the air. When he came back down the tip of his left boot caught the lip of the void. Landing on his back, his foot remained steadfast in mid-air, resolutely held by a thin strand of dark matter which stretched sinisterly from the void. Slowly it began to spread over his boot, forming fingers as it travelled over his ankle before making its way along his lower leg and gripping his calf tightly. Stardust Simpson screamed as he was whipped clear of the floor and into the air, desperately looking at Hapkido for help. When gravity regained control, his body fell, crashing down into the darkness of the void. The last thing Hapkido saw of his long abhorred nemesis were the fragmented remains of a blonde perm as it spun deep into the nucleus.

With a final push Elliott flung himself from the stage just as another shot rang out, splintering the wooden panel beside him into a thousand flying projectiles. Elliott wasn't prepared to give the shooter another chance. Running, his breathing was heavy as he navigated down the countless corridors, crashing through innumerable doors. Finally he clattered through the last one, hurling himself out into the alleyway. There, crouched, trembling on the other side, was Charlotte, looking up at him. Everything that needed to be said was there in her eyes. Elliott remained motionless as she stood, made her way over and embraced him with a tremendous sense of relief. The hug was followed by a kiss, fleeting yet passionate.

Well, thought Elliott, looks like the evening didn't go as badly as first thought.

Chapter 30

The car park at the end of the world

Elliott stood in the main car park as the hordes of police swarmed around, a blur of bustling fluorescent jackets and flashing lights. It had been nearly an hour since Elliott had escaped the main stage and burst out into the alleyway. His and Charlotte's kiss was interrupted almost immediately by the arrival of the police responding to countless reports of the rapture. Since then he had explained diligently to them that yes, he had witnessed what had happened inside. No, he had no idea where a collection of long dead despotic tyrants and 1980s wrestlers had come from. Yes, someone really had tried to kill him again. What he neglected to mention however was how events had truly unfolded. He'd already guessed that the void had been a portal of some kind, allowing evil to be swept from this world and back to where it belonged. Elliott felt the local constabulary would view this aspect of the truth with a heavy dose of suspicion. Where it was that the portal led he could only speculate. He did suspect however that it was the sort of place where an air conditioning salesman might discover a significant opportunity.

Subsequently the police entered the building and came out soon afterwards. Despite reports, all they'd found was an empty auditorium littered with hastily discarded personal items and a stage that had been wrecked by unknown means. There certainly wasn't any evidence of some of the more unusual reports they'd received. There was no Adolf Hitler, nor any sign of Gentleman Jim or the great Hapkido Valentine. They were gone, or as the police suspected, never there in the first place. Understandably they insisted Elliott clarified a few issues. Charlotte meanwhile decided to conduct her own investigation, returning forty minutes later, just as two police officers gave up trying to make sense of it all.

'So, what's the news?' Elliott asked, his arms folded in an attempt to keep warm in the chill of the evening.

'Well,' Charlotte replied, slipping her hand into his and drawing it away from his chest. 'You'll be glad to know that your assassin has been apprehended. Someone saw him run from the theatre with what looked like a gun in a bag. The police have just found him hiding at the train station down the road. Apparently he refused to answer any questions apart from those concerning the history of British Railways rolling stock. Until that is they threatened to remove him from the station before the 6:40 from Woking came through. For some reason that was enough for him to tell them everything. Anyway, to cut a long story short, it turns out he was hired by your ex-employer Carol.'

'Carol?' Elliott exclaimed.

'Apparently so.'

Elliott looked up and cast an eye over the car park. Nearby he could make out an ambulance with paramedics wheeling someone into the back, a policeman following closely behind. There reclining on the stretcher was Carol, bloodied yet still alive. Within seconds she was out of view, Elliott's last glimpse of her was Carol Swanson undoing one of the top buttons to her blouse as she winked at the policeman who followed. The doors closed and the ambulance sped away with its sirens blaring.

'I think it's safe to say she might be in a spot of bother,' Charlotte commented with a knowing smile.

'What about Bernie? Has anyone seen him?'

'Not good news I'm afraid, it seems he's done a runner. It looks like he's taken the proceeds of the ticket sales as well, all seventy grand of it. I'm so sorry Elliott, I should never have trusted him.'

'Are the police looking for him?'

'I've given them his address and that of your next door neighbour but if I know my uncle he'll be well gone by now. I wouldn't bank on seeing Mrs. Clarkson again any time soon either.'

'Oh well,' Elliott sighed, trying not to cry. 'It was only money.'

'Don't worry we'll sort something out,' Charlotte added. 'I promise I'll get you some new curtains.'

'What about Flashman? Please tell me they at least managed to catch him.'

'Sorry, not great news there either. No one's seen him and even when they do find him, technically he hasn't committed a crime. Apparently police procedures don't have anything in place for those who raise the dead.'

'There is the fact that he drugged and kidnapped me and then left me on a deserted Scottish island.'

'There is that,' Charlotte confirmed. 'Problem is, as far as I can tell your main witness to any of what happened is a ghost. Talking of which where is he? Two hours ago, if you'd told me you were in contact with Hapkido Valentine I'd never have believed you. But I saw it, with my own two eyes. Trust me to get involved with someone who attracted a spirit of a 1980s wrestler.'

'So we're involved now are we?' Elliott asked hopefully.

'Oh shut up, you know we are. Let's work out the details tomorrow but in the meantime, where exactly is Hapkido Valentine?'

Elliott shrugged.

'Truth is, I don't know. It's kind of weird, he's not here but I can still feel him. I know he's not in any danger though, just a bit busy I expect.'

'Well as far as I can gather,' Charlotte hazarded, 'and from what you've told me, he's been at your side constantly for weeks now. Perhaps you should take this opportunity for some solitude and do something useful with it?'

'Like what?' Elliott asked.

Charlotte in return fixed him with a suggestive stare.

Chapter 31

The senior citizen who loved me

Bernie Subiaco lay back on the bed, exhausted, Mrs. Clarkson perched above him, looking down. Yesterday, having secured the stolen money in a locker at Victoria station, they'd booked themselves into a low key hotel in the centre of London. Since then Bernie joked to himself that if Mrs. Clarkson tried to have sex with him one more time she'd probably end up killing him.

'Bernieboops?' Mrs. Clarkson asked delicately.

'Yes, my little pea?'

'Do you feel bad about taking the money? I mean Elliott was one thing, but your own niece?'

They both took a second to think about it before bursting out laughing.

'Nah.' Bernie chortled. 'Besides we're pensioners now. We'll need a little extra something to help pay for that winter fuel bill. Not that winter will be a problem where we're going.'

'Where are we going?' Mrs. Clarkson asked optimistically.

'Anywhere babe. There are plenty of places in the world that would welcome us and our little nest egg. All we have to do is stay shut up here for a couple more days and then we'll make our escape. Just do me a favour, give us half an hour and a bowl of cornflakes before we do it again. I'm absolutely cream crackered.'

'Of course Bernieboops, of course,' Mrs. Clarkson replied, running her fingers through his grey chest hair. 'I'll tell you what. Let me run a bath for you so you can relax and get your strength back.'

'That's a cracking idea sweet pea,' Bernie replied, watching Mrs. Clarkson sidle from the bed and walk towards the bathroom.

Bernie continued to lie there, listening to the running of the taps. Hah, he thought, I've got a sweet seventy grand stashed and a red hot lady in tow. What could possibly go wrong? Five minutes later the sound of gushing water had ceased and Mrs. Clarkson was calling him through.

'In you pop Bernieboops,' Mrs. Clarkson suggested with a wink.

'That's smashing sweet pea, top notch.'

With a few worrying clicks of his joints Bernie made his way to the bathroom. Once there he was pleasantly surprised to find a bath with bubbles spilling over the top and a suggestive Mrs. Clarkson posed against the sink. With a gesture of her arm she directed him towards the tub. Oh well, Bernie concluded, one more time wouldn't kill him. As instructed he slid his wiry frame into the bath, the water lapping at the brim. His eyes closed as to the sensation and the anticipation of the pure pleasure that was to follow.

'Oh Bernieboops,' Mrs. Clarkson murmured with her back to him as she moving around the bathroom, fiddling with something. 'What was the number of that left luggage locker again?'

'237,' Bernie replied, opening his eyes.

What Bernie saw next came as a surprise. Mrs. Clarkson was standing over the bath holding a portable heater plugged into the wall.

'What's going on sweet p...'

Bernie never got to finish.

Mrs. Clarkson let the fire drop into the bath and a sudden and murderous connection was made between Bernie Subiaco and the national electricity grid. At first he writhed, flailing desperately about in the water, opening his mouth to let out a scream that failed to follow. Then he simply decided to call it a day, the only signal of his passing that of a flickering of lights along the corridor.

'You moron!' Mrs. Clarkson snarled, doing little to conceal the murderous expression on her face.

Turning, Mrs. Clarkson made her way back over to the plug, after all, in situations such as these you can never be too careful, someone might get hurt. As she was reaching down however she noticed something. In the doorway stood a figure, neither solid nor a trick of the light. It was a woman, maybe around Mrs. Clarkson's age but her clothes were dated, reminiscent of fashion back in the early eighties. Mrs. Clarkson instantly stood up straight, terrified.

'How dare you steal that money from my Gordon and his friend!' The ghost screamed in a ghastly other worldly voice.

'But, but, but …' Mrs. Clarkson protested, inching herself away from the apparition in horror.

Mrs. Clarkson had completely forgotten about the bath behind her. She was only reminded of its presence and the danger it represented when the back of her legs pressed up against it as she backed away. By then it was much too late. The ghostly intruder let out a banshee scream that shook Mrs. Clarkson to her core and betraying her years made her leap a good foot off the ground. As she came back down, landing hard against the edge of the bath she lost her sense of balance and fell backwards onto Bernie Subiaco.

She didn't feel the electrical current streaming instantly into her body.

She didn't notice the ghost taking a few steps forward to ensure that the job was done.

The lifeless body of Mrs. Clarkson saw nothing more. Only darkness, closing in until there was nothing left to see.

Mrs. Vivian Cole, happy with what she'd achieved, disappeared back whence she came.

Chapter 32

It's good to talk (to the other side)

Charlotte came back into the front room holding two freshly made mugs of coffee and sat down beside Elliott, placing the cups delicately onto the table in front of them. Elliott in turn put the magazine he'd been reading down and turned to look at the wonderful Charlotte. Since they'd got back last night their time together had been truly magnificent. There was no need for either of them to discuss further what had happened or what the future held. Whatever lay ahead, they would face it with a sense of excitement, together.

'It says in there,' Elliott commented, pointing to the magazine, 'that the Japanese are going crazy over something called Omorashi. I was thinking, technically, I'm unemployed at the moment. Maybe that's something I can look into, you know, get in at the ground floor?'

'Haven't you had enough of dabbling in sub-cultures you know nothing about?' Charlotte asked with a warm smile.

'I suppose,' Elliott sighed, reaching for his coffee.

'What about the medium thing? You don't want to give it another go?'

'Nah, got into a bit of a mess didn't it? Those reporters are still out there you know, hoping for the big scoop on the guy who saw the spirits of the dead rise again. I could really do without all the attention. Besides, I can't do it without Hapkido anyway.'

'No sign of him then?' Charlotte enquired.

'It's the same as last night outside the theatre. If I concentrate I can sense he's still around but it feels as if the link that connected us was broken at the Apollo Rooms. Hey, not to worry though, knowing Hapkido he'll turn up again, probably when I'm least expecting it.'

'Well then,' Charlotte suggested, 'maybe next time we'll just stick to something a bit more conventional shall we?'

Elliott was just about to agree when the phone rang. Making his way over, he picked up the handset.

'Hello.'

At first it seemed like a silent hoax call but just as Elliott was about to hang up he hesitated. Listening intently to the distant hiss in the background he could intermittently make out a few brief words, barely comprehensible. Elliott listened until the words fell back and the hiss washed over the message. Finally he placed the handset back down and gave a confused look to Charlotte.

'Who was that?' Charlotte asked, curious.

'Dunno. It was really faint but I think I could hear a woman speaking. It almost sounded like she had a Midlands accent.'

'So what did she say?'

'Something about locker number 237 at Victoria station,' Elliott replied, wrinkling his nose, perplexed. 'Apparently there's something there for me.'

'Probably a crank call. Your recent actions have kind of been attracting the weirdos.'

'Still you reckon we should check it out?' Elliott asked.

'Tomorrow eh? Let's just enjoy the rest of today.'

'Good idea. In the meantime, let's see what's on telly shall we?' Elliott suggested, reaching for the remote control.

Chapter 33

Kayfabe sunset (reprise)

'Hi. I'm Travis Thornley. Welcome wrestling fans to another episode of All American Superstar Wrestling! I'm here with Chad McMannis in the Olympus Stadium located here in Texas. Hi Chad, what a series of matches we have today!'

'Hi there Travis. Greetings to all of you watching at home. Today's opening match is going to be an absolute extravaganza!'

'Who do we have fighting today Chad?'

'The champion, Bonecrusher Bobby is going up against a relative newcomer to the wrestling ranks here. He's from London, England, and goes by the name of Jeremy 'The Flash' Flashman.'

'Is it true Chad that this guy used to be a famous psychic over there?'

'It sure is Travis. In a surprise career choice he decided to give it all up to try and win the All American Superstar Wrestling championship.'

'What do you think his chances are Chad?'

'Who knows Travis? What I do know is we'll find out pretty soon. He's coming to the ring now!'

'Hey Chad, is that the music of Phil Collins he's walking in to?'

'It sure is. He's in the ring now and stripped down to his dragon motif shorts. Is that actually a medallion he's wearing?'

'The guy knows how to rock the eighties look.'

'And here comes Bonecrusher Bobby. My God Travis, it looks like he's been in the gym and really bulked up for this match.'

'I'll tell you I wouldn't want to be Jeremy Flashman today Chad.'

'I don't think anyone would Travis.'

<u>Thirty two seconds later</u>

'What the hell happened in there Chad? What was he doing? It looked like he was trying to put him in a trance just by staring at him.'

'I've never seen anything like it Travis. They're wheeling him away on the stretcher now. I'm going to try and get a word with him. Jeremy, Jeremy. Can you tell us what went wrong in there?'

'Urghhh, the power of the samurai didn't quite work out.'

'Surely that means you won't be back. You took an absolute beating today.'

'Of course I'll be back. I won't stop until I'm the champion.'

'Any last words Jeremy?'

'Can someone get me a sausage sandwich please?'

Award winning author Kirk St Moritz (Horsell village primary school under 8 division) lives on a small island in the English Channel where he divides his time between writing and working for a top-secret department of Her Majesty's government (only one of these facts is true). Born in 1974 in the suburbs of London he has lived in Australia and Norway before settling in Guernsey. Following the success of his first novel The Day Jesus Rode Into Croydon he decided to release upon the world his second novel: The Impending Sausage Sandwich Of Doom. He is currently working on his third novel but keeps getting interrupted by the various henchmen of dastardly new world orders.

As an author, the writing of a second novel came with a certain sense of foreboding. For every Nevermind there is always a To The Extreme by Vanilla Ice. The undertaking certainly would have proved more difficult without the invaluable assistance of my editor Ant Skelton. I must also thank all those who have ~~tolerated~~ gladly listened to plot ideas and an ever-changing title. Hapkido Valentine was derived from distant memories of a nine-year-old Kirk St Moritz glued to Saturday afternoon television, watching the theatrics and glamour (as glamorous as a 1980s leisure centre could be) of British wrestling. To all those wrestlers that have since left that time behind nine-year-old Kirk continues to watch in wonder.

31556170R00129

Printed in Great Britain
by Amazon